Dark Obsessions

BY DELPHINE MCCLELLAND

D1437761

DORRANCE
PUBLISHING CO
EST. 1920
PITTSBURGH, PENNSYLVANIA 15238

The contents of this work, including, but not limited to, the accuracy of events, people, and places depicted; opinions expressed; permission to use previously published materials included; and any advice given or actions advocated are solely the responsibility of the author, who assumes all liability for said work and indemnifies the publisher against any claims stemming from publication of the work.

Dorrance Publishing Co
585 Alpha Drive
Pittsburgh, PA 15238
Visit our website at *www.dorrancebookstore.com*

ISBN: 979-8-88527-434-0
eISBN: 978-1-6366-1724-4

Dark Obsessions

I would like to dedicate this book to John Voldstad. Without you, this book would not have happened. Thank you for the idea and encouragement. I would also like to dedicate this book to my family and co-workers who believed in me and pushed me to accomplish this goal. You know who you are, and I am eternally grateful to you all. Thank You for your support.

TABLE OF CONTENTS

CHAPTER 1

On the Prowl

*T*hree hundred and twenty-five miles of shoreline on the North and South Carolina border Lake Wylie was the ideal spot for relaxation and fun. The lake was picturesque, and the house was secluded, which was perfect for Kairo. The house itself was over eight thousand square feet, located in a quiet neighborhood with a private wooded lot. There were lakefront views from every room including the most spectacular views from the master bedroom with its own private patio and access point to the lake. For a human, it was the perfect place, a beautiful oasis to wash the stress of the day away, but for a three-hundred-year-old vampire, the property still needed work. Since acquiring one of the best pieces of property on the lake, Kairo was busy working tirelessly on the house that so many before him loved. Day and night delivery trucks came and went with supplies and decor for Kairo to transform his new home from top to bottom. The basement was going to be a huge part of that transformation since Kairo was turning it into his new torture chamber. For three weeks now, all the neighbors were curious about their new, mysterious neighbor.

They all wanted to get to know him and find out what he was doing to this beautiful home that had already been remodeled two months prior to him moving in. Trying to focus on the needed home improvements was hard for

1

Kairo, as he became distracted by all the alluring half naked women that came out to the lake for some summer fun. By day, the summer heat was just too much to bear, but as soon as the sun set, it was time for all the humans to play. Lake Wylie would come alive with people of all walks of life, all shapes, and sizes. While the beautiful women enjoyed lying in the sun and splashing in the lake, they were unaware that they were being watched. Kairo was there waiting and watching in the shadows like the monster he was raised to be.

Kairo was intrigued by them and would stop the work he was doing just to listen in on their conversations that were mostly about him. To the untrained eye, he was young, sexy, and single, which brought up a lot of questions for the neighboring women. They all seemed to want to know how old he was, what he did for a living, and how he could afford that house. More importantly, they all wanted to know what he was doing all day and into the night to that house. For some of the women, they could care less about the renovations. All they cared about was what type of woman he was looking for. He was the newest eligible bachelor to the neighborhood, the man that everyone wanted and believed that they all needed in their lives. He was perfect in every way.

All the women were his type simply because they were of the opposite sex, and they all contained something that he wanted, something that he would kill to have. Some were cute, some were even sexy to him, but they all would fear him if they knew what he was. Kairo imagined every one of them strapped to a different device in his torture palace. *Oh, how they would scream*, he thought. The thought of their frightened faces and screams made his fangs come free from the hidden compartment in his mouth. Kairo wanted their fears, their screams, and most of all, he wanted their blood.

As a man, a human Kairo was a good person with a loving heart. He cared about others and hurting another human being would have never crossed his mind. All that changed when he met Malachi, who changed him forever. His creator and now his friend, Malachi taught him everything he needed to know about the art of torture and pain. Kairo was a great student who was a fast learner. Where he favored psychological and physical torture, Malachi was a brute who ripped his victims apart, leaving them in pieces like the trash he believed them to be. Kairo was more like a cat, sly and smooth, stalking his victims, luring them in through the various traps he set. Kairo loved this game of cat and mouse so much that he would refer to his victims as his *little mice*. Over time he became fond of the idea of dangling the hope of freedom in front of them and watching that same hope drain from their eyes when he snatched it away at the very last second. Kairo's new private lakefront oasis was going to be great for his little cat and mouse games.

The house was enormous, providing more than enough room to house all of his medieval torture devices and giving him all the necessary space to create, for the first time, a full-size maze for all his future little mice to play in. Some of his favorite devices to use were the Breast Ripper, the Iron Maiden, and the Heretic's Fork. Each device was quintessential in slowly draining the life from his little mice as he stood by watching them bleed to death before he saved their lives and tortured them all over again. It was this sadistic ongoing psychological circle that eventually broke all his little mice. With each passing day and each new device, hope drained from their eyes until nothing was left to do but end their misery.

This was the first house Kairo put this much work into. He never stayed in one place for longer than three months. Malachi taught all his creations that a home was forbidden for them. They were not human, and therefore, they should not live as humans. For their safety it was best if they used their ability to appear human as a cover to survive. It was because of this that Kairo considered himself somewhat of a nomad. He never found that one place that felt like home until he came to Charlotte, North Carolina. Only thirty-four minutes away from his new home, Charlotte was proving to be exactly what Kairo needed. For the first time in centuries, he was thinking about defying Malachi's rules and actually putting down roots as this city made him come alive in a way no other city had ever done before. The energy that the city gave off called out to him. It was unlike anything he had ever experienced. Thoughts of the future and what was to come had to wait for now, the only thing that should be on Kairo's mind was finishing the work that was in front of him. Without his completed accommodations, his newest little mouse would have no fun at all.

Eventually, Kairo's work was completed, and he could bask in all the glory that was to come. Showered, dressed, and ready to go, Kairo grabbed the keys to his red Ferrari 458 Italia with Charlotte and the City Center in his sights. He was ready to go on the prowl in the extremely popular City Center with its two popular clubs. I-Kandies was the larger, more popular of the two clubs, and Club Luxe was a smaller more high-end nightclub with rooftop views of the Charlotte Skyline. With several other bars and lounge spots the City Center had it all, something for everyone. It was the ideal location for a vampire looking to set a trap and catch a mouse. For tonight's festivities, Kairo chose the larger of the two clubs, I-Kandies. With its line wrapped out the door and down the steps, Kairo knew that he had made the correct choice.

I-Kandies was the place to be and that made Kairo salivate at the possibilities that stood before him. He could not wait to find out just what his first mouse in Charlotte would taste like. Waiting in line was beneath him and something that he never did. Dressed in his expensive black Italian suit, Kairo walked past all the poor souls waiting in line. With a hand full of cash, a seductive smile, and a bit of persuasion, he was escorted into the club by a petite beauty who would have pleased him, but she was not what he was in the mood for. Kairo knew tonight was going to be fun as the air hummed and buzzed with electricity. The energy was off the charts and unlike anything that he had ever felt on his previous trips into the city. Experiencing this level of energy made him feel even better about his decision to pick I-Kandies over Club Luxe. *Finding my next little mouse will be effortless*, he thought.

From the outside, I-Kandies was not what you would have thought it to be. The decor made it seem like it was going to be a modern and trendy nightclub, but that was not the case at all. The décor on the inside told Kairo that I-Kandies was once a techno club and all the owner did was maybe change the name and the type of music the DJ played. For the most part, it was your typical run of the mill club but the humans loved it. I-Kandies was a two-tier nightclub where the bar, dance floor, pole, and cages were located on the lower tier and the VIP section that overlooked the dance floor was on the upper tier. I-Kandies was even outfitted with a tacky disco ball and neon strobe lights. It looked as if the club itself was still trapped in the 1980s. The humans still seemed to love it, but it was not Kairo's taste at all, and the music was trash.

Despite how he felt about the club and its décor, it was the most popular club in the City Center, so it was where he was going to stay. Club Luxe would have been a better fit for him personally, but with the higher cover charge, it was taking way too long to draw a crowd. For his first night out on the prowl, Kairo would not have been satisfied with the idea of having a long wait before he found what he was looking for. The dance floor at I-Kandies was filling up fast as new patrons to the club came in and went straight to the bar to grab a drink of liquid courage to loosen themselves up. I-Kandies would provide Kairo with a variety of mice to choose from and that pleased him.

This is going to be fun, thought Kairo as he made his way over to the VIP registration table. The club had six VIP booths that were available to be reserved on a first-come-first-serve basis. Tonight, all six booths were available, and with Kairo wanting complete privacy and no distractions to stalk his next mouse, he paid to reserve the entire VIP section for himself. Like the rest of the club, VIP could use some help as well. There was nothing to it at all but some simple black leather couches and cheap black lacquer coffee tables. The space would serve its purpose for tonight, but if Kairo was the owner, things would be changed. That line of thinking gave him a few ideas for the future. Ready to get down to business, Kairo chose the center booth, which provided him with the best view of the dance floor and the bar. For tonight there would be room for him and only one other in VIP, his perfect little mouse. All others would be turned away unless they provided something that he wanted and was in the mood for.

On the menu for tonight was a blond bombshell, petite with full breasts who knew how to use her body to get what she wanted. A gorgeous little tease who would leave little to the imagination, with more sex appeal than she knew what to do with. Not having long to wait, Kairo found what he was looking for within an hour of stepping foot into the club. She walked in like she owned the place, with this air of confidence that said she was God's gift to all mankind. Kairo would enjoy hearing her scream and beg him for her life, so *Let the games begin,* said Kairo as he watched her move through the crowd.

She was ideal in every way possible with her slim, tight body, tiny waist, and full round breasts that, to Kairo's surprise, were naturally hers. Oh, how would she scream when he ripped her large supple breast from her body with his breast ripper. Kairo could hear her screams as he imagined her in his torture chamber of pleasure. He thought about all the fun that they were going to have with a wicked smile plastered on his beautiful face. Kairo was indeed a nefarious creature, after all. His first little mouse was dressed in the tiniest black dress with matching black six-inch stiletto heels. Had Kairo been your typical man, she would have had him all over her like a dog in heat. Kairo could tell that she was so full of life, a tease who loved to use her feminine wiles to get what she felt like she deserved in life. Soon, and very soon, she would learn that she did not run the world.

Like the king of his castle, Kairo watched her mingle through the crowd while he learned all that he needed to know to set his trap in motion. Overhearing her every conversation, Kairo learned that her name was Stacee, two e's, no y, and that she was looking for a man that could take care of her every need. Taking full advantage of the pole, Stacee performed a seductive dance that made every man watching hard with a desire to bury themselves deep inside her. They all gave her exactly what she wanted, their undivided attention, as she showed them what she was working with. Stacee was like a gift to them just waiting for the right man to unwrap her, and that man would be Kairo. Once she was finished with her dance, the time had come for Kairo to catch him a pretty little mouse.

The way that Stacee held the attention of every man in I-Kandies, Kairo did the same of every female. He knew that they all wanted him, but he had eyes for only one. Walking as if floating across the dance floor to the bar, Kairo made his first move by ordering two bottles of Don Julio Real in earshot of Stacee. Kairo had the bartender chill both bottles for him and sent to his booth. Before leaving, he tipped the bartender with five crisp one-hundred-dollar bills and made his way back to VIP. His work was done, and his trap was set. Now all he had to do was sit back and wait for his little mouse to come to him, because he was the cheese that she so desperately wanted to eat. Stacee was looking for a man with money, and Kairo had just told her that he had plenty of it. She was going to be putty in his hands, waiting to be molded by him and him alone.

Stacee could not resist the man at the bar, not only was he gorgeous, he had money, and by the look of things, he had plenty to go around. Stacee was intrigued by him. He was six foot three, with honey bronzed skin, an athletic body, with shoulder length dark hair, and the most piercing golden amber eyes that she had ever seen. He had eyes that Stacee wanted to stare into, getting lost in for all eternity. His voice was like smoky honey, sweet and sexually attractive with a hint of mystery behind it. Stacee imagined all the ways in which she could please that man. He was everything that she was looking for and more. Never had she seen a man as handsome as he was. *Where had he come from and were there more men out there like him?* thought Stacee as she watched him walk away. He was just as sexy walking away as he was walking towards the bar. Stacee wanted to touch him to find out if his skin was as soft as it looked and feel his perfect lips all over her body. She imagined him naked on top of her, inside her as he made her climb mountain after mountain reaching a sexual gratification that she had never experienced before.

This was all new to Stacee. Typically, she was not one to have sex on the first night. She may have come across as a tease, but there was more to her than her sexy body. She was a smart woman who used what she had to entice men to give her what she wanted. She liked to be the one in control of the situation, making men wait and beg her for sex just because she could. Stacee knew she wanted that man, and make no mistake about it, she was going to have him no matter what. She had never been denied by a man before, and he was not about to be the first. She was positive that she had found the man of her dreams and he would not slip through her fingers. Letting her friends know that she had found her man and not to wait for her, Stacee made a beeline straight to VIP after him.

Back up the stairs, Kairo had already poured four shots of tequila for him and his guest. After his display at the bar, he was certain that Miss Stacee would be on her way up shortly. He pointed her out to the security guard letting him know that it was perfectly fine to let her up and her alone. It was not long before Kairo heard Stacee approaching, and on his orders, she was granted access to his private domain for the evening. Before Stacee reached Kairo, she had to walk past three unused booths. That was plenty of time for him to size her up and see how she would use her body to tell him all about her. As Stacee approached Kairo, she put on her best come-hither walk to mesmerize him with the sway of her hips hoping to make him melt for her.

"Hi, I'm Stacee, I saw you looking at me at the bar," she said.

Kairo smiled. "I was looking at you." He laughed, and it was the most beautiful sound that Stacee had ever heard. "No, you were looking at me, my little mouse." With a nervous giggle like that of a little schoolgirl, Stacee agreed that she was looking at him simply because he was hot. This man was beyond belief. Stacee could not comprehend how she came to be standing in front of him. Sure, she was a sex kitten, but she had never pulled a man like this before.

"I'm Kairo VanDoren, come and have a seat, let's get to know one another."

For the next hour, the two of them talked and drank as they got to know each other. Kairo learned that Stacee was twenty-seven and single and that she was an exotic dancer who dreamed of being an actress. She wanted to see her name in lights. For most of the conversation, it was all about her, what she liked, what she wanted, and her future.

In the beginning Kairo was fine with listening to her talk. It gave him time to work out the finer details of his plans for later, but after a while, he grew tired of hearing her speak. Her voice was annoying, and it was like murder to his ears. Realizing that she had monopolized the entire conversation, Stacee finally asked Kairo some questions about himself. She felt like he was much older than she was because of his maturity level. He did not act childish and goofy like most of the boys her age nor did he come across as this stuffy and boring old man. He did not look like he was much older than thirty, but Stacee could not tell for sure, so she had to ask that one burning question. Kairo wanted to be honest with his answer, so he told her the truth. He told her that he was three hundred and ten years old. Just as he expected, Stacee's mouth dropped open and she was stunned into silence.

Kairo's laughter eased her back into reality when he finally said, "I was only kidding, I'm only thirty."

Kairo took over the conversation and told Stacee a little bit more about himself. His parents had died and left him a considerable amount of money. Money that he took and made some risky but smart investments that paid off in the long run for him. Through his investments, he made millions, and instead of blowing his money, he reinvested it and continued to make money. Now he was blessed to have more money than he knew what to do with. Stacee knew what to do with all that money of his. She saw herself living the good life, the wife of this handsome rich man on one of those reality TV shows. She would have luxury yachts, expensive shopping sprees, and exotic vacations with all her friends. With Kairo on her arm and in her bed, she would be the talk of the town and she would have it all.

Kairo had already drank most of the first bottle of tequila and was in danger of finishing off the second one as well. He was still growing tired of Stacee and this charade that he was putting on. He could care less about her hopes and dreams. All he wanted was her screams and her blood. Kairo needed her to be quiet and focused on something else besides her never-ending list of questions.

Placing his finger on her lips to get her to stop talking, Kairo said, "You are an exotic dancer correct, dance for me, my sweet."

That did the trick. Stacee stopped talking, downed a few shots of tequila, and danced for him. She took this dance as the audition of a lifetime and hoped that this one dance would change her life forever. Stacee wanted this dance to help her become the future Mrs. VanDoren so she put everything that she had into that one dance. Stacee was both sexual and seductive as she danced on top of the table. As she moved to the beat of the music she removed her dress while Kairo kept his eyes glued to her. He wanted to give Stacee what she needed the most, which was his undivided attention to keep her confidence up. Kairo knew that it was her plan to use this dance to make him fall for her. This was all real to her; she wanted this dance to arouse him, making him want her more and more.

What was real to Stacee was nothing more than a game to Kairo. This was simply a means to an end. The longer Stacee danced, the braver and bolder she got. Now that she was filled with so much confidence, she was ready to take this dance to the next level. Dressed in nothing but her black panties and bra, Stacee was ready to give Kairo a performance he would never forget.

Kairo knew women like Stacee, just because she was serving him sex on a silver platter did not mean that she was going to be easy. Kairo understood that she was a tease and was used to being the one calling all the shots. As Stacee danced on top of him, he grabbed her, turning her around to face him. With just enough pressure on her wrist to frighten her a little and let her know that he was in control Kairo placed a seductive kiss on her lips. It was the kind of kiss that started a fire deep down inside of her. It was the type of kiss that told Stacee that Kairo wanted her just as much as she wanted him. Stacee even felt Kairo's fire for her as she sat on his lap enjoying that kiss. She was wrong; it was not her that lit a fire in Kairo's loins but the thought of her tantalizing blood and her fear that aroused him.

Before Kairo ruined his fun by plunging his fangs deep into Stacee's neck, he had to break away from her. "I want you, Stacee; come home with me," he said.

Stacee's head said no, but her body said yes; torn, she did not know what to say or do. Taking matters into his own hands, Kairo removed Stacee from his lap, helped her get back into her dress, and led her willingly out of the club and down to his car.

The fresh air was enough to clear Stacee's head, waking her up from the seductive fog that Kairo's kiss had put her in. She wanted to go with him, but she was in foreign territory. She was not used to not being the one in control of a situation. Somehow over the course of their entanglement, Stacee had relinquished all her power over to this striking man, and that was not like her. In that moment Stacee would have given Kairo anything that he wanted, including allowing him the pleasure of devouring her body on the first night. She had to stop this and regain control of the situation while she had enough strength to do so.

Kairo walked over to her and kissed her again to regain control of the situation. This time he looked deep into her eyes making sure that she was put under his spell. Kairo compelled Stacee to let go of all her apprehensions and give into her want and desire to be with him. Stacee who was now fully under Kairo's control, did everything that he told her to do. She was now happy to be going anywhere with him, even to his secluded lakefront home, unaware of who he really was and all the dangers that awaited her there. Kairo had set his trap and caught him a lovely new little mouse.

CHAPTER 2
A Power Within

Skylar Montgomery was not your average twenty-six-year-old woman. She was wise beyond her years, more intelligent than most people her age, and, at the same time, a bit odd. With her family name and prestige, she should have been a socialite like her mother and the rest of the Montgomery women. Skylar was far different from the world that she was born into. She only had a small circle of close friends whom she hung out with and trusted. Out of that small group of friends was Skylar's best friend Angelina. She was the best, and Skylar could always count on her. Skylar had a thing for the dead and was into the supernatural world. It was because of these strange obsessions that most people stayed clear of her. Even her family thought that she was a little bit bizarre and even abnormal. Angelina was different; she loved Skylar for who she was, weird obsessions and all. With the help of her family name and the fact that she was brilliant, Skylar had been offered the chief medical examiner position when Dr. Hayes just up and left without any explanation. Skylar had been in the position for eight months now, and she loved every minute of it.

It was early Friday morning around 7:30 A.M. when Skylar was leaving work after her third shift. She loved working at night in the morgue when most people were too scared to even be there. She felt right at home anytime she was there but being there at night was always her favorite time. Inside the morgue was the one place where Skylar felt like herself, where she felt normal. It was outside of those walls where she was certain that she would never feel normal again. It all started two weeks ago when she was in New Orleans on the Montgomery family vacation. Something happened to Skylar that she could not explain, and now her world was turned upside down.

Skylar felt even crazier than normal and needed to talk to her best friend. Angelina was the one person who was sure to convince her that she was not crazy even though there were things that she could not explain or even wrap her head around. Since returning from her trip, the energy around her always seemed to be out of whack and different. Even now as she was leaving work, there was not a soul around her, and that was odd. Typically, Skylar would run into at least four other coworkers, some who were leaving from the nightshift like she was and some who were coming in to start their day.

Today the garage was a ghost town; no one was there except Archie the night watchmen, who had a crush on her. He was always watching her on the monitors, which was just eerie. He would follow Skylar's every move all from the comforts of the security desk. That could explain why she was feeling the way she was, but then again, it could have been something else entirely. Feeling uncomfortable, Skylar hurried to her Cadillac XTS hoping that once she was back at home and got some sleep, she would feel like herself again. She hoped that she would be able to get more sleep than she had been getting over the last couple of nights.

Whatever happened to her in New Orleans was now causing her to have these puzzling dreams that kept her tossing and turning all night long. When she would wake up, she could never remember anything that happened in her dreams or what they were about. It never failed, though, whenever she woke up, she was always surrounded by an energy that she wanted to connect to but did not know how to find. It was almost as if she was having an out-of-body experience.

Back at home Skylar realized that she was more tired than she thought she was. With little effort on her part, she was asleep as soon as her head touched the pillow. At first she slept like a baby; however, things quickly changed for her. As the first hour was approaching, Skylar was met with this weightless feeling. It was as if she was floating. Then came the series of weird dreams she could never explain, even if there were parts that she could recall.

After tossing and turning for hours, Skylar was eventually forced out of bed. When she woke up, she realized that she had a pounding headache and still felt tired and exhausted. That tired and exhausted feeling was starting to become her new normal, and it was getting old fast. Like all the strange occurrences in her life, Skylar pushed this to the back burner and attempted to get on with her life as best she could.

Now that she was awake, she needed to do something to take her mind off all the unexpected vibes that she was feeling. With a quick shot of moonshine, courtesy of her father, things finally started to settle back down, and Skylar felt as normal as could be expected. She could only hope that the feeling would last, but she still needed to talk through her feelings with Angelina. Angelina was the only person whom Skylar trusted with this information. Hoping that she would be in the mode to hang out, Skylar texted her before doing anything else.

Hey wanna go to I-Kandies tonight. Skylar ended the text with the big smile emoji.

Skylar hated the décor of the club and the DJ was not always the best, but she needed alcohol and dancing, lots and lots of dancing. For what it was worth, I-Kandies seemed to always draw in a huge crowd of people from all walks of life. Skylar needed some male company since it had been a while since she was in a relationship. She was hoping that tonight would be the night where she could get close to someone without having to show her ass. Hopefully tonight her luck would change, and she would meet a decent guy that would spark her interest. Skylar typically did not have one-night stands, but with the way that she was feeling, anything was possible. A one-night stand might be just what the doctor ordered.

Knowing that Angelina was slow to respond and needing to be out of the house, Skylar decided to go see a movie. The Cineplex was showing *Blood Lust 2*, the long-awaited sequel to her favorite vampire movie. With the Cineplex not being that far away from her home, she had plenty of time to see a move and still make it back in time to change for tonight. When it came to vampires and the supernatural world, Skylar was its number one fan. Vampires, witches, and werewolves were her thing. She saw all the movies, even the bad ones, and would read just about every book. Skylar was totally obsessed. She knew it and so did everyone else that truly knew her. Over time

Skylar became used to the jokes and the freaky looks from her family and by-standers that overheard her conversations. As a child, she was taught to love herself and not care about what people thought about her. She carried that advice from her parents with her even today. Her real friends were the ones that stood by her and left her and her obsession with the supernatural world alone. Angelina was her real friend.

The theater was empty since it was still early in the day and most people waited until dark to watch horror films. Working at night had gotten Skylar used to watching movies during the day and she loved having the theater all to herself. She hated when people talked during the movie and when girls pretended to be scared just to give their dates a reason to hold them close and protect them. Skylar hated anyone that interrupted her viewing pleasure. With popcorn and drink in hand, she sat in her favorite seat at the back of the theater completely alone to watch her favorite vampire movie.

The film did what Skylar needed it to do. It took her mind off her problems for just a short while. Unfortunately, now that the movie was over, it was time for her to get back to reality. Once the lights came up so did all the stress and anxiety that had been bugging her for weeks now. Skylar grabbed her phone to check her messages, wanting to know if Angelina had responded to her text. Angelina was thrilled to have a fun girls' night out. It had been weeks since they spent time together, and like Skylar, she needed lots of dancing and good clean fun after her long week. As they traded messages back and forth, the plan was to meet at the pizzeria and then walk over to I-Kandies. With plans made for tonight, Skylar had several hours to kill before she and Angelina got their night started. Hoping to snag some eye candy of her own meant that some retail therapy was in order. Skylar was going to need the perfect outfit if she were to stand out and get noticed among all the women that would be at I-Kandies.

Skylar was never that big into fashion like the rest of the Montgomery women. She knew how to dress to accentuate her best assets without looking like an open buffet. That was one of the biggest problems that she had with the type of women that showed up at I-Kandies. They took the name literally and dressed as if they were the "eye candy" for the club. Skylar dressed sexy, but she always tried to keep something to the imagination hoping to keep the men guessing. Majority of the women that showed up at I-Kandies were the type to never leave anything to the imagination. The way they dressed always made it hard for Skylar to get noticed by any men at the club. She refused to lower her standards and display all her assets just to catch a man. Feeling optimistic, though, she hoped that tonight things would be different.

Walking through her favorite store, Skylar eventually settled on a new pair of dark skinny jeans, deep teal sleeveless shirt with cut outs along the side to show just enough skin, and black heels to showcase her long, toned legs. It was an outfit that was both comfortable and sexy, as both the shirt and jeans accentuated her curves . Tonight, Skylar planned to talk to her best friend, but high on her list was finding her a very sexy man to get close to and, possibly, underneath. Satisfied with her choices for tonight, Skylar returned home to relax, shower, and get ready for some good clean fun. She added some diamond earrings and a necklace that would sparkle and catch the light and finished her outfit off with a black clutch, a little make-up, and her siren lipstick. Looking in the mirror one last time, Skylar liked what she was seeing and was ready to have the time of her life.

Skylar arrived at the City Center before Angelina. She lived closer to Uptown in the neighboring Noda area and was only a short train ride away. She quickly noticed that the City Center was much busier than normal and that she was experiencing her new normal. For reasons unknown to her, it seemed like everyone in Charlotte chose this Friday night to come out and party. Once again, the energy was off. Skylar was feeling this buzz of electricity, a spark in the air that made her feel like she had butterflies in her stomach. On top of all of that, she felt this unnatural pull towards I-Kandies. Adamant that what she was feeling had nothing to do with her new normal, Skylar tried to ignore it as she waited for Angelina. She wanted to believe that what she was experiencing was nothing more than her excitement for tonight. While the line for I-Kandies continued to grow by the second Skylar decided to order food for Angelina and herself. The last thing that she wanted was for the two of them to be denied entry because the club reached its capacity limit.

Minutes later, Angelina came around the corner, and her and Skylar were able to get their night started. The line to get into I-Kandies continued to grow getting longer by the second, and Skylar prepared herself mentally to deal with the possibility that they were not going to get into the club tonight. Skylar was upset that she could be denied access to the club as she tried to keep her emotions in check. She did not want her bad mood to bring Angelina down and ruin their evening. It was strange, but there was a part of her that needed to get inside of that club. It was that part of her that died inside at the possibility that they were going to be turned away.

"I hope we can get in tonight," said Skylar. "I was not expecting it to be so packed."

"I know," stated Angelina, "but worst case, we can get a booth in VIP or go to Bad Dragon."

"Okay, sounds like a plan; are you ready?" asked Skylar.

Skylar and Angelina moved quickly through the ever-growing crowd of people to the line that had formed outside of I-Kandies. While waiting in line, Angelina overheard people talking about some rich guy who reserved the club's entire VIP section for himself. That did not sit well with Skylar. She did not plan for something like this to happen and was mad at herself for wanting to stop and get something to eat first. She planned on drinking heavily tonight and getting food first was a good idea at the time. By the look of the line and the number of people in front of them, they were not going to be getting into I-Kandies tonight.

"I think that we should still be able to get in; the dance floor does hold a lot of people," said Angelina.

That was Skylar's best friend, she was always the glass-is-half-full kind of thinker, and she saw the disappointment on Skylar's face. It was odd that she felt this anger and disappointment towards not getting into a club that she did not like that much in the first place. With her disappointment aside, Skylar was also dealing with that unfamiliar pull of energy that was growing stronger with every step closer to I-Kandies. Her entire body buzzed and tingled all over; her stomach grew tighter with knots and that butterfly feeling increased tenfold. Skylar was not sure what was going on with her. On the one hand, she felt like she had to enter that club, and on the other hand, she felt like doing so was putting her and Angelina in danger. Skylar was torn and did not know what the right choice was .

Thankfully for her, that decision was taken away from them when the club reached capacity and they were denied entry. Whatever that feeling was, it was something new, and not like what Skylar experienced back in New Orleans. She could not wait to get as far away from I-Kandies since something was making her feel like she was about to explode inside. As soon as she found an opening, she rushed past everyone to go down the stairs and away from the club as fast as possible. The further away from I-Kandies that she got, the better she felt or the better most of her felt. Even though she was glad to be away from the club, there was a part of her that felt sad and lost without the connection to the energy that was calling out to her. The air around her was still slightly electric, but for the most part, her emotions were getting back to normal. Skylar filled Angelina in on what happened when they were a block away from I-Kandies.

Bad Dragon was three blocks away from the City Center, and once inside, Skylar went straight to the bar. Even though she was feeling better, she needed a drink to help take the edge off. She needed something hard and ordered a double shot of 1800 tequila before ordering a round of Shirley Temples for her and Angelina. Bad Dragon was smaller than I-Kandies; it was more of a vintage arcade bar and lounge. Where I-Kandies was a place where people went to hook up with perfect strangers, Bad Dragon was more of a hangout spot for friends. Now that Skylar thought about it this was the better place to go so that she could talk to Angelina. Dancing the night away would have been great, but she knew that would have only delayed the real reason why she wanted to come out with Angelina in the first place, which was so they could talk. Angelina got seats at one of the open lounge booths while Skylar got them drinks. At Bad Dragon it was always better to divide and conquer since it was such a small location.

"So, tell me about your trip and what happened that has gotten you feeling creepy and crazy."

"Are you sure you're ready for this?" said Skylar. Angelina responded with only one word: "Talk," she said. Skylar did just that, telling her best friend all about what happened in New Orleans.

You know how excited I was to be going to New Orleans, the birthplace of all things supernatural, right? I was on Cloud nine a high I just could not explain; I had my entire trip planned out. I was going to take one of their famous tours and visit the Lafayette Cemetery No 1. There was no way I was stepping one foot in New Orleans without seeing that cemetery with my own two eyes. As soon as we landed, I was ready to do my own thing, but I had to do the family stuff first. It was fun, just not in my plans, so my first couple of days were already booked. I was able to have Thursday free and all to myself to explore the city on my own terms away from my family, since most of them think that I am obsessed with vampire lore and the supernatural world anyway. I was not in the mood to deal with them and the comments that they were going to have. So, I walked around and did my own tour. I started out by going to some of the local shops and stopping to get beignets and food, you know, the normal things to do when visiting a new city. I was scheduled to go on a witch and voodoo tour at eight P.M. At first everything was fine; it was a normal tour until we went to the Saint Louis Cemetery No1. The second I placed one foot on the grounds of that cemetery, everything I knew changed. The world around me was different; it was like I was one with nature. I could feel the power of the land everywhere I turned, and it was an incredible feeling. Strange, and a bit scary, but all the same incredible. I could feel the true power of the wind and could feel the energy in every living thing around me. I was connected to everything; even if I closed my eyes, I could still see what was in front of me based on the energies I was picking up on. As the tour guide talked and we moved through the cemetery, I felt stronger inside, like I had this power that I needed to get out. I just did not know how to release it. Soon we came to the plaque at the grave of Marie Laveau, the Voodoo Queen herself. It was at that moment everything changed; it was as if my senses became even more heightened. It was as if I could see and hear in full color, high definition. It was the best feeling in the world. For the first time in my life, I truly felt normal, like I finally fit into this world. It was as if I had finally found the one place that I belonged. As the tour ended and we started to move away from the cemetery, I started to lose that feeling. That power that I felt inside was fading away fast, and the world went back to how it was before, normal. The thing is, normal to me now is so lackluster and boring. I feel as if I am trapped in a dull gray world and all I want is to see color again. I did not experience that feeling again until Saturday when I was free to visit the Lafayette Cemetery No. 1, and just like before, I experienced the same things. This time it was not as strong as before, but it was there just the same. Like before, when I left, so did all my feelings. Since then, I have not experienced anything like it. I have what I would describe as weird vibes but nothing anywhere remotely like

18

what I experienced in New Orleans. Sometimes I feel like I am crazy, but there is a huge part of me deep down that knows what I experienced was real, but I still have my doubts. Now all I want to do is recreate that feeling and learn what it means. I need to know that it was not some smoke-and-mirrors parlor trick to mess with tourists.

"Crazy, right?" stated Skylar to Angelina. "You can go ahead and say it; I already know how it sounds."

"No, it's not crazy, and neither are you, but what are you going to do now? I know you, and you are not going to let this go that easy."

"Honestly, I don't have a clue right now, but you are right, Angie, I'm not going to let it go that easy."

Skylar did feel better now that she got that huge weight off her chest. She ordered another round of drinks, and at least for now, she was ready to put all the strange feelings behind her. For the rest of the night she only wanted to focus on having fun and not this mysterious energy that she was picking up on all the time. Skylar knew that in the morning or sometime tomorrow or even tonight when she went to bed that feeling would return and she would deal with it then. Somehow, she had opened Pandora's box and now there was no way of closing it, and if Skylar was honest with herself, she was not sure if she even wanted that box to close.

After talking through all the bizarre things that had been happening, Skylar and Angelina spent the rest of the night playing arcade games and just having fun. Angelina was the most competitive person that Skylar knew. She hated to lose at any game she played; losing was never an option for her. Angelina won in almost every game that they played. She killed Skylar in foosball and in air hockey, but Skylar was able to get the upper hand in the shooting games. It helped that Skylar's father had her shooting as a teenager, and she was an excellent shot. Skylar even walked away with a few stuffed animals from the claw game. Overall, the night was finally fun, Skylar was back to normal, and this time normal was okay. In fact, normal was better than okay.

For the first time in weeks, Skylar was truly able to relax and find herself again. She was right when she told Angelina that she needed a girls' night out just to have some good clean fun. Talking things through and just hearing it all out loud made a difference, and the alcohol did not hurt either. Things were finally looking up, until he walked in. Skylar noticed him as he rounded the corner going straight to the bar with two other guys that she did not recognize. Following her line of sight, Angelina saw whom Skylar was watching like a hawk and why her face looked the way it did.

"Of all the people to walk through the doors, why him?"

Standing by the bar was none other than Dimitri Huntington. He was a detective that Skylar met through her mother. Skylar's mother and Dimitri's mother were friends who thought the two of them should date. Dimitri felt the same way they did and let Skylar know how he felt about her and their situation every time he saw her. He was a nice guy and nice looking, but Skylar was not into him in that way.

Dimitri was a tall, dark, and handsome man, with a nice build, bald head, and plush beard, but he was just not Skylar's cup of tea. Had Skylar been another woman, she would have been all over Dimitri, but the truth was, he did not make her heart skip a beat. When it came to matters of the heart, Skylar was trapped in a fairy tale. She believed that she should feel this connection or a spark for the man that she was destined to fall in love with. Had Dimitri not been such an asshole, she may have given him a chance, but he always ruined his chances because of his big mouth.

Dimitri was a friend and nothing more. He had blinders on when it came to how Skylar felt about him. He would always try to take Skylar's no's to mean that she was playing hard to get. At first, she tried to be nice, but he would not get it through his thick skull that she was not into him in a sexual way. The other problem Skylar had with Dimitri was his possessive attitude.

Dimitri felt like since it was his job to serve and protect that gave him the right to hover around her and control her. He felt like he owned her and could tell her what she could and could not do. Dimitri never wanted to see another man look at her or even touch her. His overprotective attitude was just too much for Skylar to handle. Sometimes his attitude even made it hard for her to want to continue to be friends with him. Skylar and Dimitri had known each other for years, and ending their friendship was not a conversation she wanted to have with her mother. When it came down to it, ending their friendship could not be done that easily, and as much as Skylar hated to admit it, she did care for Dimitri but only as a friend.

Tonight, however, she was not in the mood to deal with him, his attitude, or him touching on her and asking her out for the hundredth time. After Dimitri and his friends got their drinks at the bar, they stayed out of sight. *This was new*, thought Skylar; Dimitri tried to act like he did not see her. That made Skylar angry and pissed her off. She was not sure why but being ignored by Dimitri hurt like hell. She would never ignore him no matter how bad he annoyed and upset her. *What is his problem?* she thought. Under no circumstances did Skylar want Dimitri to be up to his usual games, but to act like he did not see her at all was uncalled for. Knowing Dimitri, this was some game that he was playing, and Skylar tried hard not to fall for it. After waiting for over an hour, she was done being ignored by Dimitri and stormed over to the bar ready to give him a piece of her mind.

"Hi Dimitri, what, you can't speak now?" said Skylar. Shocked by her anger, Dimitri did not know what to say but was thrilled that his plan had worked to perfection. If he walked over and said hello and left her alone for the rest of the night, she would have been happy. The fact that she knew he saw her and ignored her drove her insane. It was destiny that they both ended up at Bad Dragon at the same time, and Dimitri just wanted to give Skylar what she wanted. She wanted to be left alone so he was leaving her alone.

"I can speak, Skylar; I just wanted to give you your space. You always complain about how I am too clingy and never leave you alone, so tonight I was not going to brother you. Although now that we both are here, can we join you?" he asked. "You did come to me and disrupt my night," he said with a sarcastic smirk. Dimitri hoped that if he ignored Skylar long enough, she would get mad at him and come to him on her own. She was, after all, a Montgomery, and as much as she claimed to not be like the women in her family, she did have aspects of them deep down inside of her. *Mission accomplished*, thought Dimitri.

Skylar had brought this on herself, had she stayed away so would he. She had just walked right into his trap, and there was no turning back. For now, she would play nice if Dimitri did not cross the line. He had a bad habit of getting a little touchy feely, and tonight, Skylar was not going to play that game with him. Before getting their night started, Dimitri introduced his two friends Mike and James. Since Dimitri was "the good guy," he had so many friends that Skylar had never met before. Immediately, Angelina took an interest in James. He was tall and blonde with green eyes, so Angelina's type. Skylar thought he was an average looking guy, but he made her friend smile and that was all that mattered. She would be keeping an eye on him just in case he shared Dimitri's same annoying traits.

To Skylar's surprise, Dimitri was not his normal self. He kept his hands to himself and never caught an attitude when other men tried to hit on her. Dimitri simply smiled and walked away each time it happened. *Could it be?* thought Skylar. *Was he finally learning his lesson?* Since he was being on his best behavior, Skylar could relax and breathe a little easier since she was the cause of this impromptu hang-out session. If Dimitri stayed on his best behavior, Skylar had no problems with him and his friends hanging out with her and Angelina.

The night was fun; they played a few doubles games of air hockey, girls versus boys. Of course, Angelina was no match for the boys, so naturally, the girls won every game. Skylar had to admit to herself that she was having fun with Dimitri. Turns out he was a fun guy when he was not being an overbearing asshole. They even shared a few dances where he kept his hands to himself and did not allow them to linger for too long on her body. Now this was a Dimitri that Skylar might consider seeing again.

Just before the DJ announced the last call for the bar and played the final song of the night, Dimitri asked, "Can we hang out again soon, Skylar?"

With a playful grin and a little tipsy, Skylar said, "Yes, we can; I had fun tonight." Seeing how Angelina had become smitten with James, she insisted that Dimitri bring him along as well. A part of Skylar was dying to know if Dimitri had seriously tuned over a new leaf or if this was all part of some grand scheme of his. Their next meeting would not be a date but four friends getting to know each other better. If Dimitri could stay on his best behavior, there may be hope for them in the future. He did not make Skylar's heart skip a beat, but he was a good man with a good heart. With one last round of drinks, all the friends said their goodbyes when Dimitri leaned in and kissed Skylar on the lips. He expected for her to slap him, but when Skylar returned the kiss, he realized that he had won. Skylar not only kissed him back, she was all over him. It was evident that she wanted him at that moment.

As the kiss deepened, something in Skylar changed. A clearer head prevailed, and she broke away from Dimitri somewhat embarrassed by her actions.

Skylar said her good-byes grabbed Angelina's hand and rushed out of Bad Dragon trying to put as much distance between her and Dimitri as she could. As shocked as Dimitri was, that kiss gave him hope and a new purpose in life. It all made sense to him. Skylar was playing hard to get this entire time. She was not drunk and therefore that kiss was not an accident. Skylar had just told Dimitri that he was the one and on their next date they would be taking their friendship to the next level. All of Dimitri's persistence was about to pay off in a big way. This time next year, there would be a Montgomery and Huntington union that would be the social event of the year. Dimitri was all smiles and had plenty of work to do before he saw Skylar again.

CHAPTER 3

Scream Little Mouse

Stacee was compelled and completely under Kairo's control and was loving every minute of the drive back to his house. Without giving it a second thought, she would have done anything Kairo told her to do. If he wanted, he could make her open the door and jump to her death. Stacee found the way that he was driving utterly fascinating. The speed and the way he moved through the traffic was unimaginable. At 150 miles per hour, he never came close to crashing; his reflexes were unlike anything that Stacee had ever seen before. The more she learned about this man, the more in awe of him she became. In less than five minutes, they were pulling into the driveway of a magnificent home. It was an all-brick mansion that sat on its own secluded part of Lake Wylie. Being the gentleman that he was, Kairo took Stacee's hand to help her out of the car as he smirked at her. "Impressed by what you see, Princess?"

Not willing to give Kairo the satisfaction of being right, Stacee played off the fact that she was very much impressed by his magnificent home. Stacee's reply came out as a weak one that Kairo was not buying at all.

"N-No, I've seen and been in bigger homes than this before."

"Duly noted," he said, not believing a single word that she was saying. "Would you like a tour of my tiny home?"

25

A tour was not what Stacee had in mind. "I want whatever you want, Kairo," she said as she batted her eyes at him seductively hoping that a tour was not what he wanted. "Good," he said, "because all I want is you."

Hand in hand, Kairo walked Stacee into the house and out to the back deck that overlooked the peaceful lake for a nightcap before his real fun began. He poured two glasses of red wine for the two of them and watched as Stacee enjoyed the stunning view in front of her. Kairo would allow her a few minutes of normalcy before unleashing the monster that lived inside of him. With her glass of wine almost empty, Kairo knew that it was time to start the show. Taking off his jacket and tie, Kairo made himself comfortable on the couch and gave Stacee her first set of orders.

"Crawl over to me, Princess," he demanded, "and take off that dress."

Without hesitating, Stacee did exactly what she was told to do. She gave into her desire to please Kairo by giving him whatever he wanted. His happiness became her happiness, and without thinking, she dropped to all fours and crawled across the stone pavers over to where he was sitting. With him watching her every move, Stacee unzipped her black dress and let it fall effortlessly to the floor. In total submission, she stood in front of Kairo waiting for her next set of orders. "Dance for me, my little mouse," he said, and again, Stacee did as she was told without question. She swayed and moved her hips to a beat that only she could hear. Stacee danced for Kairo and did not have a care in the world except for pleasing him. Free of any apprehensions, she was prepared to take this much further than before until Kairo stopped her. He handed her another full glass of wine and demanded that she finish it in one gulp. Seconds later, Stacee's head started to spin, her eyes glazed over, and everything went black. Like the poor weak soul that she was, she collapsed into Kairo's arms so the real fun could begin.

Four long hours later, Stacee woke up completely naked lying on her back strapped to a metal bedframe. Scared to death, all she could do was scream at the top of her lungs. She had no clue how, why, or who had placed her here. The last thing that she remembered was talking to the sexiest man that she had ever met. His name was Kairo, and they met at I-Kandies. Stacee spent much of the evening with him until they left the club and went their separate ways. After leaving alone, her mind went blank. She could not recall anything that happened to her after that. Her heart continued to beat out of her chest when she heard this evil and sinister laugh coming from one of the dark corners of the room. It was the type of sound that made her heart stop and her blood run cold. *What the hell happened to me?* she thought as she tried to calm her mind and piece together her memory. From that same dark corner, Stacee heard the same voice describing the device that she was strapped to.

"The method of torture that you are about to go through is called the parrilla method. Its name means the cooking grill, or barbecue," he said. "It uses electric shock as a means of torture and can be extremely painful."

The name alone made Stacee's face turn white with fear. What was this man about to do to her? His voice sounded so familiar to her even though it was dark and much deeper than anything that she could remember. It belonged to a man, a man that Stacee knew but could not place. His voice frightened her to the depths of her soul and was a voice that was made for a horror film. As he approached her, Stacee still could not place him as his black hood shielded his face from her view. In his hands, Stacee noticed that he carried an electric rod as she tried to mentally prepare herself for the pain that she was about to go through. "This particular method of torture was meant to be both physical and psychological," he said with a laugh. In that moment, Stacee knew this man was pure evil and that her chances of escaping this nightmare were slim. With an electric rod in his hand, Stacee's torturer inserted a wetted steel wool pad inside of her that paralyzed her with even more fear.

Stacee screamed, cried, and begged him to not hurt her. He laughed while turning the dial on the voltage box and placed the electric rod on her feet. With the voltage at its lowest level, the pain was there, but it was bearable. He moved the rod all along Stacee's body touching her legs, bellybutton, arms, and even her nibbles. Once he was done with his first pass, the voltage was increased, and he started his torture all over again. With each pass, the pain that Stacee felt increased. Her muscles began to constrict so violently that her bones fractured in the process. She had never been in pain like this before, and the more she begged him to stop, the more he shocked her. Stacee's skin started to bruise and blister in areas where the rod was left for too long. Her torture was unbearable and felt like it was never going to end. The minutes felt like days, and eventually Stacee had taken all that she could take when she blacked out from the intense pain that she was put through. Almost on her deathbed, Stacee's torture at the hands of Kairo was far from over. This was only round one, and if she continued to please him, their fun would not end anytime soon. Kairo forced his blood down her throat to heal her body of all the damage he had caused. In time, she would heal, and they would move on to round two. So far Kairo was loving his newest little mouse.

One hour later Stacee woke up in another strange room in what could only be described as a basement. The room was dark and screamed danger. Stacee's head was spinning as if she had been drugged, and she had no memory of how she came to be here. The last thing she could remember was Kairo, but he could not have done this to her. Nothing about him gave Stacee any bad vibes. He came across as a gentleman, a man with a good heart, so there was no way he was behind this. Stacee was going to have to figure this out and fast. As far as she could tell, she was alone but for how much longer? Stacee was scared and frozen still to the floor. Once she found the strength, she ran from corner to corner only to realize that she was trapped. There were no doors, no windows, and no way of escaping this nightmare. Panicked, Stacee screamed for help at the top of her lungs hoping that someone would hear and come to her rescue. Somewhere deep in the shadows she heard her name. The voice was one that she had known and come to love. When she heard her name once more, she was positive that the voice had to belong to Kairo.

"Kairo, is that you?" she asked. Even though she was not one hundred percent sure, her gut was telling her that it was his voice that she was hearing. *What is going on, and why does he sound so different?* thought Stacee. She was greeted with a menacing laugh followed by the sound of claws scraping against the walls. Everything about this scene made her feel like she was trapped in a horror movie. Girls like her always died a very horrible death when they found themselves trapped in similar situations. "Okay, Kairo, you win, you scared me; now stop this, and let me out of this room."

Again, she heard this dark, menacing laughter coming from somewhere in the dark; then she saw his eyes. His beautiful golden amber eyes, but something was different about them. His eyes almost glowed in the dark, and his pupils had turned into diamond shaped slits. These were the eyes of a monster, a beautiful monster, but a monster all the same. Stacee was right, it was Kairo that had done this to her, but why? This was not the same Kairo she spent time with at I-Kandies. Something was not right; he had changed, and Stacee screamed until she found her voice again.

28

"W-w-w-what are you?"

"A vampire," he said as he laughed, and Stacee screamed again.

"Scream all you want, my little mouse, no one can hear you."

Kairo looked deep into Stacee's eyes, releasing her from his spell. It all came back to her, like a pool getting filled with water. The time they spent with each other at I-Kandies, the drive back to his house, the dance, and the wine. As much as she wanted to forget it, Stacee even remembered his torture of her through the parrilla method. She remembered everything, the pain it caused, the pain he caused her. Kairo clicked a button, and a door that was not there suddenly opened. "Run, my little mouse, run," he said, "make it to the end of the maze and earn your freedom back."

For the first time in her life, Stacee did not ask any questions or attempt to fight him. She did what she was told to do and ran as fast as her legs could carry her. Her only thought was making it to the end of the maze and hoping that Kairo would keep his word and grant her freedom. She knew it was not wise to trust this monster, but he literally held her freedom in the palms of his hands. Left, right, right, left, and left again, Stacee was making her way through the maze, but she could hear that Kairo was on her heels. Even walking, somehow, he was faster than she was, and he was still laughing. This was all a game to him. Everything he did and was planning to do to her was nothing more than a game to him.

That forced Stacee to run harder and faster trying with all she had to make it to the end of the maze before Kairo caught her. Just up ahead, Stacee could see her freedom; there it was, an open door and a clear shot to escaping this madness forever. Her freedom was just another 150 feet away, and she could taste it on the tip of her tongue. Twenty, fifteen, ten, just five more feet and she was free. Inches away from the door and escaping this nightmare forever, Stacee was violently pulled back into the darkness of the maze by her beautiful monster.

Kairo grabbed her, and in the process, he broke both of her arms while he dragged her back to the center of the maze. Kairo left Stacee in the center of the maze to watch in horror as he paced around her preparing to feast upon her inviting blood. Kairo licked his lips in anticipation of tasting her blood for the very first time. Scared, defenseless, and broken, Stacee screamed again. She screamed from pain; she screamed out of fear; she screamed until Kairo sank his fangs deep into her neck draining her of almost every drop of blood in her body.

The next day Stacee was awakened by the morning sun shining on her face. Her body had been healed. The pain in her arms was gone, and the bite marks on her neck had vanished. It was as if it had never happened, but it had happened. Stacee knew that it had; she remembered every horrible detail from her last encounter with Kairo. He had fangs; he had claws; he was not human; and that was an image that Stacee would never get out of her head. Kairo was a monster, a vampire, and this was all real. She could still feel his fangs against her neck as he plunged them deep into her draining the blood from her body. The sound of her bones being broken, her screams, and Kairo's laughter were all sounds that she would never be able to get out of her head. Those sounds were worse than any nightmare that she could have dreamed up.

For Kairo's next round of torture, Stacee found herself naked and chained to a brick wall with both her hands secured above her head. Stacee could only imagine what Kairo planned to do to her now. With each hour, her torture at the hands of her beautiful monster got worse by the day. Each time Stacee hoped that she could appeal to the human side of Kairo and convince him to let her go. She was no angel, but she did not deserve what Kairo was doing to her. No one did for that matter.

Kairo appeared before her just as handsome and beautiful as the first time she saw him. That sickened her. How could she still find him beautiful and handsome when he was a monster. After all the horrific things that he had already done to her, Stacee still wanted him. The sight of Kairo made her body betray her as she became wet and aroused by him. She knew that Kairo would never let her go, so she promised that if he stopped her torture, she would willingly stay with him. She promised that she would keep his secrets and stay loyal to him always if he would just stop hurting her. For a split second, Stacee's words caused Kairo to pause and think about her offer.

Should he keep her, she would be his blood slave allowing him to feed whenever he wanted. It had been a century or more since Kairo had a blood slave to feed on and torture on a regular basis. *Intriguing*, he thought until Malachi's words rang in his head. *Humans are experts in lying; they lie so well they lie like rugs.* No, letting Stacee go was not an option no matter what she said. Kairo laughed at her again. He would not be letting her go, not now, not ever.

Oh, how he loved his latest little mouse. Stacee was amazing; she screamed, she cried, and most of all, she feared him. Stacee relinquished all her power to Kairo, and now he barely had to lift a finger to make her fear him. The mere sight of him was enough to frighten her even though she still wanted him sexually. In that regard, Stacee was far from Kairo's type of woman. The only thing she was good for was her screams, and when she no longer pleased Kairo, her time with him would come to an end. When that time came, Stacee would become another one of Kairo's dead little mice.

After Stacee realized that begging was not going to stop Kairo's torture of her, she finally noticed the new device in his hands. It was one that looked scarier and ten times more painful than the last device. Stacee knew that she would never forget the pain that Kairo was about to put her through. "What is that? she asked. "What are you going to do with it?"

With a delightful look in his eyes, Kairo said, "This is a breast ripper, and I am sure you have figured out what it does."

Kairo looked into Stacee's scared eyes and laughed that same menacing and evil laugh at her. He was clearly enjoying every second of this game of his. Stacee was turning into one of his favorite mice, because she was so amusing to him. Walking closer to her, Kairo saw the excitement that his proximity brought to her. The thought of him touching her naked body excited her. Thinking about having his hands all over her body made Stacee forget all about the device that he was holding. Kairo reached out and gently grabbed and caressed Stacee's left breast in his hands. He stroked her nipple, making it hard and stand out at attention. His hands were like magic casting spells of arousal all through Stacee's body. She wanted more than Kairo's hands on her body; she wanted to feel his mouth on her rock-hard nipples as well.

Stacee hated and loved the way Kairo could make her feel with just a simple touch. "Such a beauty," he said as he continued to massage and caress her breast with his hands. He thought about taking it into his mouth and the pleasure it would give to her. Unfortunately, Kairo did not bring Stacee here for sexual gratification. At his touch, she moaned in pleasure wanting more from him. Kairo let his hands slide down her body stopping just below her belly button. He enjoyed the thoughts that were running through Stacee's mind. She wanted him to go further and touch her pleasure center, making her explode. Stacee had this primal need for him, but he denied her at every turn.

This was all part of his sick and twisted game. He wanted to give Stacee as much pleasure as he could before the pain broke her in two. With Stacee fully aroused, Kairo had her right where he wanted her. With her on the edge, the time had come to push her over it with pain and not pleasure. Taking the device in his hands, Kairo clamped it securely around Stacee's breast.

To ease her pain and take her mind off the device, Kairo kissed her before he ripped her lovely left breast from her body. Kairo did the same exact thing to Stacee's right breast, caressing and playing with it before ripping it completely from her body. The pain was unlike anything that she had ever experienced before. She prayed to never experience that level of pain again. Being chained to the wall prevented Stacee's lifeless body from collapsing to the cold, hard floor beneath her. Kairo watched as she slowly bled to death from both of her severe wounds. Her body became Kairo's canvas, and her blood was the paint that created an irresistible picture for him to gaze upon. Kairo had to control the monster inside of him since he wanted to devour the artwork that was in front of him. This game was not about feeding; it was only about breaking Stacee's spirit and will to live. Before she took her final breath, Kairo forced his blood down her throat as he had done several times before. His blood was sweet and tasted better each time she was forced to drink from him. As the healing process was underway, Stacee was unchained and taken over to a bed where she was free to sleep until the next time that Kairo was ready to play.

Over the course of a week, Stacee lost count of the number of times that she was tortured at the hands of her beautiful monster. Day after day, Kairo did something new and equally horrible to her. He had so many different devices that Stacee lost count of them all. Each day he would break her body, her spirit, and her will to live repeatedly. Kairo loved having Stacee around, and at times he played with her more than once a day. The Heretic's Fork was one device that Stacee hated. The torture it brought was more psychological than it was physical. The physical torture Stacee could deal with, because she had no control over it. It was the psychological torture that was the worse for her.

The Heretic's Fork depended on her keeping her head up to prevent the prongs from stabbing her in the throat. For three days straight Stacee was not able to sleep as she wore the device if she wanted to avoid killing herself. Just when she had taken all that she could take, Kairo came and released her from the device. He acted as if he was her knight in shining armor coming to save her from the monster that was him. That never stopped Stacee from pleading with him to let her go and ending this nightmare she was trapped in. Every time she got the same response from him: "But why, my little mouse, when we are having so much fun?" The next day was always the same, a new device and a new way for Kairo to break her only to have the opportunity to put her back together again. Kairo would take the pain away and heal her body, but the scars and the memories would last a lifetime. If Kairo wanted to be nice, he would have made her forget all about the monstrous things that he had done to her, but he never did. No matter what Kairo said or did, he was cruel.

Stacee did not know how much more of this she could take. Kairo was successful in breaking more than her body. He had broken her spirit and her will to live. If death was the only way to end this, then Stacee prayed for death every single day. Once, she came close to ending it all herself. Kairo had become distracted and did not secure her to the bed as he had done every time before. With so much of his blood in her system, Stacee was healing incredibly fast after her torture on the rack. She was free to move around for forty-five minutes, and during that time she got her hands on a spike, which she tried to use to end her suffering. With Kairo's heightened senses, he became aware of Stacee's movements and was there in time to save her like he always did so that he could continue his twisted cat-and-mouse game.

CHAPTER 4

That Feeling Again

I kissed him; I kissed him, and I liked it, Skylar thought as she and Angelina rushed out of Bad Dragon. *This is going to be all kinds of bad,* she thought. Something changed, and Skylar had fun with Dimitri tonight, but to kiss him was not good. Dimitri had proven to Skylar that he could be fun to hang out with when he kept his attitude in check. After that kiss, Skylar was positive that she felt nothing for him. Dimitri was not her type, and they were better off as friends. Skylar hoped that her slip up would not come back to bite her in the ass and cause her more problems. The truth was she just allowed her want for a man to get the best of her. After kissing Dimitri, sparks did not fly between them. While walking back to the train, Angelina was also wondering why Skylar had kissed Dimitri. Curiosity had gotten the best of her, and she needed to get some answers.

"Why did you kiss Dimitri?"

Before answering, Skylar thought hard about the answer to that question and all she could come up with was "I was drunk." They both knew that was a lie and a poor excuse of an answer. "No, really explain what happened, Skylar."

"Honestly, Angie, I have no clue; I think that I just got caught up in the moment. It has been a while since I was with a man, and when Dimitri kissed me, he turned into Mr. Right Now, and in that split second, I wanted him."

Angelina had to be missing something. There was no way that Skylar was saying what she thought she was saying. "Wait one minute, are you trying to tell me that a part of you wanted to have sex with Dimitri, Dimitri Huntington, the same Dimitri that annoys the hell out of you every time you see him?"

"Yes, Angie, that is exactly what I am telling you. When Dimitri kissed me, it was nice, and for a split second, I wanted things to go further until I realized the full scope of my actions. Once I was able to clear my head of the fog, I knew how much of a bad idea that would have been. You and I both know that I was not drunk at all. I know that I cannot have casual no-strings-attached sex with Dimitri."

Skylar knew that going down that road would be a huge mistake and that one kiss had the power to derail their friendship.

Skylar knew this was going to end badly, but she hoped that Dimitri would not read too much into that kiss. A huge part of her knew that he would believe that their kiss meant more to her than it really did and that their friendship was going to suffer. That kiss was a huge mistake, and before the four of them hung out again, it had to get straightened out. Skylar and Dimitri were going to have an exceptionally long and intense conversation about what that kiss meant and did not mean to them. Angelina was curious about another aspect of their kiss.

"Is he a good kisser?"

Before Skylar could answer, she had to wipe the smirk off her face. "I knew you were going to ask me that, but yes, he is a great kisser; it's just that it was not the weak-in-the-knees type of kiss for me."

Skylar did not know what it was, but when it came to love and romance, she was trapped in a book. She wanted to feel butterflies in the pit of her stomach when she kissed the man that she was destined to be with. Dimitri was not her fairy tale, and Skylar was done talking about that kiss and stressing over her potential problem with him. Skylar needed to change the subject and put the spotlight on Angelina.

"So, putting my mess aside, what about you and James? The two of you were inseparable all night, and I could tell that you were smitten with him." Angelina blushed a little when Skylar brought up her and James.

"He is cute, and I really enjoyed talking to him, and I want to get to know him better."

"Good," said Skylar, "because if Dimitri and I can clear this situation up, we are planning to hang out again and I told him to bring James with him."

Angelina had the biggest smile plastered on her face when she said, "Thanks, Skylar, but you know this is not going to end well with you and Dimitri."

With a heavy sigh Skylar said, "I know," shaking her head. "This is going to be a disaster." Skylar knew that this was all kinds of bad, but she would find a way to fix things for Angelina's sack. Under no circumstance did she want their situation or Dimitri's attitude to prevent Angelina and James from having something real.

A second later the train showed up, stopping their conversation. Angelina was the first one to get on the train when Skylar was stopped dead in her tracks. There it was again, that same pull of energy wanting her to move towards the City Center and, most likely, I-Kandies. It was as if the energy was calling out to her, but there was too much interference, making it hard for her to hear it. The signal was fuzzy, as if they were on two different frequencies and the only way for Skylar to hear it clearly was for her to move towards it. Skylar had to know what the energy was and why it was calling out to her.

Without thinking or saying anything to Angelina, Skylar turned away from the train station and ran towards the pull of energy. She was unaware of everything around her except for the force that was pulling at her. There was no way that she could ignore it or deny what she was feeling. Skylar pushed herself to run faster because she had to know what it was. As soon as she reached the City Center, the energy had vanished into thin air. It was as if it was all a dream, but Skylar knew what she felt, and it was real it had to be real. One minute the energy was there, and the next minute it was gone. Skylar had no idea why this continued to happen to her, but she felt as if she was starting to lose her mind.

Now thanks to that strange pull of energy, she had missed her train and had to wait ten minutes until the next one came. The whole time Angelina was calling her like crazy trying to make sure she was okay and to find out what the hell had just happened. Her face and body language scared Angelina half to death, and she needed to know that her best friend was okay. Skylar finally answered Angelina's calls putting her mind at ease. She was thankful that her best friend was safe and still alive. Immediately Skylar filled Angelina in on everything that happened, including what she was feeling.

Skylar could not let that feeling go and finally gave into her need to go to I-Kandies, where this entire crazy night all started. For some unknown reason, the universe was pushing her towards that club. The big question was why, what, or who was inside that Skylar needed to connect with. At 2 A.M. the City Center and I-Kandies were still packed, but the source of the energy was gone. There was no buzz of energy, no butterflies, no connection at all. Everything was gone, and there was nothing that Skylar could do about it. Since being forced back to the City Center, she decided to venture inside hoping to make some sense out of what was happening.

A part of Skylar wanted the source of her strange vibes to still be inside of the club even though she was certain that it was gone. Skylar hoped that maybe something was blocking the force of the energy from her and that it was still inside that building. At the very least, she could get a drink or two to help settle down her nerves since she was shaking like a leaf. The source of the energy was gone, but the atmosphere inside the club was still off. What or whoever was giving off that energy had been inside I-Kandies for a good amount of time. After two drinks, things started to settle down again, and Skylar was calmer as everything slowly returned to normal. When she was positive that nothing was going to happen, she grabbed her phone and walked back to the train, or so she thought.

Skylar thought that everything was back to normal, but she was sadly mistaken. The universe was not done with her yet because she had one more particularly important stop to make. As Skylar was lost in thought with her mind on her most recent episodes, she failed to notice that her feet were taking her far away from the train station. She continued to blindly walk through the streets until she stopped in front of the Historic Settlers Cemetery and had no clue why or how she ended up there. *This is so strange, why am I here*, she thought while looking around trying to piece together what just happened.

Skylar was completely disorientated, and while she was standing at the entrance of the cemetery, it all started to happen again. That same hum of energy she felt for the first time in New Orleans was back. Skylar was both intrigued and thrilled by the energy as it slowly started affecting her entire body. For weeks now Skylar hoped that she would be able to experience that feeling again, and now she was. She knew without a shadow of a doubt that what happened in New Orleans was one hundred percent real. That same undeniable force reached out and touched her waking up every part of her body. With everything in her, Skylar tried to ignore the energy now that she knew that it was real, but it was strong and had a mind of its own. In the beginning what Skylar felt was nothing more than a tingle in her fingers that felt electric and alive. The energy grabbed a hold of her and would not let go forcing her to bend to its will. Skylar was left with no other choice than to let the energy guide her into the cemetery.

After taking a deep breath, she was ready to face whatever this experience was going to bring. Under the glow of the full moon, Skylar walked further into the cemetery while the pull of energy became stronger and stronger. What started out as a small tingle in her hands quickly consumed her entire body becoming a power unlike anything she had ever felt before. Skylar allowed it to drive her, guiding her through the cemetery. As the power grew stronger, she also grew stronger, and in a matter of minutes, she felt connected to the world around her. Skylar felt the energy in everything from the ground to the trees, and even the moon. She closed her eyes and let the power of the earth wrap itself around her, guiding her blindly around each grave. Each headstone became a beacon lighting her way along a dark and twisted path.

This experience was the most incredible feeling of Skylar's life. This time she was not afraid of what she was feeling and welcomed it with open arms. Not only could she see the world in high definition, but she could draw power from the moon. She was so in tune with nature that she could sense the flock of birds that were swooping around her. Eventually her walk along the dark path came to an end when she was left standing in front of a massive headstone at the back of the cemetery. Everything that Skylar had experienced was silenced by the energy that this headstone was giving off. She was completely electrified because this was where she needed to be.

Reaching out, Skylar placed her hands on the stone, and it was warm to the touch like it was alive. When she slid her hands over the etched letters of the name, a force unlike anything she had felt knocked her off her feet. When Skylar came to, she was in a different world during a different time.

Skylar was no longer in the Historic Settlers Cemetery. She awoke in a hospital with a woman crouched in a corner of the room. Rocking back and forth, she kept saying "They are real" over and over.

In mid-sentence she stopped speaking, looked directly at Skylar, and said, "Do not let them do to you what they did to me; we are one and the same. You must make them accept who they truly are." Skylar reached her hand out to touch the woman when everything faded away and she was whisked back through time.

When Skylar opened her eyes, she realized that she was back in the cemetery. *What was that?* she thought. *Who was that?* Skylar's head was foggy, and the overwhelming sense of power she felt was gone. It was as if it was all a dream, but Skylar knew what she felt was real. She would never make that mistake again. From this day forward, she vowed to never doubt herself again. Apart from what she was feeling, Skylar had bigger questions that needed to be answered like who was that woman? *Why did she say that to me, and more importantly, who am I supposed to make accept who they were?* thought Skylar.

Just out of the corner of her eye, Skylar finally noticed whose gravesite she had been standing in front of. Skylar could not believe her eyes and was sure this was still a dream. It sounded silly, but she had to pinch herself to make sure it was real. There it was right there in front of her, *Ester Annabelle Montgomery.*

The headstone that was the cause of all of this belonged to a Montgomery. Who was this woman? Skylar had never heard her name before. This woman did not exist in her family tree. The grave was over one hundred years old, but someone cared for it, loved this woman even still today. They took good care of it; the name was still visible, and there were fresh flowers placed on it. Unlike the other equally old gravesites, Ester still had family here in Charlotte who loved and cared for her. Skylar knew deep down inside of her that Ester was family, although her name had never been mentioned. It all made perfect sense; this was why she was drawn to this cemetery and this gravesite.

Curious, very curious, thought Skylar as she grabbed her bag from the ground and raced home. Armed with this new information, Skylar had a direction to explore in her quest to uncover what was happening to her. What other mysteries were hiding in the Montgomery family tree, and what part did Ester Annabelle Montgomery play in all of this?

CHAPTER 5

The Montgomery Family Tree

Nestled back at home, Skylar was exhausted and tried her best to put what happened at the cemetery behind her for now. The entire experience was unreal and crazy, but she was determined to find out why Ester was deliberately erased from the Montgomery family tree and what else her family was hiding from her. Between her late night out and her ordeal at the cemetery, it was late in the morning when Skylar was able to crawl into bed, but sleep did not come easy. Every time she closed her eyes, she was taken back to that mental hospital in a dream that seemed more like a nightmare. The scene was always the same. Ester was always the same, scared and crouched in the corner begging Skylar to make them admit to who they truly were. Whom Ester was talking about was a mystery to Skylar but one that she promised herself that she was going to solve. Skylar would not stop until the truth was uncovered no matter what, even if it tainted the Montgomery image.

When Skylar finally dragged herself out of the bed, the morning was long gone. Once her eyes opened, she realized that she was more tired and exhausted than when she went to sleep. In a matter of seconds, she was aware that nothing had changed. Between her ongoing, unexplainable dreams and dreaming of Ester, she tossed and turned all morning long. Even now the mystery that was

Ester Montgomery continued to be at the forefront of her mind. Curiosity had gotten the best of her because she was not let in on the family secrets. Skylar would not be kept in the dark any longer. It was time for her to be let into the loop. There was only one place for her to start her search, at Montgomery Manor, her childhood family home. The enormous library inside the manor contained everything pertaining to the Montgomery family. Every hospital record or news article that mentioned a Montgomery could be found tucked away in a book or folder in the library. As Skylar pulled into the driveway, she knew that beyond those walls were the answers that she was looking for.

Skylar took the stairs two at a time and hurried to the library hoping to get this mission completed before her parents caught wind of why she was there and what she was looking for. Having never heard the name before, Skylar knew getting the truth from her parents was not going to be easy. Her mother Estelle and father Jericho were extremely tight lipped when it came to matters of the family that they did not want anyone to know. This mission to uncover the truth had to stay a secret until Skylar was armed with proof that what she was saying was factual. Skylar meticulously searched through every document and piece of paper that she could find, but there was no mention of Ester in any of the files.

No birth certificate, no death certificate, no records of any kind making a reference to an Ester Annabelle Montgomery. Either Skylar was wrong, and Ester was not a member of the family, or her existence had been erased. The problem was that Skylar felt a connection to this woman. Therefore, she had to be family, and that meant someone went to great lengths to remove every trace of Ester from the family. The million-dollar question was why? What could Ester have done, said, or knew that made the family lock her away and literally throw away the key. The Montgomery's were all about family and togetherness, and what they did to Ester did not make any sense at all.

Why would someone eliminate her paper trail but leave her headstone in place? None of this made any sense at all to Skylar. Ester had been dead for over one hundred years now, but someone was aware of her existence. Ester's grave was pristine, the limestone was clean, and the engraving was fresh. Her headstone was not one that was neglected and forgotten like so many others. It was cared for and loved by someone who honored and respected her memory. Nearing the end of her search, Skylar was interrupted by her mother.

Estelle had married into the Montgomery family, and since she was the lady of the house, she took over the family history. As the oldest brother, Jericho was the heir to the family and inherited the family fortune as well as the family secrets. Estelle may have not been the one to remove Ester from the family records, but with any luck, she could help. Estelle had to know something about Ester, or at the very least she could confirm that Ester was real. With that thought in mind, Skylar was glad to see her mother. She had some questions she needed answered, and it was time to let the cat out of the bag. It needed to be known that someone else knew about Ester.

Estelle was surprised to find her daughter searching through the family records. It was not like Skylar to come by unannounced, but Estelle was pleased to see her daughter all the same. "Hey Sky, what on earth are you here looking for, honey?"

This was Skylar's chance to finally get the truth. She did not know how to open that door, and thankfully, her mother just made it easy for her.

"Hi Mom, I was looking into the family tree and could not find anything about an Ester Annabelle Montgomery. What can you tell me about her?"

That name shocked Estelle. The face she made told Skylar that she knew exactly who she was talking about. Skylar had been right; Ester was family and was intentionally removed from the histories. With a straight face and the intention to keep Ester a secret, Estelle looked Skylar in the eye and lied to her face. "Honey, I have no idea who that is. Where did you hear that name?"

The lie was written all over Estelle's face, and Skylar saw right through it. Since her mother was going to lie, so would Skylar. "Last night I went on a haunted ghost tour of the Fourth Ward and stumbled upon her headstone," stated Skylar.

"Interesting, well, I have never heard the name before, but happy hunting," said Estelle before leaving Skylar to her search. Skylar had all the ammunition she needed now that her mother had confirmed there was a story here. Skylar was more determined than ever to uncover this family secret.

Skylar's trip home was not a complete waste of time. Thanks to her mother, she knew she was on the right trail. Skylar left the house knowing for sure that Ester was a real person and a Montgomery after all. All Skylar needed was one piece of physical proof, and for that, she was going to need some help. Her mother may have been the keeper of the physical records, but it was her

Aunt Arie who was the real bone collector of the family. If there was a story here, and Skylar was positive that there was a story, her Aunt Arie was the one to go to. Before Skylar could even approach her aunt with the many questions she had, she needed to have actual proof first.

For Skylar to get to the bottom of this mystery, she was going to need the help of her brilliant and amazing friend who studied genealogy. As soon as Skylar was away from the house, she called Angelina for her help. Ester may have been erased from the records in the library, but there had to be some proof of her existence out there. The Montgomery name came with a great deal of money, power, and privilege but hopefully not enough to eliminate Ester's actual paper trail. Angelina had access to websites and materials that Skylar did not. Hopefully, she would find the proof Skylar needed to approach her aunt with. After explaining the situation to Angelina, she was thrilled to help and promised Skylar to come over as soon as she found something helpful.

Back at home, Skylar poured herself a glass of Moscato and relaxed into her favorite chair to wait for news from Angelina. While waiting, Skylar needed to keep her mind busy and did an Ancestory.com search hoping to learn something new. Again, her search came up empty. According to the universe, Ester did not exist and Skylar was having another crazy episode. Until she heard back from Angelina, there was nothing that she could do about her Ester problem. While Skylar could not fix that problem, she still needed to have an important conversation with Dimitri about the kiss that they shared.

Knowing Dimitri, he was going to find a way to upset her, so it was best that she finished her glass of wine before calling him. With more time to think Skylar knew that kiss was a bad idea, and that Dimitri was not going to take what she had to say about it well. They did not share any sparks, and it was best that they remain good friends. Hopefully, they would be able to find some common ground and put that night behind them and move on in a positive way. Then again, Skylar was talking about Dimitri, the same Dimitri who never listened to anyone and believed that he was always right. In true Dimitri fashion, he did not answer his phone. It would not have been a surprise to Skylar if he was screening his calls and did not answer her call on purpose. He had to know that she would have different feelings about that kiss. So far Skylar had two problems without any solutions. It seemed as if the only thing that she had to look forward to was more waiting. Hopefully, Angelina would come through quickly with the information that she uncovered.

It was two and a half hours later when Angelina pulled up to Skylar's house. The entire time, she was anxious and on pins and needles waiting for Angie to spill the beans. *What was she about to say?* thought Skylar. This was the perfect time for Angelina to make her suffer and see her sweat. Angelina took her sweet time walking into the living room where she made herself comfortable before allowing Skylar to know what she had uncovered. After having her fun, Angelina was ready to lay everything out on the table for Skylar. The mystery behind who Ester was had been uncovered and was about to be solved.

> *According to birth records that I found, there was an Ester Anna-belle Montgomery that was born to Wallace and Clara Montgom-ery in 1902. She grew up right here in Charlotte living in what is now the historic Dilworth Area. The trail soon runs cold; there is no mention of an Ester anywhere until she was admitted into Dorothea Dix Mental Health Hospital in 1917 in Raleigh, North Carolina. From what little records that were found, Ester was hos-pitalized for two years before her death in 1919. Her records were mostly blank only having her name and age at the top. There was no information on how or why she died. Once she enters the hospi-tal, she vanishes off the face of the earth forever.*

Skylar thought back to the gravesite she found; it was clear that someone loved and cared for this woman. The one takeaway she got from all of this was that Ester was family. Angelina had armed her with the proof that she needed to finally get the real story of who this woman was and what caused her downfall. Clara and Wallace were her great-grandparents, that was a fact. Armed now with actual proof, it was time for Skylar to find out what her aunt could tell her about Ester. The cat was out of the bag. Skylar knew who Ester was, and now she wanted the full story.

Skylar thanked Angelina for all her hard work, but this next part of the journey she had to do alone. It was time for Skylar to give her aunt a call. Aurora Montgomery was the middle sister to Skylar's father Jericho. Aurora and Skylar were the best of friends. They were more like sisters than aunt and niece, and Skylar was the only one to call her Arie. In the past Skylar could talk to Aurora about anything and hoped that easiness would continue today. Skylar had already been lied to by her own mother and hoped that things would be different with her Aunt Arie. This secret had been buried for far too long now, and it was time to shine a spotlight on it. Left with no other choice, Skylar grabbed her phone and called her favorite relative. After only three rings the phone was answered.

"Hey, Aunt Arie," said Skylar.

"Hey baby, what's wrong?" That was just like her Aunt Arie, she always had a sixth sense about things. It was unreal the way she could always pick up on Skylar's moods no matter how hard she tried to hide them. Her aunt had a way of always being able to pick up on the distress in her voice. "Nothing, Auntie, I am good. I just have a question to ask you. What happened to Great-Grandpa Wallace's daughter Ester?" There was a pause on the line before Aunt Arie started to speak again.

Oh, well, she was the oldest daughter to your great-grandparents Wallace and Clara, as you may already know. As the story goes, she was a happy and beautiful baby who grew into a well-rounded, beautiful young woman. She met this man; Charles was his name, and he was a perfect match for her. He fell madly in love with Ester and asked her father for her hand in marriage, which was granted. They were supposed to be married the summer of 1916, but things took a turn for the worse. Ester claimed that she started to feel different, like she had powers. She claimed that she was a witch. Everyone tried to talk to her, make her see reason, but she was not having any of that. She was certain in what she felt was real, and nobody was going to change her mind. Charles was still willing to stay with her and marry her until she started claiming that monsters were real. Apparently, Ester thought her new neighbors were vampires. She even claimed to have seen the male feeding from a woman one night. To the family and to Charles, Ester was completely crazy and needed more help than they could provide. They tried to get her the help that she needed by sending her away to a mental hospital, but she never changed. She always stuck to her truth that monsters were real and that she had these powers. Once in the hospital, the family left her there, forgetting all about her. While there, she contracted influenza and died in 1919. The family wanted nothing to do with her and went as far as erasing her from the family records with the hope that she would never be spoken of again. She had become a total embarrassment to the family name, and that could not be tolerated.

"How did you find out about her?" In the spirit of secrecy, Skylar did not want to tell her aunt the truth, so she told her the same lie that she told her mother, that she had seen the headstone while on a ghost tour of the Fourth Ward. Skylar told Arie that she assumed that Ester was family because they shared the same last name. Based on that thinking, she asked Angelina for help and uncovered the family connection. Skylar thanked her aunt for the information, told her that she loved her, and hung up the phone.

At last Skylar had learned the true story behind who Ester was and what happened to her. Skylar promised herself that from that day forward, Ester would not be neglected by their family. While Skylar was happy to have learned the truth, she was also extremely worried. Her and Ester's lives were similar, too similar for her liking. Like Ester, Skylar had been sensing a power and an energy that was not normal. While what was happening to her was strange and new, she was not comfortable with the idea that she was a witch. Witches were not real, no matter how much she loved the supernatural world. To admit to that was going entirely off the rails, and that was a stretch, even for Skylar. It was true that she was a bit odd and feeling this strange energy, but that was where the similarities between her and Ester ended.

Skylar understood why her family sent Ester away. The Montgomery image was everything, and they would not allow anyone family included to ruin their name. Until Skylar understood what was going on with her, she was going to have to be incredibly careful. If she was not careful, the same fate that awaited Ester would become her fate as well. Skylar's mother loved her deeply, but she was a ruthless woman when it came to protecting the family name. That made Skylar think about her most recent actions. Was she already an embarrassment to the family name with her obsession with the supernatural world? Did her obsession put a giant target on her back, and would her family really lock her up and throw away the key? From now on Skylar was going to have to keep her strange happenings and her obsession to herself. For her safety and survival, she was going to have to downplay her love for a world that did not exist. It was past time for Skylar to stop living in her dark fairy tale world.

CHAPTER 6
Monsters Among Us

Monday morning brought with it a new day and a new Skylar. After everything that she learned about Ester, she was finally ready to leave her obsession with the supernatural world in her rearview mirror. It was past time for her to get back to normal. Hopefully if she did not focus on all the strange happenings in her life, they would just go away. Looking to be normal again, Skylar was ready to dive back into the work that was waiting for her at the morgue. The weekend was not only a crazy one for her but just a crazy weekend in general. In the wake of all the craziness, Skylar had four new bodies waiting for her at the morgue. It was nice to have something normal to turn her attention towards. The first three bodies were simple, cut, and dry. All three males were murdered in what Skylar could only describe as a crime of passion. All three bodies had over fifty different stab wounds of various depths with a straight-edged blade. The cause of death was a homicide, and the killers were most likely females that were connected to each of the male victims. Based on the evidence, the females in question became so enraged by something that they stabbed their lovers until every ounce of anger left their bodies. After quickly gathering all the vital evidence, Skylar cleaned up and moved onto the final body that was going to need more of her attention.

Immediately Skylar knew that something was off with the fourth body. The look and feel of her John Doe was completely off. On her initial examination, Skylar noticed that the body was void of any death related trauma. There were no stab wounds, gunshot wounds, or any punctures of any kind that would result in the death of this man. Without cutting into the body, it appeared that he died from natural causes. Skylar, who was a young medical examiner, never made rash decisions. Where all signs were pointing to natural causes, something was telling her that she was wrong and that this man did not die in this way.

In Skylar's morgue it was common practice that nothing was ever assumed, even in cases where it was obvious what the cause of death was. Every corpse that came through her morgue was put through an intensive checklist from A to Z making sure that nothing was missed. For a man of his size, Skylar quickly noticed that the weight was off. Her best guess was that this body was missing a significant amount of blood, which likely caused his death. Had Skylar relied on her initial exam, she would have missed some vital information that could have been used to solve his murder. Skylar knew for certain that it was impossible for a body to be exsanguinated without leaving behind a mark on the body. *So how could it be that this body felt as if it were missing a significant amount of blood?* she thought. After completing her second search of the body, the results were still the same. Skylar could not find one mark that spoke to how he had been exsanguinated.

It was not her imagination; it appeared that this body was free of any marks, wounds, or punctures. *There must be a mark on the body*, she thought, *even a fictional character like a vampire would leave some type of mark on the body*. Just thinking that word *vampire* was enough to derail Skylar's entire thought process. *Could it be?* she thought. *A vampire could drain a human body quickly, but could it be done without leaving a mark?* That line of thinking made Skylar go back over the body for a third time. This time she was looking for fang marks or anything that would confirm the existence of vampires or another fictional character. This body was throwing her in a tailspin; one minute she was back to normal, and then the next she was traveling back down the road to crazy town. *Crazy town, Ester*, no, Skylar could not allow herself to fall back into that trap knowing what her family did to Ester. It was flat out crazy to think that vampires were real.

Skylar was not willing to let her imagination get the best of her. She was determined to find the true cause of death because vampires were not the answer. They were not real no matter how much she fantasized about them being real. As she examined the body for a third time, she looked at every detail no matter how small or insignificant it was. On that third search, with the help of a magnifying glass, Skylar discovered tiny single punctures along the legs and one set of parallel marks on the right foot of her John Doe. The marks were subtle and easy to miss if you were not looking for them. With a closer look, Skylar discovered slight bruising around each of the punctures to the skin from what she believed to be repeated needle use. Without running a tox screen, she could not say for certain that the needle marks were associated with drug use or something else. Based on the size and shape of each puncture, Skylar believed that one or multiple twenty-five-gauge needles were used repeatedly to drain or inject something in the victim's legs and feet. Skylar hoped the marks were from some type of drug use. Any other outcome would have sent her falling down the rabbit hole again. When the tox screen came back clean, Skylar was back on the crazy train. There was no real reason for a human to use several needles to drain the blood from a body.

Immediately Skylar's brain took her down a path that she did not want to go. The parallel marks on the foot were the ones giving her the most trouble. To a super fan like Skylar, the parallel punctures screamed vampire bites. Everyone knew that vampires favored the carotid artery in the neck and not the arteries in the feet. From Skylar's medical training, she knew of several major and minor arteries that carried oxygenated blood from the heart to the legs and feet. The dorsalis pedis artery would work as a replacement artery for vampires to feed from. It made sense to Skylar that if vampires were real, they would change their habits to stay hidden in plain sight. Puncture wounds on the neck, like what you see in movies, would cause a believer to think vampires were real, but not on the feet.

Skylar just so happened to think on a different wavelength than others. This was all starting to sound crazy to her. This was bad, and she knew it, but she could not stop herself from going down that road. It was just yesterday that she had promised herself that she was putting crazy on the bus and leaving it there. Now she could not be sure if the wounds were from a needle, fangs, or both. She was spiraling out of control fast. In truth, what did she really know about vampires?

Everything Skylar knew about vampires came from the many movies she watched and from the fictional books she read. Vampires were creatures created for scary stories and intended to keep people up at night. Skylar never knew where those myths and ideas came from, but she was sure that vampires were not real. She had no way of knowing what was real and what was not. As of right now, everything that she was thinking was pure speculation. It was all starting to be too much for her to handle and was giving her a massive headache. Skylar was a scientist; she followed and trusted facts, not myths and stories. Right now, all she was doing was letting her delusions of grandeur get the best of her. The only way she was going to get a clear picture of what happened was to open this man up. This entire time all she was doing was letting her imagination run wild. She had to focus on the facts that were in front of her and nothing else. What Skylar needed was some time away from the situation and some lunch to help clear her head.

Skylar was wrong; eating lunch did not help to clear her mind at all. Her brain kept flashing to images of vampires gently breaking the skin on the feet of their victims to feed and then using needles to drain them dry. Since lunch was not helping, Skylar was done eating. She could no longer let her mind wonder, and she needed real answers. It was time to prove to herself that this was not a vampire killing. After performing the standard Y incision into the chest and cracking the body open, Skylar learned that she was correct in her previous assessment. Her John Doe was drained of two-thirds of his blood supply, which was the cause of his death. Removing some of the skin around the wounds of the feet and legs, Skylar was able to determine that the marks were, in fact, from a needle. She was relieved to learn that the marks were from needles and that her crazy vampire theory was not correct. Whoever this killer was, he had some serious patience to drain a body in this manner. That made Skylar wonder if this was the first time a body was killed in this way. If she found another body killed like this one, that could mean that there was a serial killer on the loose in her beloved city, or something worse. A serial killer could go on killing this way for years and never get caught. Skylar almost missed the signs herself, as the bruising was minimal and almost hidden to the naked eye.

With both exams completed, Skylar started looking through old records to see if another body came in with similar wounds like her male. After searching through a couple of records, Skylar found not one but two more bodies like her male victim six months ago. One female victim and one male victim with the same type of needle marks on their legs and feet. The bruising was the same, small and minimal, and would have been missed if you were not looking for it. According to the previous medical examiner, Dr. Hayes, the cause of death was a heart attack in both cases, but he never noted any damage to the heart muscle. Dr. Hayes also made no mention of the puncture marks on the legs of either victim.

Now that Skylar knew what to look for there was no mistaking the wounds anymore. It was strange that Dr. Hayes would not check the heart when ruling that the cause of death was a heart attack. Not willing to let this go, Skylar searched through all of Dr. Hayes' records. He only worked for the morgue for two years before he quit without any notice. Skylar may have been young and new to the job, but she was aware that Dr Hayes' reports were wrong and missing some important information. In the two years he ran the morgue, Skylar uncovered the death of twelve men and women in the same manner. The cause of death in every case was listed as heart attacks or "natural causes."

Thankfully for her Dr. Hayes took the required photos of each body since all the remains were cremated. In every photo Skylar noticed the same type of bruising in the same exact spot along the legs and feet of each body. In each case Skylar assumed that the slight bruising came from the same repeated use of a twenty-five-gauge needle. There was no more denying it; the pattern was staring her right in the face. Every two months there was one male and one female victim that was found clothed among the trash in different neighborhoods all throughout the city. They all had similar bruising, and Skylar could only guess that they all were missing a significant amount of blood. In every case Dr. Hayes did a basic exam and ruled that each person died from natural causes. With the help of Facebook, Skylar was able to question the case of death in a few of the victims. It was clear that they were in the best shape of their lives; they ate right and exercised on a regular basis. Based on their social media pages, it was hard to believe they died from a heart attack.

Each report read the exact same. It was as if all Dr. Hayes did was change the date, gender, and body location of each victim. Skylar could not believe what she was looking at. She was positive that she had uncovered a serial killer in Charlotte. From the look of things, Dr. Hayes was trying to cover it up until he just left the job. *But why would he help cover up these murders and then just leave the job?* thought Skylar. As bad as having a serial killer on the loose was, it was better than the alternative, unless the serial killer was not human. *How on earth would I stop a nonhuman serial killer?* The loss of blood was still upsetting Skylar; what was a human doing with all that blood? Not knowing what was happening to the blood kept the vampire angel alive and well in the back of her mind. She kept imagining an incredibly old vampire drinking the blood from a crystal goblet. No matter what Skylar did, she could not get that image out of her head.

Skylar could not get a clear image of what was going on because her picture had some major holes in it. If she was going to get the entire picture of what was truly happening, she was going to need some help. Good thing for her she knew a detective on the force, even if he was annoying and drove her crazy. Dimitri had to be informed of this and soon, because somewhere in the city there might be a killer on the loose. If the killer kept to the same pattern, that meant a woman was next in line to die by his hands. After making copies of all the reports for Dimitri, Skylar rushed over to the station to inform him of what she found. Like herself, Dimitri could not believe what he was reading and the implications that it was making. Was there truly a serial killer in Charlotte? Dimitri thanked Skylar for the files and for letting him know what she had found out. Just before Skylar walked away from him, Dimitri made his move.

"So, you owe me a date, Skylar," he said. Calling it a date was a bit too formal for Skylar. She did promise to see him again, and she wanted Angelina and James to get better acquainted. Even now, Dimitri was being his best self. Skylar thought she would reward his good behavior and give him what he wanted.

"Fine, Dimitri, we can hang out again," she said, "but first we have to talk about that kiss."

Dimitri was all smiles. "Yes, that kiss was amazing. I think that we should do that more often," he said.

Skylar knew that kiss was going to bite her in the ass. "No, Dimitri, that kiss should not have happened; it was a mistake, and we are just friends and nothing more."

Dimitri walked closer to Skylar. "Are you sure about that, Skylar? You look like you want to kiss me now."

"I am sure, Dimitri; we had fun, and I want to keep my word and hang out again, but you have to understand that WE ARE JUST FRIENDS," she said while screaming at the top of her lungs.

"All jokes aside, I know, Skylar, we are just friends, so can I see you this weekend?" he asked once more. "I promise to be a good boy unless you choose to cross that line again," he said.

Skylar felt that this was going to be a bad idea, but she wanted to give him a chance. "Yes, Dimitri, we can hang out, but please bring James with you, okay? And you better keep your promise."

Again, Dimitri smiled. "Cross my heart, Skylar. I will see you this weekend in that purple dress perhaps." Skylar just shook her head, laughed, and got back into her car.

Skylar did not know what to expect from Dimitri this coming weekend. She hoped that he heard her and understood that they were just friends and nothing more. She really was doing this for Angelina since she wanted to see James again. Angelina was going to owe Skylar big if things did not go well between her and Dimitri. At least I-Kandies was a huge club, so hopefully she would be able to lose Dimitri in the crowd. The best thing about this visit with Dimitri was that he promised her that he would investigate the murders that she uncovered. With any luck, he and his department would find the human killer and save the city.

CHAPTER 7
Disposal

Kairo held Stacee captive for just over a week now. In the first five days he could not get enough of her. Stacee was ideal; her screams were everything to him. She had been a great little mouse in the beginning. Kairo enjoyed her so much that he increased his playtime with her more and more each day until she changed her behavior. Stacee may have been a blonde, but she was far from a dumb woman. She quickly came to realize that Kairo favored her screams and the fear that he saw in her eyes over her actual torture. Not giving into him was what Stacee needed to do if she wanted to stop the pain Kairo was putting her through. That was the hardest thing she ever had to do. Whenever she refused to scream and play his little games, he became upset and incredibly angry with her. He would try even harder to break her and he would become frustrated every time she resisted him.

On more than one occasion, Stacee wanted to give into Kairo and give him what he wanted, her fear and screams. That was all he cared about, but when Stacee fought him, her torture was worse but always shorter. The more she resisted him meant that he was having the least amount of fun with her. Stacee was almost at the end of her rope and wanted to end it all. Then again, there were times where she was determined to win at all costs, hoping that Kairo would have mercy on her and let her go.

On the eighth day of Stacee's captivity, Kairo finally lost all interest in her. He tried several times in the morning to give Stacee one last chance to save herself. All she had to do was play correctly and let him hear her screams. Kairo wanted so much for her to show him her fears and she would be safe for one more day. Stacee finally lost all interest in pleasing Kairo, and for that mistake, she had to pay the ultimate price. She had succeeded in ruining his game of cat and mouse, and for that, she had to die. There was no way around it because Stacee could not be trusted to continue to live while knowing his deep, dark secrets.

Over Kairo's three centuries, he had killed many people; killing had never been a problem for him. There were times when he did not want to kill but he had to kill, and there were times where he killed for the fun of it. Killing was always easy for him, but now he had a major problem. The area of disposal had always been Malachi's job, because he had a love of ripping their victims apart for the shear fun of it. When Kairo and Malachi went their separate ways, killing was not a part of Kairo's plans until he linked back up with Malachi.

Charlotte was intended to be just another stop on his journey across the country looking for new cities for him and Malachi to play in, but Charlotte was different. On Kairo's first day in the city, an unknown force grabbed a hold of him, and it would not let him go. The energy was unreal, something Kairo could not shake. He could not leave the city until he knew what that energy was and why it was calling out to him. Until that day, this city would become his home despite everything Malachi had taught him to believe. Thinking of Charlotte as his home was a problem for another day. Before Kairo did anything else, he had to figure out how he was going to dispose of Stacee's body without making Malachi suspicious of his actions.

After his last attempt to play with her, Kairo left Stacee sleeping and tied to the bed. He would never again allow her to freely wander after trying to end his game on her terms. Stacee was a decent beauty when she was quiet and sleeping, and a tiny part of Kairo did not want to kill her. In that moment she was his sleeping beauty, while he watched her deciding on the best way to end her life. Her blood was average at best, but it would serve its purpose in making him stronger. Kairo circled Stacee's sleeping body once more, licking his lips when he decided that draining her dry was best for them both. Kairo transformed and scared Stacee awake, getting a small taste of what he wanted all along. His voice was dark and menacing as he violently shook Stacee to get her to wake up.

"Wake up, Stacee," he said while he freed her from her chains.

The fear Kairo saw in her eyes pleased him but only for a second. Once Stacee's eyes focused on him, she knew this was not going to end well for her. Before today Stacee hoped and prayed for this ending, because Kairo had successfully broken her spirits. There was no way that she could live with the memories of what he had done to her day after day, or so she thought. When she was looking death in the face, everything changed for her. She realized that she had been lying to herself and did not want to die. All she wanted was for her torture and pain to stop. Somehow, she had to convince Kairo to spare her life.

"Please, Kairo," she begged. "I promise to keep your secrets; I will stay here with you; I will do anything for you, just don't kill me please."

Stacee was too late, and now there was no stopping Kairo. His mind was already made up now that she had ruined his game. Stacee had to die, and she had to know that she brought this on herself. Had she been Kairo's perfect little mouse and given him what he wanted; they would not be here now. Kairo grabbed Stacee up by the neck, choking the life out of her, before sinking his fangs deep into her neck. With a gleam in his eyes, Kairo relished in the taste of Stacee's blood as he pulled every drop from her body. In a matter of seconds, his game of cat and mouse was over, and he was thankful for Stacee and for her blood. He would always remember the fun that they had and rank her high among his other little mice for her lovely screams. With Stacee gone, Kairo had an opening for another mouse, one he hoped would be just as fun as Stacee had been.

Without Malachi here and the device that he created, Kairo had no way to dispose of Stacee's body. For now, she had to be put in the freezer until Kairo could get in touch with Malachi. It was Kairo's intention to keep Stacee around until he contacted Malachi for his device and found her replacement. As the newest and most eligible bachelor in town, Kairo was planning one killer housewarming party with the hopes of finding him a new little mouse. The women of Lake Wylie were curious about his newly remodeled home and itching for the chance to meet him. This party was a win-win for both Kairo and the neighboring women who had an interest in him.

Over the course of Kairo's existence, Malachi had become more than just his creator, he was his friend. Where Kairo had an evil streak, Malachi was a hundred times worse. He allowed his past to taint the way he saw humans today because they were the real monsters that needed to be feared. Malachi saw them all as merely food and the occasional plaything. His hatred towards them allowed for him to create a new method of disposal. With vigilante groups operating in the world like the Council of Truth Seekers, it was more important than ever to keep their existence a secret. The world needed to continue to believe that vampires and other ethereal beings only existed in pop culture. Malachi and the other three originals developed the perfect way to get rid of those vile creatures. A way that would keep their kind safe, allowing them the freedom to feed and play without worry. It was a way for Malachi's kind to be free to be themselves.

With the help of modern technology, the autopsy process had evolved, and it was just a matter of time before the humans figured out they existed from the blood loss of their victims. Something had to be done to give Malachi's kind the freedom they craved. Malachi called it promession; it was the process of freeze-drying human remains into a powder. It was the perfect means of getting rid of a body without a single trace being left behind. In order to do this, Kairo needed a special machine that would freeze the body with liquid nitrogen. Then through vibrations from the drum, the body would be shaken into a dust that could then be placed inside a small pouch. Malachi was the only one of their kind Kairo knew who could get him one those devices. The problem was Malachi was off in Europe having his own fun, waiting for Kairo to join him.

Kairo needed that device not just for Stacee but for all his future mice since he did not have any plans to leave Charlotte. For those that knew the real Malachi knew that he could be an evil man to those who betrayed him or broke his trust. He would never harm a member of his family if they all followed their number one rule, which was Keep Their Existence a Secret. A vampire could travel the world and kill everyone in sight if he or she kept their existence a secret. Kairo had to get his hands on one of Malachi's devices if he wanted to continue to be his last living creation. Having a device of his own was a must if Kairo was going to stay in the city for a while and continue his game of cat and mouse. Kairo called his longtime friend who was thrilled to help after getting over his initial shock that Kairo would not be joining him in Europe. Malachi assured Kairo that the device would be delivered in two days, and the timing could not have been better. The device would arrive just in time for Kairo to claim a new mouse. Out with the old and in with the new.

Kairo even told Malachi about Charlotte. It was a city he had never been to before, so he could understand why Kairo chose to stay for a while even though it was odd. Malachi was happy to hear that Kairo was doing well and living up to his potential. He almost felt like a proud father since Kairo had not let their time apart make him go soft. That was a problem Malachi had with a few of his kind. After living for so long, most of them became tired of the killing and wanted to live as humans with humans. While Malachi was pleased to provide Kairo with a device, something about the way he described Charlotte made him curious. *What is Kairo up to in Charlotte, North Carolina?* he thought. That really made Malachi think that maybe it was time for him to leave Europe and make a surprise visit to Charlotte and check up on Kairo.

While Malachi was away, it seemed like Kairo was busy making this city his new home. With a device of his own and a plan to be free, Kairo was on top of the world. It seemed as if everything was falling into place perfectly. All that was left to do was plan one killer party allowing the people of Lake Wylie the chance to peek into his world. It was time for Kairo to get to know his neighbors.

CHAPTER 8

An Old Friend Comes to Town

Two days later Kairo had everything set up and ready for his housewarming party. The buzz around town was all about him, the very handsome bachelor who was throwing an amazing pool party at his home. Everyone was invited; the more people that came, the better, and Kairo needed for everything to be perfect. For him, this party was only meant to be exploratory. While his guests mixed and mingled and enjoyed themselves, he would be in search of his next little mouse. Between the pool and the lake as well as the dance floor, surely Kairo would find something to satisfy his taste. The summer brought out everyone, and Kairo made sure all the residents and their guests would be welcomed. While going over the last few details to make this night perfect, there was a knock on his door. However, a knock was a bit of an understatement.

Kairo walked over to the door ready to kill whoever was banging on his door like they were crazy. Thinking that it was stupid kids playing some stupid game, Kairo was ready to teach them that they were playing around on the wrong door. Over the past two days, Kairo's mind was focused only on his party and nothing else that he completely forgot about the phone call he made to Malachi requesting the promession device. Opening the door, Kairo discovered that it was not teenagers playing but the device Malachi had promised to send him and the man himself. That was a surprise for Kairo, as Malachi was the last person he expected to see.

"What, are you not going to invite me in?" Malachi laughed as he made fun of the human theory that their kind could not enter a home unless they were invited.

"Oh, by all means, you may enter," responded Kairo. "I thought you were in Europe stirring up trouble?"

"I was until I got your call; you gave me a reason to leave. As you know, I have never been to North Carolina and was dying to learn more about this new city of yours."

"I think that you will find this city very enjoyable," said Kairo.

"Great," said Malachi, "and the council is not here yet." They called themselves the Council of Truth Seekers, but that was not who they were. They were a group of humans who knew vampires and the supernatural world existed based off stories passed down from their ancestors. They wanted nothing more than to rid the world of them all. Simply put, the members of the Council hated anything that was not human and believed that they were doing the world a great service by killing all ethereal beings no matter if they were good or not.

Malachi was not your typical vampire. He was only five foot four inches tall, which was small for someone who was as strong and powerful as he was. Malachi was one of four surviving original ethereal beings that walked the earth. Words like "vampire," "bloodsucker," and "supernatural creatures" were all human terms. Long before they knew of the existence of humans, ethereal beings walked the earth. They were one with nature and lived in perfect harmony until humans came along, and jealousy and hatred changed everything. It was during that time Malachi and the other beings learned that hate was a powerful force among the humans. That was when things changed for the worse. Kairo did not know the full story of Malachi's past, but he knew it was not a happy story.

What Kairo did know was that whatever happened between their kind and humans changed who Malachi was. He was once friendly and loved humans, and one day, it all changed. Malachi was laced with a hate so deep that he passed it along to everyone that he created, and he never talked about his past again. Malachi suppressed it all and moved on with his life, because dwelling on the past made him weak. From century to century, Malachi spread the same hate that laced his heart to all manner of ethereal beings. Kairo was the monster he was today because of Malachi's teaching. Malachi was the monster he was today because of the treatment he received.

Malachi even allowed his past to dictate his outward appearance. It was believed that he was a monster, the thing that kept humans awake at night and looking over their shoulders. If that was what he was supposed to be, then that was how he was going to look every day of his existence. Malachi wore his hair in locs that fell past his shoulders to the middle of his back. At times he would twist his hair back to look like two horns. As a nod to his love for blood, he would sometimes dye the tips of his hair a blood red. With his impeccable eyesight, he wore solid gold round-rim glasses tinted dark to add a bit of mystery to his face and hide his eyes from the world. It always delighted him to see the shock on his victim's face when they saw his eyes. They were a deep slate gray color with vertical pupils. They were the eyes of a cat. Malachi's skin was dark and smooth, like the color of onyx, allowing him to blend into the night and go completely unnoticed. Malachi worked diligently to make himself look as if he were a monster straight off the set of a movie. He felt he was only giving the world what the world had given him. Pure evilness and hatred.

Walking around Kairo's residence, Malachi took everything in before he spoke. Kairo's house was telling Malachi a much different story than what he was saying. Everything that Malachi noticed was filed away to be used later.

"I'm feeling parched; how about you be an excellent host and take me out for a drink or two?"

"There is no need for that, Malachi; in another hour I will have the drinks coming to you. I'm having a little housewarming party tonight, and everyone is invited."

"Excellent," responded Malachi, "then let the drinks flow."

"Yes, they will, but tonight all we do is drink, browse the menu, if you will. I know nothing about our guests yet."

"I will try," said Malachi with a shrug of his shoulders and matter-of-factly. "You know how hard it is for me to stop once my interest has piqued."

"You must," said Kairo. "I am only following your rules, after all. There is the chance some of these humans will be missed. I have not been here long and do not know these humans well enough yet to start making them disappear."

"Fine, you win for now, Kairo, but remember, I taught you everything you know."

"I am aware of that, Malachi," said Kairo. "Find yourself a room upstairs other than the master bedroom and relax until our guests arrive." Malachi was gone before Kairo could say another word. Tonight, he would not only have a taste of Lake Wylie but also start to uncover the truth Kairo was hiding from him.

Malachi's arrival had been completely unexpected, but at least Kairo had the ball rolling on the party. The only thing left for him to do was sit back and wait for his guests to arrive. With Malachi here and his open palate, Kairo was happy that he left the invitations open. Malachi's tastes changed about as much as he changed his clothes, so having a variety of drinks to choose from was going to be great. Kairo still planned on playing the young, successful thirty-year-old angle. He was looking for something young and sweet. Malachi could play this several ways. He may choose to be the distinguished gentleman looking for something older and more refined, or he may choose to find something young, wild, and free.

The room Malachi picked fit his personality nicely. Its decor had a masculine feel to it with a hint of mystery behind it. It said a lot that Kairo, a nomadic vampire had decided to decorate every room in this house. That piece of knowledge was added to the rest as Malachi started to piece together what was really going on inside Kairo's head. After a shower, Malachi realized that Kairo was right. Tonight, had to be only about a taste and nothing more. *Kairo is smart; you raised him right*, thought Malachi. As much as he had grown to like Kairo over the last three hundred years, if he were ever responsible for exposing their kind, he would share a similar fate to many others before him. Malachi put his dark thoughts behind him for now. He was eager to sink his fangs into some new blood. Just as Kairo said, within the hour Malachi heard male and female voices coming from outside and downstairs. It did seem like the entire neighborhood had come to Kairo's little party.

Malachi was not like Kairo at all. He never had a problem feeding from males. When it came to his "food," Malachi was an equal opportunist. Blood was blood if it was fresh and filled his body, keeping him strong. At times Malachi even enjoyed the fight he would get from men since they assumed he was an easy target with his small stature. *Indeed, this was going to be fun.* Thankful for the call, Malachi realized that he needed a change in scenery. He had not realized just how bored he had become with his time in Europe.

Most of the guests were females and males between the ages of twenty-five and thirty-five. Women hoping to snag the handsome eligible bachelor, and men who wanted to be his friend. There were a few older women, "cougars," if you will, who thought Kairo needed more experience in his life. Those women Kairo would leave for Malachi since they were not his type. Happy with the turn out, Kairo was positive that he and Malachi were going to enjoy all this night had to offer. Malachi came downstairs dressed in a European cut suit getting looks from both the women that wanted him willingly and the ones who were not sure if he was safe to be around. With a glass of champagne in hand, Malachi made the rounds as well as Kairo. They were both in search of their first taste of the night.

Kairo found his first taste quickly. She was a young twenty-two fair-skinned female with short dark hair and green eyes. Kairo approached her, and they did the small talk for a while before he had her in the corner with his fangs deep in her neck. Sticking with the rules for tonight, all Kairo did was take a taste of her before sliding his tongue over the wounds to seal them with his saliva. Kairo compelled her to forget everything that happened between the two of them before leaving her and moving on to his next taste of the evening.

Malachi quickly found his first taste of the evening as well. She tried to move through the party without drawing too much attention to herself, but she caught his eye. Her name was Karen, and she had overheard her neighbors talking about the party. They were all cougars eager to meet the handsome young man who had just moved in. Karen was just looking for a reason to get out of the house and try to start living again. She still looked good for her age, with her toned body and dark skin and blood that smelled divine. Malachi followed her, almost stalking her as he lingered in the shadows waiting for the perfect time to strike. It was Karen's intention to come over, have a few drinks, and leave the party. Turns out, she was noticed by the worst monster in the room.

Karen was taken aback by Malachi when he walked up to her and introduced himself. She was shy and not sure of herself, but something about Malachi told her that he could make her feel good again. As they talked about everything and nothing at all, Malachi never took his eyes off her. Karen told him how lonely she was now that her daughter was grown and had a family of her own. That was when Malachi knew she was perfect. He placed a chased kiss upon Karen's lips and took her by the hand and led her upstairs to his room. Like the gentleman he pretended to be, Malachi took his time with Karen. He made her feel alive, more alive than she had been in the last five years. Malachi kissed her gently again while unzipping her dress.

Karen felt bold and powerful in Malachi's presence. She stood to allow her dress to fall to the floor like a puddle of crystal-clear blue water. She wanted this, as she needed to be back in Malachi's arms. Malachi wanted something entirely different. He took Karen back into his arms kissing her once more before releasing his fangs plunging them deep into her carotid artery. Malachi had broken the rules for tonight and taken more than a taste. He quickly drained Karen of all the blood in her body before ripping her into pieces. Like he did with all his victims, Malachi left Karen in a pile on the floor. Wiping his mouth, he looked at what was left of Karen, locked the door, and went in search of his next taste. Hoping he would be lucky enough to find another who could go missing just as easily as Karen had.

The entire time that Malachi and Karen were talking, Kairo was watching. He stood by and watched as Malachi escorted his first victim upstairs. Knowing that this was a bad idea, Kairo hoped that Malachi would follow the same rules he expected them all to follow. It was not like him to put them in danger, even if the Council was not here yet. Malachi had never put them in danger before, so Kairo hoped that he would not do it now. It became clear what happened in that room when Malachi came back downstairs alone. Kairo immediately pulled him to the side and questioned him about what he had just done.

"What were you thinking? I told you tonight was only about a taste and you go and kill someone."

Kairo was irate and forgot who he was talking to when he reached out and grabbed Malachi. Malachi, not liking Kairo's tone or the fact that he had touched him, reacted badly. Before Kairo had the chance to fix the situation, Malachi had already crushed his right hand. The murderous look in his eyes told Kairo that he had crossed the line.

"How dare you talk to me like that and put your hands on me; have you lost your fucking mind? You think you have the authority to speak to me like I am a child and tell me what I can and cannot do. This may be your residence, Kairo, but never forget, I made you. I will not hesitate to end you and all these people if you cross me again. I taught you; therefore, I would NEVER put us in any kind of danger. She will not be missed; nobody knows she was here; her own child does not come to visit her."

Malachi said his peace and left Kairo to deal with his own injuries. He needed blood to heal faster and not draw attention to his crushed hand and forearm. Kairo compelled the first woman he saw. He needed fresh blood and could care less about what she looked or smelled like. Kairo did not bother with the small talk. He simply ordered her to not move and stay quiet while he fed from her and healed his injuries. Kairo would never make the mistake of questioning Malachi or putting his hands on him again. For the rest of the night, both Kairo and Malachi kept their distance from each other. Each one of them enjoyed the party as they both made the rounds. Between the two of them, all the women in attendance had an experience with one of them. Everyone except for Karen went back to their lives as if nothing out of the ordinary happened. All they would remember was that they experienced one of the best parties of their lives.

After the party, Malachi went back to his room to deal with the mess he left behind. He gathered what was left of Karen, placed her into a box, and took her downstairs to get rid of her for good. Not that Malachi cared, but Karen's death was a peaceful one. She died with a smile on her face because she was finally given what she wanted. She was free of her sad and lonely existence for good. In hindsight, Malachi was the best thing that had ever happened to Karen. Malachi had given her the best five minutes of her life. He took the pieces, threw them into the drum, pressed the button, and waited until there was nothing left of her but a small bag of dust. For the next couple of days, Malachi would keep an eye on the news just in case there was news of Karen's disappearance. He was certain she would not be missed, but still, he would make sure just in case there were loose ends to tie up.

Kairo returned to his room to finalize the last-minute details for his business meeting in the morning. He was in the market for a new business, an extremely popular club in the City Center. Until he figured out why the energy was off around him, he was not going to be leaving Charlotte. This second part of his plan was going to have to stay a secret now that Malachi was here. The way Kairo was feeling went against everything Malachi had taught him. In three hundred years, Kairo had never gone against Malachi or his teachings.

This was all new territory for him, and after tonight's episode with Malachi, Kairo knew it was not wise to anger him.

"I am sure that you are planning something while you are in this city. You can fill me in on that plan tomorrow. I think that I am going to love this city you have found."

Kairo agreed. He, too, was going to love this new city of his. Kairo had this feeling inside of him that was telling him it was time for him to put down roots. Deep down, Kairo knew he had finally found his home, and that could prove dangerous for him now that Malachi was here.

CHAPTER 9

A Place to Call My Own

The next morning could not come fast enough. Kairo hardly slept last night after his amazing party and encounter with Malachi. It was never Kairo's intention to upset him. This was the first time Malachi had ever turned his wrath towards him. The last thing he wanted was to have an angry original living in his home. The power they possessed was out of the ordinary. Kairo had only witnessed a small taste of the power Malachi possessed and the things that he could do. Worse than upsetting Malachi was underestimating him simply because of his small frame. Kairo naturally thought he would follow the same rules he expected them all to follow. Since the first day of his transformation, Malachi beat that one rule into his head. *Keep our existence a secret.* Malachi would not allow Kairo to explore his new form until he understood and followed that one simple rule. Kairo knew he would have to fix the tension between the two of them at some point, but that was going to have to wait. He had more important things to do today. He had an important meeting with a man about a club.

Every time Kairo drove into the city, that energy was there, sometimes stronger than others but always there. What did not make sense about the energy was that Kairo could never find it. As a vampire, he should have been able to track where it was coming from, but he could not track it. He could not track it nor could he ignore it, but it was changing him deep down inside. Kairo could never tell this to Malachi, but deep down, he wanted this city to be his new home, his forever home.

That was something that Malachi did not want them to have, a place to call home. Malachi's home was taken from him a long time ago, and he never recovered from that. A home, love, true happiness, they were all human ideologies that only served to make their kind soft and fragile. With the way he was feeling, Kairo would have to be incredibly careful around Malachi from now on. If he ever suspected or even noticed the slightest change in Kairo, that could be the difference between life and death. Purchasing a club might just be the answer that Kairo was looking for. He needed to give Malachi something else to focus on instead of focusing on him and why he was staying in Charlotte longer than normal.

The idea popped into Kairo's head on his first trip to I-Kandies when he met Stacee. On that first night, he wanted to taste her, a sampling if you will. Not knowing where the cameras were or if the club even had cameras meant that Kairo could not be his true self. Now, if he was the owner of that club, he would have free reign to be himself and do as he please. Kairo and his people would be free to be themselves in a city that was not infested with the Council. For the first time in centuries, they would be free again and free to feed in peace without having to look over their shoulders. Private VIP booths were the answer to all Kairo's problems.

Kairo did not just want any club; he wanted I-Kandies. The layout was perfect, and with his enhancements and style I-Kandies, would become the best club in the city hands down. Looking into who the owner of I-Kandies was, Kairo came up with a name. The current owner was a man by the name of Alvin Jackson, who also owned a few smaller clubs on the eastside of town. Alvin was not what Kairo was expecting. He assumed that the owner would be older, but Alvin was not it. Not only was he older, he was also balding and, from the pictures, a poorly dressed man. Alvin had the look of being a pushover, and Kairo knew that this was going to be an interesting meeting. His endgame was to compel Alvin to sign over the club to him, or to "John Smith." The plan was to meet Alvin at Montecristo's, a cigar lounge that just so happened to be located across from the club that Kairo planned on taking from him.

Alvin had arrived early and ordered a Robusto cigar and a double shot of whisky while he waited for "John" to arrive. Just as Kairo expected, Alvin was smug and had this air about him that said he was better than everyone in the room. Before getting down to business, Kairo ordered a double shot of tequila, his drink of choice. He needed to take the edge off so he did not lose it and kill Alvin right where he was sitting. Their meeting had not started yet, and Kairo hated everything about this man. Kairo needed this meeting to be over as quickly as possible before Alvin forced his hand and made him do something that he would regret. All Kairo needed was just one minute of Alvin's time. After that one minute, he would be walking away with the deed to I-Kandies in his hands. Once Kairo finished his drink and was in a better state of mind, he was ready to get this meeting started. Sitting across from Alvin, Kairo avoided the small talk and got down to business.

"I want to purchase your club, so what is it going to cost me?"

Even now, Alvin continued to display that same smug attitude as before. "I will sell you Flamez for a million five," he said.

Kairo looked confused. "Flamez, why are we discussing Flamez? I want to purchase I-Kandies."

The look on Alvin's face said it all. He was not prepared for Kairo to want to purchase his most popular club. That was the shock Kairo was looking for. It may have been shock or pure anger, but whatever it was, it caused Alvin to remove his sunglasses and look Kairo directly in his eyes.

"You want my cash cow? Well, that is going to cost you heavily."

The thought of losing his most popular investment did not sit well with Alvin. He would sell but only if the price were right. Alvin thought of the most ridiculously high number he could come up with hoping that he and John would meet in the middle. I-Kandies was worth close to three million dollars, and if Alvin played his cards right, he could walk away with a nice-size profit. After taking another minute to decide on a number, he leaned forward, looked Kairo in the eyes, and said, "I will sell for six and a half million and not a penny less."

That price was ridiculous, when the club needed some major renovations, but Alvin had done exactly what Kairo needed him to do. Kairo just smiled knowing he had already won. Alvin was in the perfect position for Kairo to compel him to sign away his cash cow without ever getting one red cent for it.

"Deal," said Kairo, while looking into Alvin's eyes he continued, "you will sign I-Kandies over to me, John Smith, and you will forget that we ever had this conversation."

Without hesitating, Alvin signed the deed to I-Kandies over, drank the rest of his whiskey, and simply walked away. It all took about six minutes. It was easier than Kairo expected it to be. He was now the proud owner of one of the hottest nightclubs in the City Center. So far, today was a good day. *Mission accomplished*, thought Kairo as he grabbed the keys and the deed to I-Kandies and walked over to his newly acquired club.

Kairo had won. He set out to purchase a club and walked away with the best. Kairo knew he was going to have to tell Malachi soon, but he still had some time to kill. Even now, in the City Center, the energy was affecting him. With the meeting over, he was now able to focus on that energy and the way it always lingered around him. Today it was not as strong as it normally was, but Kairo could still feel it all around him pulling at him. The problem was, he still could not pinpoint in what direction it was coming from. There was no way for him to know if it was coming from a person, a place, or a thing. What Kairo did know was that this energy was affecting him, and Malachi was the only person he knew that could help him make sense of it all. Bringing this to Malachi was a big mistake, and one that Kairo could not make since his life depended on it. This was his problem, his secret, and he was going to have to push it to the back of his mind and deal with it another day. One way or the other, Kairo was going to figure out what it was, come hell or high water. His hope was that Malachi would become bored with his new city and leave sooner rather than later. As of now, Kairo had something much bigger to focus on.

His new club, I-Kandies, was going to need a ton of work before it would be perfect for his kind. Alvin's current floor plan and flow was off, and the décor was in bad shape. Before this club would open again with Kairo as the new owner, it was going to have to be renovated. Walking around the club, Kairo studied the current layout while making mental notes of the changes that he was going to make. Finally, Kairo's kind would be able to feed in peace, find sexual gratification, and for the ones that were like him and Malachi, they could safely find their next playthings. Kairo had a lot of work to do, and he was excited to get started.

Since the flow was off, the first change Kairo would be making was switching the location of the bar and DJ booth. It did not make any sense to him to have the DJ booth more towards the front of the club and the bar towards the back of the club. With an improved sound system, the DJ could play from any corner of the room. Kairo's patrons needed to have easier access to the bar and all the new top-shelf liquor he would be providing for them. The bar would be stocked with more tequila than ever before as well as several new spirits. The upstairs was going to receive the bulk of the renovations, since that was where Kairo and others like him would be spending most of their time. Kairo, Malachi, and any other vampire that might stop by would be needing more privacy. To provide his non-human guests with the privacy they required, Kairo would be installing private VIP booths with two-way glass. This way they would be able to entertain their current guest while searching the crowd below for their replacements.

For any human lucky enough to reserve a space, they would just think that the two-way glass was an awesome touch. Kairo would do the same thing with the owner's office. The wall that faced the dance floor would be taken out and replaced with the same two-way glass. Kairo thought, *Why stop there?* The floors, paint, and overall décor would change as well. He thought the eye candy cages were a bit primitive, so they were going away as well. Today's women were into poles, aerial rings, and aerial silks, not cages.

Apart from the club renovations that had to be done, Kairo had to deal with the staff. He thought about hiring a brand-new staff, but that was going to take some time. Kairo was not in the mood to deal with interviews and all the paperwork and everything else that he would have to do to keep everything looking normal. He just needed to have a mandatory face-to-face meeting with them or Malachi would. Kairo was strong and gifted, since he was transformed by an original, but he could not compel that many people all at one time, but Malachi could. The entire staff was going to need to disregard everything they would see while serving in VIP. In the end, it was a good thing that he had to kill Stacee and call Malachi. He was going to be needed after all.

After making phone calls to the hardware stores to get the supplies needed to renovate, Kairo was almost ready to get to work. With his speed, he would have all the work completed in a day or two. News from the glass company was not what Kairo wanted to hear. It would take about two weeks for the two-way glass to come in, so I-Kandies was going to be closed. Closing his newly purchased club for two weeks was not part of Kairo's plan. There was just no way around it; the club was going to be closed since Kairo could not utilize VIP the way he needed to. With the help of Malachi, the actual work would only take a couple of hours, but none of that mattered until the glass came in. There was nothing left to do but plan one killer-ass Grand Reopening party.

Malachi woke refreshed and ready for a new day. He was eager to see all that Charlotte had to offer, and what was keeping Kairo here. Malachi missed nothing, and Kairo should have known that. From the minute he saw Kairo, he knew that he was keeping something from him. If Kairo thought Malachi would not look around his residence while he was away, he was sadly mistaken. Kairo had become Malachi's favorite, and he knew how he felt about them *finding a home* and trying to live this human life. It was fine for them to attempt to blend in and hide in plain sight, but they were not human. There was no place for their kind in this world; humanity made sure of that a long time ago. Malachi had taught Kairo well, and all his hiding spots were the same as his. Malachi was aware that there was more to the basement than what could be seen. Behind the false walls, Malachi found all Kairo's devices and the full-size maze that he created. It was clear to him that Kairo was making plans to make North Carolina his permanent home. That thought alone made Malachi's blood boil. Not only was Kairo displaying human thoughts, he had the nerve to look him in the eyes and lie to him. This was not the Kairo that Malachi knew, and one way or the other, he was going to figure out what Kairo was really hiding from him. Perhaps that secret was the real reason why he wanted to stay in North Carolina. From this day forward, Malachi was going to have to keep a close eye on Kairo if he wanted to uncover what his real plans were.

On the other hand, Malachi could understand why Kairo chose to live here on the lake. The house and the location were beautiful and peaceful. With all the violence their kind dealt with every day, a peaceful place to lay your head was always good. However, they were not human, and humans did not understand who and what they were. The large, lush green trees around the house, the lake itself, and the way the sun shone through the trees was breathtaking. It was all magical and took Malachi back to a time that he never wanted to revisit. His past was painful for him to remember. No matter how much he wanted to forget his past, those memories would never go away. Centuries later, Malachi was still haunted by the memories of his home and his beloved Rose. It was a different time, and he was a different person. Malachi was weak, and Rose was brutally taken from him by a group of evil humans. Their actions alone planted a seed of hate so deep inside of him that he fed on it every day. If Malachi were a different man, he would consider staying here himself. Thinking about the past made Malachi vulnerable, which was something that he vowed to never be again.

Until Kairo returned, Malachi needed a distraction. Thankfully for him, Kairo had a massive television set mounted to the living room wall. Nothing could take your mind off your own thoughts faster than American TV. Humans loved to display their problems on television for the world to judge. Like always, the shows were hilarious and did exactly what Malachi needed them to do and took his mind off his problems and the past. Malachi watched TV for another hour before he heard Kairo approaching the house in the distance. *This had better be good*, he thought. Malachi understood Kairo was still hiding something from him, but he knew that he was working on a plan for them here.

As soon as Kairo stepped through the door, Malachi demanded that he tell him why he was there. Malachi was not a fool; he knew that Kairo was not just passing through, but he wanted to give him the chance to tell him the truth. Not wanting to anger Malachi and not really in the mood to heal from whatever damage he would inflict, Kairo told him everything. "I own a nightclub in the City Center," he said. "It will provide us with many different tastes to choose from." Kairo knew Malachi had to agree with him and see the benefits that the club would provide.

Malachi was quiet for a few minutes processing everything that Kairo said. "So, tell me," he said, "will this be a place where I am free to be me or just another front for our kind to pretend to be human." Kairo had hoped that Malachi would just accept this idea of his without any questions. Questions only meant that he noticed that things were off with him.

"No, Malachi, this club is for us to play and have fun; I will be running things, so nothing will happen." Again, Malachi was silent as he pondered everything that Kairo was saying. *This is it*, thought Malachi. *Kairo just walked into my trap.*

"Does this mean that the great Kairo VanDoren is going soft on me?"

Kairo had to play this cool and not give anything away. "No, not at all, Malachi; I can and will be in charge of the club from a distance, and if necessary, I will have a second in command."

Malachi was clever, but he had no real way of proving that Kairo was lying, but he would find out soon enough. Malachi was pleased with this plan of his. For once, vampires like him would have a place to be free and feed on any human that they pleased. Typically, when their kind opened any establishment, it was forbidden for them to be themselves. Hurting the humans was off limits since they chose to live as humans themselves. Kairo had come through for their kind in a huge way, but Malachi wanted the complete truth from him. Malachi knew Kairo was keeping something else from him, and he wanted to know if Kairo would tell him what that was.

"I love this plan of yours, Kairo," he said. "Is there anything else you want to tell me?"

With a straight face, Kairo looked Malachi dead in the eye and said, "No, I have nothing else to tell you, Malachi."

Kairo knew that it was a bad idea to lie to Malachi, but he just could not tell him the truth not just yet. Kairo still did not know what the energy was or what it meant to him, so it was best to keep Malachi in the dark for now. When, and if, the time were right, he would tell Malachi the truth, no matter what the consequences were going to be.

CHAPTER 10
A New Little Mouse

*I*t was offical I-Kandies would be closed for two weeks. That fact alone drove the humans crazy. Where were they going to spend their weekends now? The word on the street was that they all were extremely angry but looking forward to all the new changes the new owner was making. As the rumor mill went into overdrive, everyone had an idea of what the club needed or what the new owner should change. To keep them happy and to ensure all the regulars and even some newcomers would show up, Kairo promised an hour of free drinks and some other giveaways, including a private party. The hour of free drinks did the trick in pleasing the locals. Kairo was positive they all would be in attendance when the doors reopened. The closing of I-Kandies turned out great for the other bars in the area. They had the pleasure of gaining the I-Kandies crowd and being jammed packed for two weeks. Malachi had come through in a huge way and talked with the staff, making sure they were all on the same page. All the pieces were falling into place, and the last thing that Kairo needed was for his glass to arrive.

Malachi got his hands dirty and helped with the renovations since he had a valid interest in seeing the doors back opened sooner rather than later. Kairo was on the phone everyday with the glass company trying his best to get the glass in sooner than the scheduled two-week timeframe. Malachi and Kairo started the renovations by painting the boring white walls that were now dirty and brown. For the walls, Kairo wanted something that was interesting to look at and would hold up against all the traffic. For paint, he decided on a stain-resistant mixture of light and dark greys to create this marbled textured look.

Kairo wanted the walls to catch your eye and entice you to look around and see all the other changes that were made. After the walls were painted and dry, the entire lighting system was overhauled. First on Kairo's list of things to remove was the tacky, outdated disco ball. Kairo's club would not be stuck in any time period, especially the '80s techno area. To bring in some much-needed visual interest in the lighting, Kairo installed 3D LED color-changing tube lights. The lights were amazing and could be displayed in different patterns and shapes to match any vibe the club was trying to set.

The walls and lighting were completed quickly and next on the list was the flooring. Malachi had to get something that he wanted, so he chose a black aspen oak with wood grain that was laid out in a herringbone pattern. It was durable and would hold up to all the patrons that would be tearing it up on the dancefloor and stage. For that reason, Kairo chose to use the same flooring in the VIP section and his office. The next big renovation was the bars, which were moved from the back of the club and repositioned more towards the front of the club. The bars would be the first thing you saw when you entered the club. They were sleek, long LED bars with glass bar tops and lighted shelving to display the new top shelf liquor.

To finish off the downstairs renovations, the new and improved stage was outfitted with two poles and an aerial ring to replace the primitive "eye candy" cages. I-Kandies would not be the same without a place for the brave to showcase their talents. Malachi was eagerly anticipating seeing a perfect beauty utilize either one of the poles or the aerial ring. Kairo was more interested in who would be bold enough to give the ring a try over the ones that chose the pole. Anyone could dance on the poles, but the aerial ring would require someone with talent.

With four long, slow days of renovations behind them, Kairo and Malachi were done pretending to be two humans working on their club. They had done as much as they could until the two-way glass came in. Kairo could not speak for Malachi, but he needed a new little mouse to replace Stacee, and this time he wanted someone that aroused him sexually. Stacee was fun, but she was missing that one key component when it came to being his perfect little mouse. Had she appealed to him on a sexual level, he may have kept her around longer. What Malachi was into was a totally different thing. He may want a female for sexual pleasure or a male because they provided more of a challenge, and he loved a challenge. Keeping their plans to themselves, both men had quite different ideas of where they were going to find their next playthings.

Malachi knew that Kairo was lying to him about something, something that he would figure out in due time. Seeing as how Kairo had his own little secrets, it was only right that Malachi have secrets of his own as well. Malachi had a hatred for all humanity, and now that he was here without the prying eyes of the Council, he was thinking about staying for a while. Currently there were no available properties for purchase on the lush lake, but Malachi did have his hands on a good size estate. It was an estate that once belonged to Karen. Since her death, not a soul had come to look for or even asked about her. Malachi was right, Karen was not missed at all. With a house of his own, Malachi needed his own victim for both blood and fun. Having a house was also going to come in handy when he discovered what Kairo was hiding from him. Malachi already had an idea of what that was. He was going to sit back and let Kairo hang himself first. Until then, he would start to unleash his brand of evil on this enigmatic city.

Malachi opted to be a man of mystery tonight. He was dressed in all black from head to toe, allowing him to blend into the shadows all night long. He was ready to hit the streets and find his next victim. Karen was easy and brought no enjoyment to his life at all. She welcomed the death that he gave her because she was sad and lonely. Malachi freed Karen from a life that was not worth living anymore. Tonight, he needed someone with a spark of life still in them, someone whom he could force that light from their eyes. Malachi had done his research; Club Luxe was more to his liking, but it was extremely hard to take someone from there and still be able to enjoy them the way he wanted to. Bad Dragon was smaller and too close for Malachi to linger in the shadows, so it was out. That left Studio21, an '80s and '90s club with a layout like that of I-Kandies. With their club shelved for two weeks, Studio 21 became the newest hotspot in town, so that was where Malachi was meant to be.

Forcing the bouncer to forget he even saw him, Malachi casually walked into the club, being sure to stay in the shadows. As he moved through the shadows, he was able to hide in plain sight until he was ready to strike. Malachi and Kairo were different on many levels. Where Kairo cared about the physical appearance of his little mice, Malachi only cared about the smell of his victims. The smell was everything to him, the sweeter the scent, the better the blood. Only a vampire's soulmate's blood would smell and taste the sweetest. The scents that filled the club were average at best until he walked in. He was a man of average build, tan with dark hair and brown eyes. He had a scruffy beard, and his hair was put up in a messy man bun. By the attention he received, he was classified as a sexy man. Malachi loved today's sexuality; everyone was so fluid making it that much easier for him to rid the world of all humanity. *Yes*, he thought, *he would do just nicely*.

The night was in full swing, and with I-Kandies closed, the City Center was alive and spilling over with tons of people. Club Luxe was looking more and more enticing without I-Kandies being opened. For once the energy around Kairo was normal, so normal in fact that he did not know how to take it. For the first time since coming to the city, Kairo could honestly say he missed that feeling. Without that pull of energy to make him come alive, he felt dead inside. Until it resurfaced, he was just going to have to find a new little mouse to make him feel normal again. Kairo was torn between Club Luxe and Studio 21. The '80s was never a decade Kairo enjoyed, so for his taste tonight, Club Luxe would have to do.

Malachi found his target, and he was not going to bother with small talk or any other human pleasantries. Hiding in the shadows, Malachi waited for the perfect moment to take Max. When the time came, he emerged from the shadows to compel Max to leave the club for the evening. Unlike other vampires, Malachi did not have to look into his victim's eyes to compel them. He had the power of suggestion through touch, and in a matter of seconds, Max was under his spell. There was the possibility that Max could vanish without a trace and the possibility that his disappearance would not go unnoticed. For now, Max would be just for fun and the occasional drink, and if his disappearance could go unnoticed, then Max would become just another one of Malachi's victims. Until that decision could be made, Max would remain under Malachi's control believing whatever story he decided to tell him.

Max did exactly what he was told to do. As if he had become bored with the scene at Studio 21, he walked out of the club and back to his car. Keeping to the shadows, Malachi followed him the entire time. While under Malachi's control, Max drove his car to a bad part of town and left it there. Under his own power he walked over to Malachi and willingly climbed into his trunk. The drive to Malachi's borrowed residence only took a few minutes, and in two more minutes, Malachi had Max screaming for dear life on his makeshift rack. Malachi had never played this little torture game of Kairo's, but he was enjoying it to the fullest. The pain and fear in the eyes of the almighty humans was like music to his ears. He understood why Kairo enjoyed hearing his little mice scream so much. It was a joy to be heard, and Malachi was fully enthralled by this new game of his. Sadly, it was growing late and past time for him to return to Kairo's house. His fun was going to have to be put on pause until the sun set on another day. For Malachi to uncover Kairo's secrets, it was important that he play the part of the perfect house guest. Malachi would be seeing Max again very soon.

Club Luxe had worked out perfectly for Kairo. After a few hours he finally found what he was looking for. She was tall, almost as tall as he was, with long red hair. She had brown eyes and creamy caramel skin and smelled divine. Kairo was going to have her. Again, he played the part of the handsome, rich bachelor to win her over. Unlike Stacee, Monica was not into a man for his money and all the things that he could do for her. Kairo and Monica partied and enjoyed each other's company for nearly two hours before Kairo had her in his car heading back to his home. At first, Monica was going to be Kairo's new little mouse, but something about her made it hard for him to torture her like he did with Stacee. Kairo fed from her and tortured her through sexual bondage for hours but something was off with her. Monica served her purpose; she pleased Kairo sexually and physically through her blood, but she still could not fill the void that he had. Monica would be one of only a few humans whom Kairo had let live. After their time together, Kairo did not care what happened to her. He compelled her to leave his house forgetting all about him and how she ended up on Lake Wylie. Knowing his neighbors, Kairo was sure that someone would come to her rescue. Monica satisfied the itch that he had, but she was not what he wanted. Kairo realized he was missing the connection to the weird energy that always made him come alive in the City Center.

When Malachi returned from his night of fun, Kairo's night was already over. It had been hours since Monica had been ordered to leave his home, leaving him curious about Malachi's night. After the last time that Kairo questioned him, he was smart enough not to ask him where he had been. Never again would Kairo question him about anything he did. After not getting fully satisfied, the only thing left for Kairo to do was plan for the grand reopening of I-Kandies. Kairo wanted everyone to be there. *The more the merrier*, he thought. More importantly, Kairo wanted the owner of that energy to be there. Even though he could not be sure, it felt like the energy belonged to a person. Hoping that person was an attractive female, Kairo was busy doing everything within his powers to make sure that all of Charlotte came out to the reopening of the city's favorite club. Knowing that the club would reach its capacity fast, Kairo had a plan to keep everyone that was turned away as happy as clams also.

Keeping everyone happy, Malachi included, was going to be a very taxing job. That meant tomorrow Kairo had a million phone calls to make. First thing first, he was going to need a large supply of alcohol on hand. With the hour of free drinks and the crowd that Kairo hoped to bring in, having plenty of spirits was a must. The last thing he needed was to run out of alcohol and have to kill everyone in his club. Kairo also needed to call all the local radio stations to promote the club's giveaways. As Kairo was making notes of his final details, Malachi came in. "Were you able to get the glass in sooner?"

"No, not unless I drive to the warehouse and do some persuading. Where did you disappear to?"

"I visited Studio 21; they had some interesting aromas there but nothing worth bringing back with me. I think the club should stay closed for the two weeks; it will give me more time to explore the city." That plan worked for Kairo, with more time he could make sure everything was perfect and in place for the reopening party.

"That works for me," said Kairo before Malachi returned to his room for the night.

Over the course of the next week, both Malachi and Kairo worked by day to finish the renovations and get the club back opened. Once the glass came in, the renovations could be completed and I-Kandies was ready for the grand reopening the following weekend. The buzz around town was everything Kairo wanted to hear. All around the City Center, I-Kandies and the reopening were the only things on the tongues of the masses. All the hard work Kairo and Malachi had been doing was about to pay off. The radio broadcast was a huge success as well. With all the positive publicity that the club was receiving, Kairo knew that the turnout was going to be huge. Either he was going to find him a new little mouse, or he was going to locate the source of that energy.

While Malachi was helping with the renovations, he would disappear from time to time. He would never say where he was going or when he was coming back. Little did Kairo know, he had Max to return to. Malachi kept Max on the rack for a week as he slowly stretched and ripped his limbs from his body. In true Kairo fashion, he healed Max only to place him on something equally heinous, the Judas Cradle. Malachi had Max bound at the hands and hooked to a pulley system where he was able to lower and raise him onto the cradle. Max's screams were a thing of beauty for Malachi, but he was done with this game. Kairo always kept his mice around for way too long, and that was not Malachi's end game. Max disappeared, and no one cared. If he had family left, they were not in Charlotte or they just did not care about what happened to him.

Malachi was not the only one that found additional pleasure over the next week. Things had finally started looking up for Kairo even though he still had not felt that pull of energy. He was starting to believe that the energy was gone forever. It had been almost a full week since he felt it last. It was gone, and he had to get on with his life. The only positive thing out of this was that Kairo could stop lying to Malachi. With the energy gone, he had no reason to stay in Charlotte. He would get someone to run the club for him while he moved on in search of something new. Without the energy, Kairo was back to his old self, even though that hole stayed with him. He found him a new little mouse, and like Malachi, he skipped the small talk and got right down to business. All he cared about was hearing her scream.

Kairo's process and demeanor had changed slightly since Malachi was around. Kairo did not want to look weak in the eyes of his creator, so he was somewhat done with his game and chose not to keep his mice around long. Over the course of the following week, Kairo went through five little mice not caring to keep any of them around for longer than a few hours at a time. During his time with them, Kairo brought out the breast ripper, the iron maiden, and the head crusher. Three devices that made Malachi extremely happy to see in use. They both ended the week off on a high note when they both ended their playthings and looked forward to the reopening of I-Kandies. With Friday night just around the corner, they both knew the real fun was about to begin.

CHAPTER 11
Drawn to Each Other

*F*or the past week and a half, Skylar was off the hook with her so-called date with Dimitri. Her job sent her to Tennessee to help with a huge case they had. The thought of not having to see Dimitri made her happy, but at the same time, she was nervous about leaving the city. *What if my new normal shows itself; what will I say if people think I am crazy?* Despite all of her thoughts, the decision was not hers to make. It was either lose her job or go and lend a helping hand. Tennessee was nowhere near as bad as she thought it was going to be. The landscape and weather were like North Carolina, the people were friendly, and they loved their orange. All in all, it was good to get away. While work kept her busy, she could not help but notice that her life was normal. The entire time she was in Tennessee, she never felt that strange pull of energy. Those first couple of days without that energy, she was fine; it was good to feel normal again. As the days went by, she realized just how much she had missed her new normal and that she was right all along. That "normal" was boring and not how she wanted her life to be. The energy made her feel alive, and without it, she felt alone, like a part of her was missing. She was so ready to go back home, until Dimitri's phone calls started. Dimitri called her every day until she finally agreed to meet up and hang out with him. Angelina had filled her in on all the latest news, news that was mostly about I-Kandies. Turns out, it had a new owner who closed the place for some major renovations. There was a huge grand reopening party this coming Friday.

Skylar had only been back in Charlotte for a few hours before Dimitri was calling her again like crazy. She had already agreed to meet up with him, so there was no need for him to call her like this. The way Dimitri was acting about this friendly date was making her regret ever agreeing to it. For Skylar, keeping her word was a big deal. That was really all this so-called "date" was, just her keeping her word. For Dimitri to show her this side of himself again was not working out in his favor. This was more proof that they were not meant to be together. They were just friends, and that was how it was meant to be. Dimitri was even more annoying than ever before, and Skylar could not deal with him. Come this Friday, she would keep her word and, with some luck on her part, get him to finally understand that they were only ever going to be friends.

Over those last couple of days, all anyone could talk about was I-Kandies. Skylar hoped that with all the buzz and excitement she was hearing that the club would be a packed house. She desperately needed it to be filled with people so that she could lose Dimitri among the crowd after she upheld her end of the deal.

The other reason that Skylar agreed to this "date" was to help Angelina out. She wanted to see James again, and since they did not exchange numbers, the only way for their date to happen was through Dimitri. Playing nice with him was the only way for Skylar to get what she needed, and she would make sure not to lead Dimitri on or confuse him. Skylar wanted her best friend to have a genuine connection with James. Hopefully, they would decide to take things to the next level. One of them should be happy and in love, and since she did not have a potential man in mind, all hope fell to Angelina. High on Skylar's list of things to do tonight was to have some girl time with her bestie. They had a lot to catch up on, and nowhere in those plans was Skylar making a love connection with Dimitri. His latest actions told her he would never change. If they were to get together, it would only bring out the worst in him.

From the flyers that were released, I-Kandies' grand reopening was going to be wild. The new owner was entering everyone into a drawing for a private party on a day of their choosing. The winner would have complete access to the entire club, the staff, and all the food and drinks they wanted. That alone was enough of an incentive to bring out people in drones. With a new owner and new decor, I-Kandies was sure to have a new vibe, and that was something Skylar was looking forward to. She was thrilled that someone had finally changed that outdated club. As a fan of the club, it was a great hang-out spot, but its decor was stuck in a bad techno era. Skylar hated the so-called "eye candy cages," some of the music that was played, and, most of all, the tacky disco ball that hung above the dance floor. By making these simple changes, I-Kandies would be by far the best club in the city, hands down. Like everyone else, she was intrigued to see the new reveal.

As the minutes ticked by, it was time to get dressed and for Skylar to meet her friends for a night of fun. Feeling the need to cause a little trouble and be a thorn in Dimitri's side, Skylar did something she normally would not have done. Looking in her closet, her purple dress screamed, *Wear me, wear me.* This was the same dress Dimitri had requested to see her in and would make him drool at the sight of her in it. Hopefully, the dress would have the same effect on someone other than Dimitri. The dress was amazing; it clung to Skylar in all the right places and showed off her best assets, her long, toned legs. To add to the drama of her dress, Skylar added her five-inch heels. The dress and heels added just enough sexy to get her noticed and, at the same time, keep something to the imagination. Tonight, was going to be all about her and what she wanted or, more importantly, whom she wanted, and Dimitri Huntington was not on that list. With one last look in the mirror, Skylar knew that tonight was going to be fun as she grabbed her keys and black clutch.

The crowd did not disappoint, as everyone came out for a seek peek of the new I-Kandies night club. The renovations and all the incentives the new owner put out did the trick. The line was wrapped down the stairs and around the City Center. I-Kandies was going to be an extremely popular club for the next several weekends until that new smell wore off. Dimitri had already anticipated that the club was going to be crazy. He was not taking any chances tonight. Skylar had already rescheduled their date because she had to be out of town for work. He was not about to let the possibility that they did not get into the club be another cause of delay for their date.

Thursday evening, when the website went live, Dimitri logged on quickly to reserve a booth in the new VIP area. He could care less about the renovations to the club. All he cared about was getting Skylar alone and picking up where they left off. Kissing her was high on his list of things to do, kissing her and so much more. Tonight, Dimitri was not going to let Skylar label their connection as just friends. That was a lie. She was too flirty with him, flirtier than a friend should be. With a little persuading and some time alone, Dimitri was sure he would get Skylar to see things his way. Dimitri arrived before his party to check into his VIP booth and set the vibe for the night. Of all the renovations, he liked the new additions to VIP the best. The booths were much nicer than before and offered him more privacy, which was a bonus.

He loved the new two-way glass the most. It was a nice touch to the new VIP booths. He and Skylar would have the privacy he wanted and still feel as if they were a part of the party below. Getting James to take Angelina to the dancefloor at some point would not be a problem at all. Tonight, was going to be his night. He and Skylar would be taking their friendship to the next level. Knowing the kitchen might get backed up, Dimitri ordered two bottles of White Grape Cîroc, a round of tequila shots, and two orders of lemon pepper wings. He did not want Skylar to come up with yet another reason to leave him alone in VIP. Dimitri had thought of everything. He made sure that everything was perfect and exactly what Skylar would have wanted. Tonight, he was finally going to get the girl.

Somehow Skylar had managed to talk Dimitri out of picking her up like this was a real date. Letting him drive her to the club was opening a can of worms that would have been impossible to close again. It helped that Angelina told him that she and Skylar had some girl stuff to take care of first. It was their plan to meet each other outside of the club before meeting up with James and Dimitri. They had to get their signals together just in case Skylar was going to need Angelina's help tonight. She hoped she would not need to use any of the signals, but with how Dimitri was acting, she had to be prepared for anything. Skylar did not want to ruin a good night by having to kill Dimitri if he was not on his best behavior.

The club was incredible, much nicer than Skylar would have imagined. It was sleek and sexy. It was as if the new owner was inside of her head. Everything she wanted to change was changed. To her amazement, the stupid eye candy cages were replaced with an aerial ring that she planned to use if she consumed enough liquid courage . Having on a dress was going to make it somewhat difficult to perform on the ring, but if the occasion called for it, then it was going to happen.

With all the new changes, it was hard for Skylar to walk away from the dance floor. The entire vibe of the club had changed, and the music was the best part. Dancing was all she wanted to do. She deserved a night of dancing since her plans a few weeks ago got derailed. Looking in the direction of the new VIP booths, Skylar knew that up there Dimitri was waiting for her but so was James. Leaving the dance floor now was for the best. Skylar's only comfort was that it was going to be packed, making it that much easier for her to lose Dimitri later. Like clockwork, Skylar felt that slight tingle in her gut and realized just how much she missed that feeling. It was like what she had been feeling, but at the same time, it was different. Skylar ignored those feelings since she was already on edge waiting for the time when Dimitri got under her skin. For now, she was going to play nice and play this little game with him if he stayed in his place. When Angelina saw James for the first time tonight, she was all smiles. He did look nice in his simple dark jeans and white button-down shirt. James appeared to be right for Angelina, and Skylar hoped that things worked out well for them.

Dimitri was another story; like always, he was trying way too hard to impress her. He wore a three-piece suit. *Who does that?* thought Skylar. Granted, I-Kandies was much nicer than before, but it was not the suit type of club. Skylar loved a man in a suit, but Dimitri was not doing it for her. Now that everyone was there, the plan was to just hang out, chill, and catch up with each other. They all lived busy lives, and it had been a while since the four of them had seen each other. The conversations were going great, and Dimitri was being on his best behavior so far. It did annoy Skylar that he sat beside her and tried to act as if they were together, but at the very least, he was keeping to himself, so it was okay.

Skylar hoped this would continue all night long. She did not want to be the cause of any drama tonight. Sitting around and talking was starting to be a big problem for her. That butterfly feeling increased, and she had this pent-up energy that she needed to dance away. The other problem Skylar was having was her dress was meant to be seen and not hidden away in VIP all night long. After sitting around and chatting for about an hour, Skylar was over it all.

"Can we please go downstairs?" She was met with an unhappy look from Dimitri, but at this point, she did not care. Aside from just dancing, she needed to put some distance between her and him. Skylar knew it was only a matter of time before he returned to his overbearing, annoying self. Before things got out of hand, Angelina and James both backed Skylar's suggestion to move this little gathering downstairs for some more fun. Dimitri was the only one who had a problem with this suggestion, but he was out voted.

The new DJ was great, as he kept the vibe high and everyone dancing. This was Skylar's chance to ditch Dimitri and find someone who sparked her interest. As far as she was concerned, she had honored her end of the deal. She spent over an hour in VIP with Dimitri and now her hands were clean, and their "date" was over. This was her time to put her dress to some good use and find her some eye candy of her own.

It was completely astounding how free Skylar felt when she was away from Dimitri. That butterfly feeling she had in her stomach slowly started to fade away, and she was ready to party. Every song the DJ played was better than the last one. It was a great mix of old-school hip-hop and today's hits. The DJ played "Raise Up," the North Carolina anthem of 2001 by Petey Pablo, which just so happened to be one of Skylar's favorite songs. She was not able to resist the urge she had to dance as she made her way to the most crowded part of the club. Skylar was a great dancer, and everywhere she looked there was an equally handsome man who wanted to dance with her. This was what she had been missing while sitting in VIP. She made it a point to dance with every one of them until she was tired and needed a drink. The bar was just as nice as the rest of the club. It was stocked with several different kinds of tequila. Again, Skylar was like a kid in a candy store with all the options that she had. As more of a hardcore drinker, she ordered a shot of Sauza Tres Generaciones, which was her favorite brand.

Two shots later, Skylar was finally spotted at the bar by Dimitri. *So much for getting away from him for the rest of the night*, she thought.

"There you are," he said from behind her. "You are one hard woman to find; why did you leave me?" Skylar could tell that Dimitri was somewhat angry and annoyed by her disappearance.

"Dimitri, I have told you a thousand times, we are not together. I can go where I damn well please."

"Feisty," he said. "I know that, Skylar, I am just trying to look out for you and keep you safe; there could be a killer on the loose and it is my job to protect and serve."

There was a chance that Dimitri could be right, but still, Skylar did not care. That was not a good enough reason for her to stay by his side the entire night. Skylar could protect herself. She was trained in Krav Maga and did not need a man to save her. From behind her, Dimitri massaged her shoulders, moving down her arms. He took her hand in his and asked, "Can I have one dance, please?" he said with those big puppy dog eyes of his.

"Just one dance, Dimitri," said Skylar as he flashed that big boyish smile of his. Somehow that one dance turned into several, as Dimitri would not let Skylar go. He even had the nerve to side eye every man who looked at her, giving them the impression that he was her man. Skylar should have known that he would not keep his promise and keep his hands to himself. The thought of punching him just so he would have to take his hands off her crossed Skylar's mind several times. Somehow, she needed to get away from him before she did something she would regret. Thankfully, her prayers were answered when she saw Angelina and James making their way towards them.

They were a godsend when Skylar was minutes away from going crazy on Dimitri. Like so many times before, Angelina was coming to the rescue when Skylar was minutes away from losing her temper. What she was planning on doing to Dimitri would not have been a pretty sight. She was happy to see that Angelina had been having such a great time with James. The excitement was written all over her face, but Skylar still noticed that something was off with her friend. Angelina walked over and grabbed Skylar by the arms and said, "We need to talk, now." Those words were the best words Skylar had ever heard. She wasted no time in wiggling out of Dimitri's grasp to get some alone time with her friend. Unfortunately, Dimitri was not about to let her out of his sight for another minute. He quickly grabbed her arm, pulling her back by his side. James, of all people, came to the rescue.

"Let's give the ladies some time to talk; we can watch over them from the bar while we have a few drinks and catch up."

Angelina mouthed a soft "Thank you" to James before taking her best friend deeper onto the dancefloor far away from Dimitri.

"By the look on your face, it looks like I got there just in time."

"You did, I was about two seconds away from breaking his nose. Let's not talk about it. What about you and James?"

"Well, I like him well enough; he is not the overbearing asshole that Dimitri is. I am not sure how they are friends. He is a nice, sweet, respectable guy, but there are not any butterflies or sparks or anything like that between the two of us. Don't get me wrong, I think he is handsome, but he is not who I see myself with when I close my eyes."

"Well, we don't have to talk about him right now either; let's just dance and have as much fun as we can."

"You're right, but first we need a drink." Angelina quickly went to the bar and returned with two whiskey sours now that the bar was open for its free hour of drinks.

Skylar and Angelina put all conversations aside and focused on dancing the night away and releasing some much-needed tension. For the rest of the night, their plan was to have fun and not worry about anything else. About ten minutes into their fun, both James and Dimitri rejoined them wanting to get in on the fun that they were having. Whatever James had said to Dimitri worked; once he was back around Skylar and Angelina, he seemed to be calmer and more relaxed. He was no longer the same overbearing, controlling ass he was before. From this point on, Dimitri did not exist to Skylar. She was a single woman who was going to do as she pleased no matter what. Under the annoyed and watchful eye of Dimitri, Skylar danced with every guy who came her way. Her actions were upsetting to him, but she no longer cared about him or his feelings. When Angelina suggested that they go to the bar for more drinks, Dimitri reared his ugly head once more. As if he could control her, Dimitri tried his best to stop them from getting more drinks.

"I think that you have had enough drinks, Skylar."

Fed up with him and his attitude, Skylar was about to give him a real piece of her mind. As she was about to tell him where he could stick his two cents, Angelina beat her to the punch.

"Please shut the hell up, Dimitri; no one here needs or wants you to take care of them; trust me, we got this." Skylar loved Angelina; she may have been small, but she had a bite that was vicious.

Needing to lighten the mood, they ordered two Shirley Temples this time. Believe it or not, but they knew their limits when it came to drinking, and they would never cross that line. Sitting at the bar with its new plush seats, Skylar could see James and Dimitri approaching from the left. In that moment, Skylar decided that she was done giving Dimitri all her energy and all her time. This was her night to have fun and enjoy herself. Without warning, that butterfly feeling she had earlier returned in a huge way. Skylar felt weird and somewhat queasy inside. The energy in the room was off the charts as it appeared to spark and buzz around her like she had Spidey senses. It was the strangest feeling in the world, totally unreal. *Why is this happening to me?* she thought as she looked around the room trying to find the cause of the strange energy. Not sure what she hoped to find, but everything stopped the minute she laid eyes on him.

It was as if they were the only people in the room, the only people in the world. The music stopped, all the voices were silenced, and the lights dimmed everywhere except where he was standing. Like the Statue of Adonis, he was magnificent, a beautiful God for Skylar's eyes only. Instantly, she had this possessive spirit that came over her that screamed "mine" while her eyes were locked onto him. She could not focus on anything but him, his toned body, chiseled, bronzed chest barely hidden behind his half-unbuttoned shirt and his amazingly kissable lips. His golden amber eyes sparkled and shined bright like the aura that surrounded him. *Was anyone else seeing this magnificent and bewitching man besides me?* thought Skylar. She was afraid to blink or even take her eyes off him as she feared that he would vanish into thin air.

He could have his pick of any woman in the world, and Skylar was concerned that she was not his type. While she was pretty and full of confidence, she did not fit into that "bad body" category that men like him wanted. His eyes were locked in her direction, but that did not mean he was looking at her. *Is he hypnotized by me?* she thought. Or *is there some superficial female in the distance that has caught his eye?* Completely overwhelmed by the energy pulling her towards him, Skylar was about to leave her seat at the bar when Angelina finally regained her attention.

"Hello, Earth to Skylar, come in, Skylar," said Angelina as she reached out and touched her friend bringing her back from the trance that he put her in.

"What are you starring at?" Angelina asked as she looked in the direction that held her attention for so long.

"Huh, what were you saying?"

"What or who took your attention away?" Angelina asked again as she looked around trying to figure out what had gotten into Skylar.

Skylar looked again, and he was gone. *What the hell?* she thought. *Am I going crazy?* Angelina did the same looking again where Skylar's eyes went to. "He was right there," she said. "I swear, he was the sexist man that I have ever seen."

Still looking around for him, Skylar was positive he had to be close. She could feel that strange energy pulling her towards the stage and aerial ring. Every fiber of her being wanted to go in search of him, to be touched by him, and loved by him. Angelina had to see him for herself to know that he was real. It all felt like a dream, a crazy, wonderful dream.

Skylar was determined to find him at all costs and prove to Angelina and herself that she was not crazy. Finally, after what felt like forever, her search could come to an end. Skylar spotted him by the stage hiding in the shadows, and Angelina saw him with her own eyes. That gave Skylar an idea.

"WOW, he is fine," said Angelina, "and as far as I can tell, he cannot take his eyes off you." That was hard for Skylar to hear.

"Wait, what?" she said as she looked again in his direction. For the second time that night, it did look like he was staring at her and only her. Knowing that gave Skylar the motivation she needed to put her plan into motion. Dimitri was distracted, and for once, his focus was not on her. This was Skylar's only chance to do something bold and equally amazing. She was sure of what she had to do. Rising from the barstool, she walked with a purpose over to the aerial ring.

"What are you about to go do?"

With a sly smile, Skylar said, "Give him the best show of his life."

By the time Skylar got over to the stage, he was gone again. This time, Skylar did not bother looking for him. She knew he was close since she could still feel that pull of energy. Still concerned that she was not his type Skylar had to show him just how talented she was. She needed him to know that those other women had nothing on her. It had been six months since she performed on the ring last, but it was like riding a bike. Skylar knew it would all come back to her. The fact that she was not dressed appropriately was a little concerning, but deep-down, she had to do this. Nothing else mattered but her, the ring, and the fact that he was somewhere in this club watching her every move. As if on cue, the DJ started to play Lil Wayne's "Make it Rain." Up there on that ring, Skylar was free, free from herself, her fears, just free, and she loved every minute of it. This had been her best performance in a long time, and she was beyond happy.

After the second song, Skylar came down from the stage feeling great. She had all eyes on her and knew that somewhere in the shadows he was also watching her. That freeing feeling that she had quickly came to an end as Dimitri approached her. He was furious with her and had lost his mind when he grabbed her, pulling her off the stage.

"What the hell was that, Skylar? How could you go up there and show your ass to everyone in here?"

Skylar was shocked and too pissed off to give Dimitri an answer. What she did was of no concern to him. She did not do this for him, and she did not care how he felt about it. When she refused to answer him, that level of disrespect drove him mad. He had lost his mind when he slapped Skylar hard across the face. Dimitri wanted a reaction from her, and he was about to get one. In the blink of an eye Skylar, punched him in the face. She was not sure if she broke his nose or gave him a black eye. All she cared about was that he felt that punch and that she was not playing with him anymore. Before Skylar could hit Dimitri again, Angelina and James rushed over to break things up. Skylar was fuming; she could not believe Dimitri had done that, and as Angelina was pulling her away, she yelled, "PUT YOUR HANDS ON ME AGAIN AND I WILL KILL YOU!" James helped his friend make sure his nose was not broken before taking him in the opposite direction to calm down and figure out what was going on with him.

Angelina took Skylar back to their VIP booth to calm down and ask her own set of questions.

"What was that all about?"

"I don't want to talk about that right now," said Skylar. "I can't believe that bastard hit me," she said as she drank the last of the Cîroc.

"Calm down, Skylar, and talk to me; what was up with that performance?"

"I don't know what came over me. When I saw him by the stage, I had this overwhelming feeling inside of me that pushed me to do something amazing for him. I wanted to give him a performance he would never forget so that he would not forget me."

"Well, I'm sure you did that; you were incredible up there," said Angelina. That was a side of Skylar she had never seen before. The one thing that they could agree on was Dimitri and how wrong he was. As crazy as the night was, Angelina still felt like there was more to the story, that Skylar was leaving a big part out. Angelina was not the type of friend to push, so when Skylar was ready to talk about it, she would listen and be the friend Skylar needed.

"One thing for sure is that you know how to piss Dimitri off."

"Well, that is not my problem; it is his. I have told him a thousand times that we are not dating."

After all the fireworks, the ladies really did need to relax, and thankfully, James nor Dimitri came back to the VIP booth for the rest of the night. After what Dimitri pulled tonight, Skylar was not sure if their friendship could be fixed. Tipsy and hungry, they ordered some much-needed comfort food, loaded cheese fries and soft drinks. As things started to settle down again, Skylar noticed that her butterflies and that overall weird feeling were back. This time the feeling was off, and she could not tell if it was from him or her fighting with Dimitri. For starters, what Skylar was feeling was darker and angrier than it was before. It was not that light and airy feeling she had become used to feeling. Maybe it was her body telling her that Dimitri was close by; this was his VIP booth after all. Just because it looked like he and James left did not mean that they did. Skylar was happy Dimitri stayed away. She was not in the mood to deal with him, hear his excuses, or accept his apology. At least not right now anyway.

Skylar and Angelina spent the rest of the night in VIP talking and laughing until the DJ called for the final song of the night. For the last two hours, they did not hear from James or Dimitri. To completely disappear was not like him at all. Anytime they had a disagreement, Dimitri was quick to seek Skylar's forgiveness. In the back of her mind, Skylar knew that something was wrong. She tried to stay positive and hoped that Dimitri just needed more time to gather himself and say he was sorry. This was the first time that he had ever hit Skylar, or any woman for that matter. Angry or not, Skylar hoped to at least hear from him or James at some point tonight. She needed to know that Dimitri was okay and that he did not go and do something stupid because he was upset.

CHAPTER 12

She Belongs to Me

*I*t had been a long two-week process, but the end was finally here. It was Friday night, and Kairo could reopen I-Kandies. The buzz and overall human curiosity had worked out in his favor. Everyone was making plans to attend the grand reopening of one of Charlotte's favorite nightclubs. It seemed like all the work Kairo had done was paying off. He was sure that the hour of free drinks and the chance to win a free party helped their cause out a great deal. Humans were so predictable; they loved anything that was free. For the suggestion, Kairo owed Malachi in a huge way, and tonight, he would repay him for that kindness. Tonight, Malachi would be the guest of honor. According to gossip that Kairo would start, Malachi was going to play a rich and handsome prince who was here in America looking for his bride-to-be while out having a night of fun. By doing this, Kairo was ensuring that Malachi would have his pick of the litter and hopefully be too preoccupied to be concerned with what he was doing tonight. If more women were like Stacee, everyone in the club would be dying just to get close to Malachi. It had been a while since Kairo had his hands on a proper little mouse, a mouse that was as much fun as Stacee had been. Malachi did not approve of his cat and mouse game, so things had to change for a while. Tonight, however, they both were going to get exactly what they wanted.

Now that Malachi was all set to be a prince, there was no telling what he was going to be wearing. Knowing him, it was going to be something flashy to match the grand entrance he was planning to make in hopes of catching the eye of all the beautiful women. Kairo had already played the role of the handsome rich man, so tonight, he was simply going to be himself, his human self, who was the owner of the club. He needed a change since he was not feeling like himself lately. Without that pull of energy, life seemed dull and boring to him. He did not have the time nor the energy to create this elaborate story about who he was. In continuing the trend of keeping things simple, Kairo wore some black slacks paired with a white button-down shirt, which he left halfway unbuttoned. It was important for him to give the ladies a sneak peek at his body in the hopes to have them drooling all over him. As the saying goes, *Less is more*.

In keeping with the theme of simplicity, Kairo's red Stingray was the vehicle chosen to get him to the club two hours ahead of the scheduled opening. Kairo wanted to take some time for himself and be there to witness everyone's arrival. He just wanted to be alone for a few hours hoping that the energy would return. It was paramount that he kept Malachi off his scent and happy tonight. Malachi preordered six bottles of Johnnie Walker Blue Label Ghost and three bottles of pink Moscato for the ladies. With his booth setup and the seed planted, Malachi was all set for the evening.

Walking around his now empty club, Kairo had to pat himself on the back. He had truly outdone himself. With its new face lift, I-Kandies was nothing short of spectacular. It spoke to who Kairo truly was as a man. It was bold and sexy, and Kairo could not wait for the doors to open and for everyone to see it. The doors were scheduled to open at eleven and not a minute sooner. The vibe in the air told Kairo that things were looking up as he felt that slight pull of energy. For reasons unknown to him, the pull was not as strong as it had been, but it was there all the same. Kairo had to admit that he was proud of the work he and Malachi had done while he was sitting in his office waiting for the doors to open. In a matter of time, more of his kind would be able to come and pay him a visit and play in peace. This idea of his was going to work, and Kairo would have the first vampire club where his kind could be themselves. No hiding, no compromising, just free to be themselves no matter how dark and twisted they were.

Kairo had the best seat in the house, his lavish leather chair offered him a great view of the entire club. The massive two-way window allowed him to watch over the fruits of his labor. From there, he could see every inch of the dance floor below, so finding his next little mouse should be easy. From up there, everything was amazing, a visual feast for the eyes. The LED bar and lit shelves created a warm and inviting space that would draw in all types of people. The drinks would overflow as they celebrated his new establishment. The only way this night could get any better was to have someone test out the aerial ring above the stage. The ring required skill and talent, so it was not for the faint of heart. Kairo watched the clock as the minutes slowly ticked away and neared time for the doors to open.

Just as he had expected, when the doors opened, it was as if the floodgates had been opened. The line was steady and moved until the club was filled up with partygoers ready to let loose and have fun. A few of the patrons had been smart and had already reserved them a booth in VIP to ensure that they would be spending the evening here for the club's grand reopening. There were three VIP booths that were available tonight. The largest one with the best view had already been reserved for Prince Omari and his royal party as well as two others that were reserved on Thursday. Many of Kairo's guests were hoping to go ahead and take advantage of the hour of free drinks only to be disappointed. Kairo's guests were going to have to spend some of their own money before they got something for free. The DJ would be making that announcement at 12:30 am. The new DJ Kairo hired was a hit, as more and more people hit the dance floor and refused to leave it. Kairo was pleased with how everything had turned out.

As expected, within the hour I-Kandies had reached its capacity limit, and as a man of his word, everyone that did not get access to the club tonight was given a golden ticket that guaranteed them access on Saturday night. No matter where they were in line, they would be the first ones in as long as they had that golden ticket with them. Kairo heard from his staff that all the golden ticket holders left I-Kandies with a smile on their faces, so his plan worked, and they would be back. Everyone was happy, and soon, some were going to be on cloud nine if they were one of the lucky ones to get a chance to spend the night with an "actual prince." Checking his watch, Kairo was aware that within the next thirty minutes, Malachi and his entourage would be arriving.

After what happened at his housewarming party, Kairo made sure Malachi would be happy. He double checked Malachi's booth one last time to ensure that everything was laid out according to the wishes of the prince. In due time, Malachi would have his own playthings, and it was time for Kairo to find him a new little mouse.

In true fashion, Malachi made a grand entrance. He stole everything from an old American movie that he was watching about a prince. Malachi even compelled some lovely ladies to walk in front of him dropping rose petals at his feet. The whole thing was comical and made Kairo and a few people in attendance laugh. Kairo was safe since Malachi did not see him laughing, but as for the others, they may not be so lucky. The chance that Malachi would kill them all was high, but for now, he had his eye trained on someone else. With his unique look and mysterious allure, Malachi had both women and men checking him out. Everyone wanted a chance to get next to the prince, and knowing Malachi, everyone that wanted that chance would be granted access to him at some point. It was unclear what flavors among the crowd would appeal to him, but he would know it when he smelled it. Kairo was fine with whatever he did if he stayed out of his way and was happy. With the turnout, Kairo knew it was only a matter of time before he found what he was looking for as well.

Malachi worked fast; within the first thirty minutes, he had already picked out three beautiful young women to accompany him to his VIP booth. As promised Kairo had given him the best booth for tonight and everything was perfect. Keeping to his story, Malachi toasted with his guests to finding his future bride and to enjoying all that America had to offer. There was no doubt in his mind that Malachi would be happy and satisfied. Malachi was one less thing that he had to worry about. There was nothing left for Kairo to do but focus on setting his first trap of the night. His office provided the best view since all the VIP booths had been reserved. It was from here that he would watch from above until he found what he was looking for. Kairo watched and waited and waited and watched.

Something was off; Kairo had spent hours in his office, but nothing piqued his interest. He thought the energy was back, but it was all wrong and not the same as before. *Perhaps this energy I am feeling is not the same*, thought Kairo. That did not sit well with him. Tonight, he was supposed to locate the source of that energy. That was why he did all of this in the first place. Kairo believed that his night was going to turn around, so he gave it some more time. He continued to search for his next mouse, but nothing caught his eye. More time was not what he needed. The energy was starting to be very frustrating for him, and Kairo was starting to wish that he never felt it in the first place. Having these types of feelings was a huge risk, a risk that was going to get him killed. From Kairo's view from the top, everyone was having the best night of their lives. He even heard from the staff that Malachi had men and women coming and going from his booth, so he was happy. While some thought the prince angle was fake, there were several people who believed every word of it. Malachi chose his favorites to stay with him in VIP and to accompany him back to his place. I-Kandies provided Kairo with all types of women, but sadly, none of them were special. Everything about them was average to him, even the way they smelled. Kairo was bored with all of them, and that was completely out of character for him.

A night that started out perfect was quickly ending on a sour note for Kairo. Hoping that once he left his office things would look up. Finally Kairo made the move hoping that a change in scenery would change his mood. Before going down to the dancefloor and getting closer to the action, he checked in on Malachi. He might have a morsel or two that would get Kairo's spirits back up. Typically, they did not share treats with each other, but Kairo was hopeful that Malachi had something he did not want. There was no one that could read Kairo's mood the way Malachi could. Even before he walked into Malachi's booth, Malachi knew that there was something off with him.

"Have you not found a mouse yet? I have plenty; do you see anything you like? I have not touched them yet."

Kairo looked around and there were plenty of women for the taking, but still, no one jumped out at him until he finally felt it. That tingle of energy turned into a full force of power that pulled at him stronger than ever before. At that moment, Kairo knew that the source of that energy was close by. He had to find it before it was lost to him forever.

"No, that is okay. I think I will have a look around downstairs," he said. Finally leaving his office was about to pay off. This was what Kairo had been waiting for as the energy in the club became electrified and alive to him. He could not get away from Malachi fast enough. As always, Malachi had already picked up on the change in his mood.

"I see you have picked up on something you like; well, go and enjoy. I know I will," said Malachi.

Kairo gave into the energy, letting it consume him as he let it drive him straight to the stairs that led to the first level. Standing on the landing at the top of the stairs, Kairo looked out into the crowd in search of the source of energy that called to him. One look in her direction and everything changed. Kairo was unaware of anything or anyone other than her. She was stunning and unlike anything that he had ever seen. She lit up his world and eclipsed everything around her. She was a vision in purple, and she was his, all his. Had Kairo not been able to feel her, he would have believed that she was not real. She was, hands down, the most beautiful creature that he had ever seen. She was incredible, and Kairo needed her, wanted her, and was going to have her no matter what. Her hair was like black silk that came to the middle of her back; her skin was like creamy milk chocolate that he wanted to taste. Her eyes were luminescent and exotic while at the same time sweet and mischievous. Her body was naturally curvy. Everything about her was natural, real, and succulent. Her dress hugged every curve of her body as it showcased her perfectly long, toned legs as she sat at the bar. She had legs that Kairo wanted to kiss all the way to her juicy sweet center. From clear across the room, her scent was intoxicating. Kairo had to have her and taste her. She belonged to him, and soon, she would be put to the test as his newest little mouse.

For the first time in all his existence, Kairo was frozen in place when they locked eyes with each other. As they were totally connected with each other, she smiled at him. It was a smile that could easily light up the darkest room. She was like the sun after a rainy day; one look at her and the darkness was gone. Kairo was completely in tune with her every move. They were like one body moving together in perfect harmony. Everything and everyone around them disappeared. They no longer existed. Kairo was even unaware of Malachi watching the two of them closely from behind him. The seconds seemed like hours to him, as he could stay like that forever.

Kairo was in pure nirvana until her friend regained her attention. She called her by her name, *Skylar*, and it was the sweetest tasting sound to ever grace Kairo's lips. With his exceptional hearing, he was pleased to learn that he affected her the same way that she affected him. She thought that he was sexy and even tried to deny the fact that he was looking at her. Kairo wanted her blood, and to hear her screams of both pleasure and pain. Sensing that she was about to walk over to him, Kairo had to move quickly. Now was not the time for the two of them to share a space because he was losing control fast. It was not safe for them to share the same space, surrounded by so many on-lookers, because Kairo wanted to devour her. He was quickly losing control of the monster that lived inside of him. With all these people here and Malachi, that would not have been a good idea. Her scent was now embedded into every fiber of his being, so he would find her again.

In a split second, Kairo was gone from her view, and that annoyed her. Skylar thought she was going crazy, and it was killing Kairo to torture her like that. He did not like it, but he had to hide from her since their safety was paramount. The distress that Kairo was putting her through was unbearable, and it forced him to come out of his hiding spot. That was exactly what she needed, as his presence put her at ease and, at the same time, put the two of them back in harm's way. Kairo watched in amazement as Skylar walked towards him with a newfound purpose. She was approaching the stage, and that filled him with so much joy and excitement. *Is she about to do this?* he thought. Skylar closed her eyes and took a deep breath allowing for Kairo to hide deeper in the shadows to watch her perform. This time, Skylar did not look for him, as her mind was focused on the ring in front of her. Keeping to the shadows, Kairo found the perfect spot to watch his mouse. He put enough distance between them to allow him to drown in her delicious scent while keeping a safe distance from her. Outside of VIP, I-Kandies was just too public of a place for Kairo to play with Skylar the way he wanted to. With Malachi here, he had to keep his wits about him and not do something stupid.

As Kairo looked at her friend, she was thrilled at what was about to happen. Kairo and almost everyone in attendance was excited to watch Skylar perform. There was one man who was not so happy about her decision. Kairo could read the disappointment and anger that was written all over his face. *Who is he; what is his connection to my Skylar?* thought Kairo. If they were together or if he thought they were going to be together, that was going to be a huge problem. Kairo had already decided that Skylar was his, and he always got what he wanted. She was going to be his in every way possible until he was bored with her. That was something that she did not have a choice in.

Her performance was astonishing. She was utterly incredible; magical was the best way to describe it. For Skylar's first performance, she danced to Lil Wayne's "Make it Rain." It was such an appropriate song since Kairo wanted to do just that. He wanted to give her whatever her heart desired. Her second performance was even better than the first. She finally let go of all her nerves and was free as a bird in flight. Her strength and flexibility were impressive, and Kairo knew that she would be a fun little mouse. He could not take his eyes off her. She changed his mind; of all the additions that he made to the club, the rings were his favorite by far. Just out of curiosity, Kairo looked in the direction of the angry male only to find that he was furious and heading straight for her. Everything was fine until he put his hands on her. Who in the hell did he think he was touching what did not belong to him? Skylar took Kairo by surprise when she punched him in the face and threatened to kill him.

Do not worry, my love, he will pay for putting his hands on you, thought Kairo.

They were both in agreement; he would turn up dead if he ever touched her again. Kairo needed to calm down, as he was enraged by this man's actions. Kairo was positive that Dimitri was not Skylar's boyfriend, and therefore, he would learn not to touch her again. He had better pray that Kairo would allow him to continue breathing after what he had just done.

If it were not for the fact that Kairo did not want to see Skylar harmed in any way, he would have emerged from the shadows and ended Dimitri right there in the middle of the dance floor. That would have been a huge mistake with Malachi here. As of right now, they were safe. The Council was not located in Charlotte, and if they did not draw unnecessary attention to themselves, they were fine. Dimitri would have to wait for now. Kairo needed to see Skylar to calm down; he needed to see for himself that she was okay.

It only took a matter of seconds before Kairo found Skylar back in the VIP booth that Dimitri reserved. That angered him all over again. He was aware of why Dimitri had reserved them a booth in VIP. It was his plan to be alone with Skylar and do inappropriate things with her. Kairo was seeing red all over again, but the silver lining was his connection with Skylar. Somehow, he could feel her emotions, and while she was still angry, this new connection between them caused Kairo to forget about Dimitri. This was something new for him and something that he was growing to love. It took every ounce of force he had to stop himself from knocking down that fragile wall that stood in between him and Skylar. Her voice, her scent, hell, everything about her made him come alive in a new way. This woman made him crazy, and he needed to get away from her, and at the same time, he could not stand to leave her side. *Soon, my little mouse, you will be all mine. I will hear you scream*, he thought. Before he could claim Skylar for his own, he still had the matter of Dimitri to deal with. It was hard, but Kairo walked away from Skylar and left the club in search of Dimitri. It was time he learned a valuable lesson.

CHAPTER 13

An Unforgettable Night

Skylar was still fuming after what Dimitri had pulled at the club. She could not believe that he put his hands on her. Skylar touched her face where he had slapped her, and her cheek was still sore. In all the years she had known Dimitri, she had never seen this side of him before. Dimitri was not the type of man to hit a woman no matter how mad or upset he was. Who was this man, and what had he done to the Dimitri she had known for years? Dimitri was lucky that Angelina got her away from him before she did more than just punch him in the face. The night started out great and ended badly very badly. Angelina called James again and finally got in touch with him. James told her that as far as he knew Dimitri was fine, but he was still angry and upset. The last time they spoke he left him alone to cool off in the alleyway behind the City Center.

Even though Skylar was still angry with Dimitri she was thankful to know that he was okay. The ball was in his court now. It was up to him to reach out to her and apologize to her for what he had done. Their friendship was going to be up in the air for a while, and if they were going to have a friendship in the future, Dimitri was going to have to understand where she stood. This game of theirs was going to end before one of them got hurt. It was clear to Skylar that she was going to have to call Dimitri out on his jealous behavior. She was not attracted to him in that way, and she would never be. Dimitri was her longtime friend, and his current actions were threatening to end their friendship forever. He had crossed a line that was going to take her some time to get over.

Now, that man she locked eyes with and performed for was a totally different story. Skylar would be whatever he wanted her to be, no questions asked. He did things to her without having to touch her. With one look, he made her feel things no man had ever made her feel.

It had been such a long night, and Skylar did not want to be alone. She begged Angelina to stay the night with her since she had so much that she wanted to talk to her about. With Skylar's persuasive speech, Angelina could not resist the idea to stay the night with her friend. Truthfully, she wanted to talk to her about that mysterious man and the things he had her doing. They both were tired, but sleep was going to have to wait for a few more hours.

Just as their LYFT ride pulled up in front of Skylar's house, the skies finally opened as the long-awaited storm hit the city. Skylar had known all along that it was going to rain at some point today. She felt it deep in her bones. She was glad it waited until they had ended their night out. Immediately inside, Angelina went straight to the questions.

"So, what was that all about?"

With a guilty look and a smile that said it all, Skylar said, "What?" like she was some innocent schoolgirl.

"Oh no, you are not getting off that easy, start talking."

Skylar did not know where to begin or how she could explain something that she did not understand herself.

"I honestly don't know how to explain to you how I was feeling and what actually happened.

"When I first laid eyes on him, something inside of me changed. The energy in the room was different; it was as if we shared this connection. He made me feel things I have never felt before. The thought of losing that connection drove me mad. I had to do something to keep his eyes on me and that connection between us alive. I wanted him to be mine mentally, physically, and sexually. I still want him now that I am thinking about him, but what am I supposed to do, stalk him every night at the club? I cannot describe to you how he made me feel with just one look. He was across the room and made every cell in my body come alive. I can only imagine how good he could make me feel with just one touch if he were to be inside of me. You know me, Angie, I am far from a shy person, but the thought of talking to him scared me to death. Performing on the ring gave me the confidence I needed to be able to approach him, until Dimitri ruined everything."

Angelina understood where Skylar was coming from, even though it sounded crazy to them both.

Angelina was at a loss for words and just accepted Skylar's answer and did not push her for anything more than what she offered.

"I have to admit, though, he was fine," stated Angelina. "I almost wish that I had seen him first because I would have been all over him."

Skylar laughed, trying to hide her true feelings about what Angelina had just said. The thought of her best friend anywhere near him filled Skylar with so much rage that she thought about fighting her over that comment. Skylar did not know why but she felt very possessive of him; he was hers.

"What? I was just playing," Angelina said with her hands up as she backed away from Skylar. "I saw that look you gave me, and I was just playing; you are my best friend, and I would never do that."

Skylar knew that she was losing it, what was this man doing to her even now.

"Sorry, Angie, I don't know what is going on with me; the thought of someone else with him makes me angry. I wish that I were able to talk to him and find out what his name was."

"As far as I can tell, it sounds like you REALLY LIKE this man," Angelina said. That thought threw Skylar in an even bigger tailspin than she was already in. How can someone like a man that they do not even know? Skylar knew nothing about him. She never spoke one word to him, but was it possible that she liked him in the way Angelina was suggesting? This was all too confusing and was making her head hurt.

Skylar needed a night cap and some sleep. This conversation was supposed to help, not leave her with more questions than she started with. It should have brought her some clarity, not muddy the waters even more. After one more drink, Skylar was ready for bed, as was Angelina. Skylar could not talk about that man anymore or her potential feelings for him. Tonight, was fun before all the crazy things started to happen. Maybe it was all the strange energy that was floating around tonight that caused Dimitri to act out of character. Thinking of Dimitri made Skylar call him one last time because she felt like something was wrong. There was still no answer, so Skylar left a message hoping to at least hear from him soon.

Not long after Skylar's head hit the pillow, she was fast asleep. It appeared that she was more tired than she thought. The strangest thing was that no sooner had she fallen asleep, she awakened. The bed Skylar was in was not her own. It was a massive four-poster bed with crisp white sheets that smelled of warm spice. It was like the scent of her favorite brand of tequila. The only other furniture that was in the large master bedroom was a matching dresser and black leather armchair. Lying in that bed with its expensive sheets made Skylar want to stay there forever. Also in the room was a set of double French doors. Just through those doors was the most breathtaking view of the lake. It was so tranquil that Skylar never wanted to leave that house. She wanted to see that view every day for the rest of her life.

Slowly the night came back to her. She was at I-Kandies with her friends and left with Angelina after the night turned bad. She should have been waking up in her home in her own bed, but that was not the case. She was still dressed in the same purple dress she wore to I-Kandies and that gave her some comfort. The cool breeze off the lake caught Skylar's attention again, forcing it away from her current surroundings. At that time of night, the lake was peaceful the way it reflected the full moon back on its crystal-clear water. The view was all that Skylar could think about even though she should have been scared or, at the very least, a little bit worried. It was clear to her that she had been taken from her home, but she had not been drugged. She felt normal and was without any of the leftover effects that said she had been drugged. She had not been restrained, so why was she here? The only thing that made sense to her was that she never wanted to leave. Skylar truly felt right at home here.

Completely focused on the view in front of her and lost in thought, Skylar never heard him walk up behind her. He was quiet as a mouse and moved like a cat stalking his prey. Skylar felt his hands and warm, spicy breath against the back of her neck before she ever heard his voice. His hands lingered along her body and caressed her breasts as his silky, soft lips rained kisses down the back of her neck. "That view pales in comparison to you, my love," he said while his hands continued to explore her body. He allowed his hands to trace over every curve of her body. His touch was like magic as he made every cell in her body come alive. "Don't move," he said taking his hands from her and leaving Skylar dying without his touch. "I want to look at you."

Taking his time to face her, Skylar was curious as to who this man was. When their eyes locked onto each other, she was taken aback. It was him, the man from the club, but how could that be? None of this made any sense. *How did he find me?* Everything about him was inviting, and Skylar missed the feel of his hands and lips on her. *Was this about to happen?* she thought to herself. "Who are you?" she asked. The smile that came onto his face was paralyzing, locking her body in place in front of him.

Just before she was about to open her mouth again, he beat her to the punch. "Don't speak, love," he said while placing his finger on her lips. His hand brushed along her cheek. His touch instantly ignited a fire deep inside of her. After what felt like hours, he finally gave in to his need to taste Skylar by claiming her soft, supple lips with his hungry mouth.

The kiss started out slow and chaste before he laced it with more passion and desire. In that kiss he put enough raw passion in it to make Skylar's knees weak and buckle beneath her. His hands continued their exploration of her body, sending waves of heat all through her. Every inch of skin his hands touched continued to add to Skylar's growing blaze. He slowly and gently parted her lips enough for his tongue to enter her mouth. Their tongues intermingled, engaging in the perfect dance working together as one taking Skylar higher. Time stopped while he sent shockwaves all through her.

His hands finally made their way to the zipper of her dress. *Finally*, thought Skylar; this was the moment that she had been waiting for. Slowly he unzipped her dress, exposing more of her sensual body to him. Sweeping her hair away from her neck, he began to trail kisses along her neck and collarbone. Keeping with this method of torture, he kissed Skylar down her spine and back up. His hands found her breasts, caressing them through the thin lace material of her bra. Holding her securely in front of him, his hand lingered down from her breast to the exposed skin of her stomach. With just the tip of his nails, he stroked them across her body, sending waves of pleasure all through her. Skylar was on edge not knowing how much more of this she would be able to take. With just his touch alone, she had been climbing the mountain and was close to the summit. He slowly walked his fingers down her stomach and stopped just above her panty line. His hands stalled there to torture Skylar more. She almost begged him to continue when his hand finally found her vertical smile. Skylar was taken to heaven on a wave of pleasure as his touch made her wet. He quickly turned her to face him again because he needed to taste her sweet lips.

Skylar wanted nothing more than to feel him inside of her. Her hands lingered along the strong muscles of his neck as they traveled down his body. Her fingers found their way under his shirt massaging his toned abs and rock-hard chest. Skylar became aware of his need for her through the growing bulge in his pants. His clothing was a barrier between them working against the fire that he was igniting within her. It was now or never, Skylar had to free him, allowing her hands to linger around the button to his pants. Before she was successful in achieving her goal, his hands firmly grabbed hers by the wrist.

"No, love," he said before sliding his hands inside her bra to please her supple breast. With fingers like magic, he caressed her nipples. With his thumb, he drove her wild with these circles that heightened her arousal. Working from the top of her breast, he bit and nibbled his way back to her waiting mouth. Each bite contained just enough pressure to force the softest *yes* from Skylar's perfect lips. His kisses were directed to her ear where he slid his tongue on, under, and around her earlobe. Taking it between his lips, he sucked on it slowly, finding her spot. Skylar was on a wave of ecstasy that she rode to the mountain top. His tongue was mind-blowing, and she wondered what else it could do to her. Her body was screaming for him, calling out to him, for him to extinguish all the fires he started. He was enjoying the torture he was putting her through. His hands circled every inch of her body. They found their way between Skylar's legs again to rub against her through her panties. With his touch against her precious center, and his tongue working on the sensitive parts of her neck and ear Skylar was close to being pushed over the summit. Knowing that he was close to pushing her over the edge, he walked away from her leaving her wanting more.

The scent of her arousal lingered in the air and along his fingers. Skylar was an exquisite creature to toy with, and he was enjoying every minute of it. She affected him in the same way. He had this primal need to bury himself deep inside of her juicy center. Soon he would get lost inside of her, but first, his torture had to continue. Skylar could no longer allow him to continue his torment of her body. Her frustrations had reached a point of no return. She needed this man now, and she would not wait another second. He was an arsonist who set her on fire only to watch her fires burn. Skylar was done waiting on him.

She was going to be in charge now. She walked closer to him to reclaim his hungry lips. As planned, his hands were busy as they laid claim to her body once again. Knowing how it tortured her and drove her body wild, he dragged his nails across every inch of her skin. In between kissing him, Skylar released the most delicious sounds he had ever heard. Her moans and breathing increased with each touch of her electrified body. He had her where he wanted her, and she had him right where she wanted him. For the second time, her hands found their way to the button on his pants, and for the second time, she was denied. "You don't listen, do you, love? For that, you will be punished."

Skylar's punishment intrigued and excited her. How many more ways could this magnificent man punish her? With one hand, he took possession of both of hers. With his other hand, his sexual assault of her body continued. While her breast were still protected by the fragile material of her bra, his fingers tortured her again. He drove her wild as he traced small circles along her breasts and nipples increasing her arousal. With each stroke of his hand, her nipples became harder against the fabric. He placed his hand inside her bra needing to feel the taught skin around her nipples. His mouth took over where his hand left off. Her arousal increased as she fought to get her hands free of him. He still had not penetrated her yet when his touch finally allowed her to achieve her first climax. Now it was time to take things to the next level.

With her hands secured behind her back, Skylar was picked up and carried over to his bed. Her chocolate skin was breathtaking against the soft, crisp white sheets. She instantly became even more beautiful to him. With his most wicked smile yet, he secured her hands to the headboard and covered her eyes with a blindfold. Starting at her feet, he worked his way up to her mouth, kissing and biting on every inch of her savory and mouthwatering skin. He spent time on her inner thighs giving them both some much needed attention. He worked from left to right and back kissing and licking the most sensitive parts of them. Skylar arched and moaned with pleasure fighting against her restraints. More than anything, she wanted to touch him and lay her eyes on him once again. Through her panties he kissed her already moistened center before moving the rest of the way up her body. Skylar was already past the point of no return, and the smell of her arousal made him harder.

She felt his lips and warm breath against her ear when he said, "You are beautiful Skylar, and you belong to me now." With a quick swipe of his hand, he made little work of her bra finally freeing her voluptuous breast.

His mouth was spellbinding as he bit on her sensitive and hard nipples. As his mouth claimed each areola, his tongue and teeth worked simultaneously, sending wave after wave of pleasured pain through her. With him, pain and pleasure went hand in hand as Skylar continued to fight to free herself. Switching between his sensual tongue and biting on her made Skylar scream out. He reclaimed her mouth again muffling her passionate screams. Kissing her had become his favorite thing to do. Releasing her mouth, he kissed back down her stomach to her lovely, dripping center where he finally freed her of her last article of clothing.

Before officially tasting her sweet nectar, he kissed around her pink panther torturing her more. His sweet kisses turned into slow, long licks of his tongue against her clitoris. Skylar was taken to heaven again. Her moans became more intensified as she begged him for more and not to stop. Her wish was his command. He rewarded her with more of his tongue exploring all the inner folds of her lower lips. He plunged his tongue deeper inside of her as he searched for that spot that would send her back over the edge. His mouth was phenomenal, causing Skylar to buck and pull against her restraints. Her "punishment" was true torture for her. He took her to heights she had never reached before. He made her wetter than she had ever been with each stroke.

He was not done with her yet. She tasted like a fruit salad, so sweet and delicious that he would never get enough of her. To enhance her pleasure, he added two of his strong fingers inside of her to accompany his tongue. They worked in tandem to push her over the edge. Starting out slow, moving in and out of her, his fingers worked faster to cause her another explosion. He played Skylar like an instrument where her moans and screams created the words to his favorite song. He played her harder and faster searching the deepest parts of her. In a matter of minutes, she was going to give him a full taste of her sweet nectar. He wanted this, and she wanted this as he found a way to invade her deeper, harder, and faster. Skylar was going to be unleashed in three, two...

Skylar woke up back in her house in her bed alone. He was not there invading her body with his delicious tongue and strong fingers. It was all a dream, a great and an amazing dream. It felt real; Skylar wanted it to be real, but it was not. The things that he was doing to her were out of this world. Skylar was still on fire from what she had dreamed. She needed a cold shower. Somehow, she was going to find that man and give him permission to do all those things and more to her. The last words he spoke to her played over and over in her mind, *You belong to me.* Deep down, Skylar wanted those words to be true. She wanted to belong to that man in every way possible.

CHAPTER 14

Lesson Learned

Kairo could no longer stay at the club hovering by Skylar's side. Dimitri was a problem and had to be dealt with as soon as possible. Skylar's scent was now embedded inside of him and Kairo would be able to find her again easily. There was no one in the world who smelled as sweet as she did. Dimitri, however, was a different story. The longer Kairo waited, the harder it was going to be for him to pick up on his aroma. Kairo had to deal with him immediately, because he needed to understand that whatever connection he and Skylar had was now over. She belonged to him now, and he needed to know to never touch her again. It was like torture for Kairo to leave Skylar's side, but it was a must. He told himself that by leaving her side he was keeping her safe. It was strange how it happened, but her safety and happiness were the only things that mattered to him.

Kairo had been right, Dimitri's foul scent was fading fast. Had he stayed by Skylar's side any longer, Dimitri's trail would have run cold. Taking only a minute to find it again, Kairo followed it and another scent that he assumed belonged to James. Both trails lead him out the side door of I-Kandies and down the street to an alleyway just behind the City Center. Things could not have been any better when Kairo found Dimitri and James. The alley was dark and private and the only two people around were James and Dimitri. James was a non-factor since he did not have any interest in Skylar. He would be given the chance to escape this lesson if he did not interfere in Kairo's business. James was trying to be a friend as he tried to understand what just happened and why Dimitri slapped Skylar. In the year he had known him, James had never seen this side of Dimitri before. Nothing had ever made him so upset that he would even think about hitting a woman, let alone hitting Skylar. James knew that Dimitri cared about her, but he had just taken things too far.

"What the hell are you thinking?"

Dimitri needed a minute to think. He could not believe what he had done, and he did not have an answer for James. Kairo also waited. He, too, wanted to hear the answer to that question. *Yes, what reason did you have for hitting my Skylar?*

Dimitri was still angry and upset, more so at himself and a little at Skylar. He felt that she was making him look bad and that she had disrespected him in front of the entire club. Dimitri's ego was hurt; he was, after all, a Hunting-ton. He was a great guy, and anyone, including Skylar, would be lucky to be with him. They were on a date, so why would she give that performance in a dress when she was there with him? To Dimitri, the answer was simple. Skylar was drunk, and all he was trying to do was keep her safe, even if he had to keep her safe from herself. Dimitri could not get James to understand where he was coming from. He of all people knew how he felt about Skylar. Dimitri loved her, and he would never intentionally hurt her. James had known that Skylar liked to play hard to get. Dimitri had explained all of this to him after their last get together. This entire night was nothing but a game to Skylar. She kissed him the last time they were together and still agreed to this date. Dimitri told James that he knew Skylar loved him, and he was tired of this game that she was playing. It all just finally exploded when she got up on that ring.

Laughing, James knew his friend was crazy obsessed with a woman that was not into him. It was obvious to everyone except Dimitri that Skylar did not feel the same way he did. Dimitri was still on edge when he completely lost it on James and lashed out at him. That angered James, and before the two of them got into it, he had to walk away, leaving Dimitri alone in the alleyway to deal with his temper. James was done with the entire conversation, and for the time being, he was done with Dimitri. He was a big boy, and he could fix his own problems, so James left his friend alone with a monster hiding in the shadows.

Kairo thought the entire exchange between James and Dimitri was funny. He blamed Skylar because of her performance, a performance that was for him and not this clown. This poor man thought that Skylar loved him. This "date" of theirs was so her best friend could meet up with James again. Skylar did not want anything to do with him in a romantic way. Kairo watched and waited for the perfect moment to address Dimitri. As Dimitri paced up and down the alley, he was confident he would get Skylar to forgive him. He would admit that he was wrong for hitting her and shower her with gifts. He would get her to understand how sorry he was even if it meant letting go of the idea of the two of them being together romantically. Skylar had never been this upset with him, and if he ruined their friendship, that would be the worst thing in the world. After hitting her, Dimitri knew to never put his hands on her again. When she punched him, it hurt like hell, and he was glad that she did not break his nose. Looking at his watch, an hour had gone by. Dimitri was running out of time to fix things with Skylar. The club would be closing soon, and she would leave without saying goodbye to him. After what he did, he had to talk to her in person, face to face. This was also Kairo's last chance to deal with this situation tonight.

After watching and waiting, it was time for him to strike. Just before Dimitri could walk past him and leave the alley, Kairo emerged from the shadows. He startled Dimitri and even laughed when he jumped and stepped back. Standing there in front of that man brought everything back to Kairo. He saw it clear as day, Dimitri's right-hand slapping Skylar across her beautiful perfect check, and he instantly saw red. Kairo had to take a deep breath and clear his mind. Killing Dimitri was not the answer, because he did not know anything about him. Killing him could bring up a ton of questions and cause the Council to move into the city. That would be disastrous for Kairo, and Malachi would kill him or, worse, kill Skylar and make him watch. Once Kairo was calm again, he asked Dimitri two questions. "Why did you slap Skylar, and what is your connection to her?"

Dimitri looked confused; who was this pretty boy, and why was he asking him about his connection to Skylar? Furthermore, what concern was it of his that he hit Skylar. Yes, he was wrong, but that should not have been this guy's concern. He did not even know Skylar, and as far as Dimitri was concerned, he was just some guy trying to get into her pants. Dimitri's refusal to answer only added more fuel to Kairo's flames. He was only going to ask him one more time, "I said, why did you slap Skylar, and what is your connection to her?"

Dimitri was bold and full of himself when he said, "Man, fuck off," as he tried again to walk past Kairo. He did not have time for this; he had to get back to Skylar. Kairo was no longer playing with Dimitri. His refusal to answer his questions pushed him over the edge.

Kairo grabbed Dimitri by the throat and threw him against the wall of one of the buildings in the alleyway. Before he could start his assault on Dimitri, Malachi appeared next to him, stopping Kairo in his tracks.

"Who is this human that you want to kill so badly, Kairo? Does this have anything to do with that pretty little mouse you were watching tonight?"

Kairo was at a loss for words. *How did Malachi find out about Skylar?* He must have been watching when he realized that Kairo had picked up on a very tantalizing scent. Unaware of what he may already know, Kairo told him a portion of the truth.

"Yes, Malachi, I did find me a lovely little mouse, but this human disrespected me, and I just want to teach him a lesson."

Malachi understood he would never allow a human to disrespect him, but he had just one more question before he left Kairo to handle his business. "What do you know about him?"

"Nothing," said Kairo.

"Do as you must, but do not kill this human until you know more about him." Those were the last words Malachi said as he turned back into vapor and disappeared. Malachi was right; Dimitri could not die just yet, but a lesson he was going to learn.

The exchange between Malachi and Kairo only took a few seconds. Dimitri was still trying to regain his balance. He was not sure what just happened. How this guy was able to throw him like that blew his mind. Dimitri knew he had to be smart about this. This guy was strong and extremely fast. To give

Dimitri a fighting chance and make this fun, Kairo slowed his speed down. He easily had the upper hand throughout the fight as he connected with Dimitri's face and body with each punch he landed. This was so much fun for Kairo. Dimitri broke out in a sweat and became more and more frustrated with his lack of success during the fight.

He was a trained officer, and it was not like him to get beaten this badly in a fight. Dimitri could only connect with air as each punch that he threw failed to connect. Kairo wanted to give him one last chance to save himself from this lesson. He asked him again, "Why did you hit Skylar?"

Kairo knew he loved her, but he wanted Dimitri to be smart and tell him the truth, that there was nothing between the two of them. Making that confession was the only way for Dimitri to stop this and have any hope of walking away unharmed. Dimitri had the nerve to laugh in Kairo's face. "You are not her type; she wants a real man like me and not some pretty boy like you."

Dimitri had just made the biggest mistake of his life. He unleashed a monster that he was no match for. Kairo fully transformed, and his eyes changed in a way that they had never done before. His golden amber eyes were tinted red as Kairo experienced a new kind of rage. This fight had just turned from a game into the real thing. Now, with each punch that connected with Dimitri's body, bones were breaking. First it was Dimitri's ribs as Kairo connected with body shot after body shot. For Dimitri to protect his ribs, he exposed his face and arms to Kairo's beating. Kairo pounded him into a bloody pulp as he landed blow after blow onto his body and face.

Dimitri's face was completely unrecognizable, as Kairo used it for his very own punching bag. He did not let the fact that he had already broken several of Dimitri's bones stop him. For another five minutes, Kairo continued his dangerous assault on a defenseless Dimitri. When the dust had settled and the beating was over, Kairo had broken almost every bone in Dimitri's body, including puncturing his lungs. Kairo had lost track of his true objective. He was only supposed to teach Dimitri a lesson, not beat him to an inch of his life. The wheezing sounds Dimitri was making told Kairo that he was clinging to life. If he did not do something soon, Dimitri was going to die.

Kairo had just screwed up and made the ultimate mistake. Malachi warned him not to kill this human until he knew who he was. This was not supposed to be a beating, it was only supposed to be a lesson. When the long-awaited storm finally hit the city, it washed away the blood from Dimitri's body. Kairo's mistake was staring him in the face, and he could no longer deny what he had done. It was bad, and there was only one way to save both their lives. Without knowing much about this man, Kairo could not be certain he could clean this mess up. What would he tell Malachi if Dimitri died, if he let Dimitri die? There was only one option. Kairo had to save Dimitri's life by having him drink his blood. All it would take was a simple bite to his wrist and just a few drops of his blood to make this nightmare go away. Once that happened, this entire night would be over. Kairo could grab Skylar and enjoy his newest little mouse.

It was such a simple thing to do, but Kairo could not bring himself to save this human. In the end, Dimitri was always going to be a problem for him. The friendship he and Skylar shared was known by too many people. It was just too risky to try and compel them all to forget that Skylar and Dimitri knew each other. Kairo wanted him dead, and therefore, he could not bring himself to heal Dimitri and save his life. Dimitri was fading fast, and Kairo needed to decide quickly. He hoped that American medicine was as good as they said it was. Kairo picked Dimitri up and ran with him to the nearest hospital, hoping that they would be able to save his life. Staying in the shadows the entire time, Kairo made it to the hospital in time and unnoticed. He dropped Dimitri off in the ER, yelled for help, and disappeared. It was up to American medicine now. They had to save Dimitri's life.

Clinging to the shadows again, Kairo made it back to the club to get his car. What was he going to tell Malachi when Dimitri died from his beating? Would the cause of his death be suspicious? "Fuck!" shouted Kairo; this was all bad, unbelievably bad; even if he still had the body, he could not get rid of it without Malachi knowing. Malachi's senses were unmatched by anyone; he was an original, and there was nothing that he could not hear, see, or smell. Kairo had to focus on the positives, for now, Dimitri was not dead. He was successful in getting him to the hospital while he was still clinging to life. Dimitri had a fighting chance, and Kairo could survive this.

The alley did not have any cameras, and James left the area before the beating happened. The only people who knew about the beating were Malachi, Kairo, and Dimitri. Kairo nor Malachi would be saying anything about what happened that night. After that beating, if Dimitri survived, there was the chance he would not remember anything, and if he did, Kairo could fix that easily. The storm washed away any evidence that may have been left on Dimitri's body or along the street. Everything was going to be fine as long as Dimitri did not die.

Things were going to be okay, and soon, Kairo would have his Skylar all to himself. "Fuck!" shouted Kairo again, Skylar, the club, and that dance. Would she put two and two together and believe that he, *the mysterious man* from the club, could be capable of hurting Dimitri? Kairo believed that Skylar felt the connection between the two of them. She had to know just how bad he wanted her, and she knew how jealous and protective Dimitri was over her. This had the potential to be bad, and Kairo had to get in front of it. There was no way around it, as soon as he arrived back at the house, he had to fill Malachi in on everything. This was the only way to keep the two of them safe. Should Skylar give the police his description, they both would be in danger. Malachi would clean this mess up even if it meant killing them both and leaving Charlotte behind for good.

Where Skylar was concerned, Kairo was left with only one option, and it really was not an option at all. He could compel his lovely little mouse to forget she ever saw him that night. Just thinking about erasing their connection drove Kairo mad. *Would she be able to feel our connection when our paths cross again?* Making her forget that night was not an option, the risk was just too big for Kairo to take. Their connection was the best feeling in the world, and he could not lose that. Kairo loved the way in which he could feel Skylar's emotions, the good and the bad. He felt how free and alive she was when she was putting on a show for him. He also felt that dark side of her, the rage and anger she felt when Dimitri hit her. Kairo's actions after that were all on him; he would not blame Skylar for what he had done to Dimitri. The entire night had been a total disaster. Depending on what happened with Dimitri, things could only get worse. *What have I done?* thought Kairo. *I was supposed to be protecting Skylar, not putting her in more danger.*

CHAPTER 15

The Investigation

There were a million and one things running through Kairo's mind as he drove home. It was of the utmost importance that he spoke with Malachi immediately before he heard anything about what he had done on the news. Everything Kairo had to do now was about damage control and keeping Skylar safe. He did not care so much about himself; it was all about keeping her safe. Kairo knew Malachi, and he could be evil and sadistic, even more so than he was. Malachi would take great pleasure in hurting Skylar just to watch the horror and pain it would cause him to see her hurt by someone other than him. Skylar was to be his, and if she were hurt, it would be by his hands and his hands alone. Kairo hoped Malachi was busy having a great night, because if he were in a good mood, it would be easier to talk to him.

Pulling up to the house, Kairo sensed that Malachi and four others were inside. Unaware of what he would find, Kairo eased into the house already knowing that Malachi knew he was back. Inside, Kairo found one male dead on the living room floor, two other females clinging to life on the couch, and, by the sound of things, a third female being sexually satisfied by Malachi upstairs. This was great; Malachi had been too busy to care about what Kairo had done to Dimitri. Kairo was up the stairs quickly standing outside of Malachi's door waiting for him to finish his extracurricular activities. It would be an even bigger mistake to interrupt him before he was finished.

When there were no more sounds coming from the other side of the door and Kairo was positive that Malachi was finished, he knocked on the door. Kairo had to get this conversation over with fast. The last thing he wanted was for Malachi to find out what he had done before he had the chance to tell him.

"Malachi, I need to speak with you, it is extremely important that I do so now." Within seconds, a fully naked Malachi was standing in the doorway looking highly annoyed at having been disturbed.

"What is so important, Kairo, that you would interrupt me when I was about to have a drink."

"You could have put something on first," Kairo said.

"You said it was highly important."

"It is, but you could have gotten dressed first; please meet me downstairs."

"No, I will put something on, and we will speak right here." A second later Malachi was standing back in front of Kairo. "Speak," he said. Kairo quickly told him most of what happened tonight. Fearing for Skylar's safety, Kairo kept her name out of the conversation. With each passing second of re-telling the story, Malachi was becoming more and more angered by what he was hearing. By the end of the conversation, Malachi was beyond furious by what he heard from Kario . He was in a full rage seeing red and would have ended Kairo, but he wanted to see if he was going to tell him the full story. There was just something off about his story that made Malachi know he was still lying to him.

"How stupid can you be? Do you know who he is?" Knowing that things were about to go from bad to worse, Kairo just shook his head.

"He is a well-respected and decorated detective who has been on the force for fifteen years. Should he die, the investigation into his death will not end until someone pays for it. Did you not think about that and the Council? This type of investigation will bring them here."

"I know, Malachi, that was stupid on my part, but I will clean this up," said Kairo.

"Whatever comes from this mess, Kairo, you will fix it, do you understand me?"

"Yes, Malachi, I will fix this no matter what; nothing will come back on us, and he may not die."

"You better hope so" were the last words that Malachi spoke to him before vanishing back into his room since he still had a fresh drink waiting for him.

Hoping to learn something helpful, Kairo turned his attention to the television and the news. He had to know what was going on. During a news broadcast about the near-death beating of a cop, the story was interrupted with new details in the case. It was announced that Dimitri Huntington had died from his injuries after his vicious assault. As of right now, the authorities had one person of interest whom they needed to speak with. They hoped that that person could shed some light on the events of the night and paint a much clearer picture of what happened. Kairo needed more information since that person of interest could be James or Skylar, or him for that matter. He needed to get to the bottom of this investigation. Kairo had to know what evidence they had and where the investigation was going.

The only way for him to get that information was to go to the police station, and for that, he was going to have to be extremely careful. The station was crawling with people all angry and out for blood for the killer of one of their own. Kairo had to play this smart since he could not transform to vapor to gain access to the information he was after. Walking into the station was also out since he did not have Malachi's unique ability to fool the mind of so many at one time. For this mission, Kairo needed an officer that would not draw attention to themselves. Finally, he found a rookie officer who was perfect for the job. With her help, Kairo learned that Skylar was the person of interest they needed to speak with. Due to who she was, her family's ties to the community, and the nature of her relationship with Dimitri, they were playing this by the book. The officer also told him that they had a video of her threatening to kill Dimitri if he ever touched her again, and she was the last person to call him. A witness from I-Kandies came forward with the video and an interesting account of what happened at the club.

Kairo was furious with himself and could not believe he had let this happen. This entire time he was so concerned about keeping Skylar safe from Malachi that he forgot about the threat that she made to Dimitri. This was his fault, and he had to fix it for her. Thankfully, the police had an anonymous call-in line where he could give a description of the person that he saw in the alleyway with Dimitri. Kairo would create a person the police would never find, and with any luck, the investigation would run cold and eventually go unsolved like so many other cases.

Back at the house, Malachi had cleaned up and was waiting for Kairo to return. The second he walked through the door, Malachi started to question him and his actions over the last several hours. "Tell me the truth, Kairo, does this have anything to do with you wanting Skylar all to yourself?"

For the second time in Kairo's existence, something caused him to be frozen in place. Not only had Malachi known about Skylar, somehow, he learned of her name. Just when Kairo thought that things were finally looking up, Malachi had to go and throw him into yet another tailspin.

"No, Malachi, he simply disrespected me. I know I should have saved him myself, but I wanted him dead, end of story."

Malachi simply looked at Kairo one last time and walked out of the room. It did not sit well with Kairo that he knew so much about his Skylar. More importantly, Kairo was concerned that Malachi knew he was lying to him about the entire situation. On top of everything else, now Kairo was going to have to find out what else Malachi knew. This was just one more item to add to his growing list of things that he had to keep an eye out for. The first thing on his to-do list was finding Skylar. The only way to keep her safe was for him to claim her as his. Once he took possession of her, then he could figure out the meaning behind the connection that the two of them shared.

After awakening from her intense dream about the man she saw and most definitely wanted from the club, Skylar found it difficult to fall back asleep. Her mind was stuck on him and all the amazing things he was doing to her. Hoping to clear her mind of him, Skylar turned her attention to the television since she did not want to wake Angelina up. She was also not ready to talk about that dream or what she wanted from that man. Skylar knew Angelina would ask her questions that she did not have the answers to. Of course, Skylar found it impossible to find anything good on TV at such an early hour.

For the next several minutes, Skylar found herself channel surfing. She flipped through channel after channel until she saw Dimitri's picture on the news. Stopping, Skylar tuned into the broadcast as she mentally prepared for the worse. In that moment, she realized she had never heard from Dimitri, and that worried her. Seeing his picture on the news was not a good sign. Skylar did not want to believe something bad had happened to him, but her gut was telling her another story. She was mad at Dimitri, but never in a million years did she want something bad to happen to him.

When the news reported the death of Detective Dimitri Huntington, Skylar was shocked to say the least. According to the story, he was brutally beaten to death and left at the hospital where he later died from his injuries. The entire story was crazy. Who and why would someone want to kill Dimitri? Immediately Skylar knew things did not look good for her even though she had an airtight alibi. She was furious at Dimitri for hitting her and was aware that people saw the exchange between the two of them. She assumed she had to be the person of interest the police wanted to speak to. Before doing anything crazy, Skylar wanted to play the night over again in her mind.

Dimitri never got physical with anyone, even though he was eyeing every man who looked at her. Skylar wondered if one or more of the men from the club followed Dimitri out back and did this to him. It was true that Dimitri could come across as an asshole, but underneath all that bravado, he was a sweet guy who did not have any enemies. Skylar was certain that whoever had fought and killed Dimitri was from the club and that it had to be more than one person.

Before doing anything else, Skylar had to contact her lawyer. She needed to be advised on what the best course of action was. She did have to protect the family name after all. Anyone who knew Skylar knew that she would never do anything to hurt Dimitri no matter how mad she was at him or how many threats she made against him. After speaking with her lawyer, Skylar learned they were on the same page. He advised her to get some sleep and give her statement first thing in the morning. For the second time, Skylar went back over the events of that night hoping that she did not miss anything. As she lay back down to get some sleep, a thought made her jump out of bed.

That mysterious man she saw on the stairs. He was the reason for her performance on the aerial ring that upset Dimitri in the first place. Skylar wondered if he saw the two of them arguing because they had such an undeniable connection to each other. Skylar felt like he wanted her just as much as she wanted him, and for the rest of the night, she felt that familiar pull of energy. The only thing Skylar knew for sure was that she never saw him or Dimitri again after their altercation.

The next morning came around faster than Skylar would have liked, and she hardly got any sleep. She could not stop thinking about Dimitri and why someone would kill him. The *why* was the hardest part to answer. Skylar had known Dimitri for a long time now and she was positive that he did not have any enemies. After Angelina woke up, Skylar filled her in on everything that had happened. Without thinking, she even told her about the amazing dream that she had. Angelina was just as shocked as Skylar had been when she heard about Dimitri's death. At the behest of her lawyer, Skylar and Angelina went over their stories again to make sure that they were on the same page. Skylar was thankful that Angelina did not bring up her mystery man, as she felt like he did not play a part in what happened to Dimitri. That gave Skylar hope that she may be wrong about him. How could she have a connection to and potentially be in love with a killer?

At the station Skylar gave her statement to a detective named Michael Cobb who was the lead detective on the case. He knew Dimitri well and made it clear to Skylar that he would not rest until Dimitri's killer was caught and brought to justice. Skylar told Detective Cobb everything that she knew starting at the beginning with her serial killer theory. Her thinking was that she may have put Dimitri in danger by having him investigate those murders. He could have easily come across the killer in his investigation, and that led to his death. Detective Cobb felt like Skylar was way off base with her theory, but he was going to investigate it and every other tip that came in no matter how crazy it was. Dimitri was one of them, and they would turn over every stone to find his killer.

Detective Cobb was more interested in the events of the other night at I-Kandies. They knew that the club was the last place that Dimitri was seen alive. Again, Skylar told Cobb everything that happened. She mentioned the way Dimitri looked at every man that got near her even though she never saw him have a physical altercation with anyone. Skylar even told Cobb about Dimitri hitting her and about her reaction to what he had done. Cobb had already known all of this. He even had video evidence of Skylar punching Dimitri and the threat she made to him. More than anything, Detective Cobb wanted to know if Skylar went through with her threat and had someone kill Dimitri on her behalf.

Skylar could not believe that they thought she could kill Dimitri or that she would pay someone to kill him for her. To prove her innocence, Skylar produced her receipt from I-Kandies that proved she was in VIP until they closed. She also gave Detective Cobb her LYFT receipt that proved what time she returned home. There was no way she could have been in that alley when Dimitri was beaten and killed. Once the detective received her phone records, he would know that she did not hire someone to kill Dimitri. Skylar was an open book and told Detective Cobb everything that he wanted to know, but she kept him out of the conversation. Dimitri was her friend, and she wanted more than anything for his killer to be caught if it was not that man. Skylar felt very possessive of him, and she had this overwhelming need to protect him at all costs. She felt like it was her job to keep him safe.

On Skylar's way out of the station, she spotted James, who was coming in to give his statement as well. James was the last person to see Dimitri alive, but a witness cleared him. There was no way he could have been in the alley when he was four blocks away at a diner. For now, the trail had run cold. It was as if a ghost had done this to Dimitri, a ghost or something much stronger, more brutal, and ten times scarier. Again, Skylar's mind took her down a very dark path.

CHAPTER 16

The Sweetest Scent on Earth

The morning sun hit Kairo like a blaze of fire awakening every dark corner of his room to its lovely warm glow. Of all the myths about their kind, this was Kairo's favorite. According to the movies, "vampires" were not free to walk around during the day. They were one hundred percent creatures of the night. Like so many untruths about him and his kind, this, too, was false. Kairo loved the sun, he always had, even before his transformation three hundred years ago. He loved the way the sun's rays broke through the sky and how it still warmed his skin even today. It was not the same as it was before his transformation, but the sun still made his skin warm. It was past time for him to wake up, get out of bed, and get on with his day. The events of last night had stressed him out and caused him to rest longer than usual. Today Kairo had to find out where the police were in their investigation, and he still had to locate Skylar. If things had gone according to plan, the police should be chasing down the false lead that he gave them. In the end, Kairo was happy with his decision and the fact that Dimitri was dead. Now he would never touch his Skylar again or come between their connection.

Today was supposed to be only about finding Skylar, but that was going to have to wait. To keep Malachi content, Kairo had to make a stop by the station and seek out Amy, the rookie cop he enlisted for help. With one look in his direction, Amy's compulsion would take over and she would tell Kairo everything he needed and wanted to know. As expected, the station was busier than normal, as it seemed as if every officer on the force was called into work. Besides that, the station was also crawling with reporters all hoping to get the exclusive story of the slain detective. Kairo hid in plain sight among the crowd and waited for Amy to lay eyes on him.

It did not take her long to spot Kairo as she rushed to his side to tell him everything. Their conversation was short and sweet. Kairo learned that Skylar had already been to the station and given her statement. The proof she provided was more than enough to clear her of any wrongdoing. James and Angelina were both cleared of any involvement in the crime as well. Amy also told Kairo that, as of right now, the trail had run cold, but the tip line provided them with a very promising lead. Currently the entire force was in search of a man that a witness had seen with Dimitri in the alley. Finding that man was their one and only objective. The tip line had been great, but now they were getting a lot of useless information that did not pan out at all.

Kairo was happy things were looking up. Malachi would be happy to learn that he was in the clear as well, that is, if he were not already aware of what was going on. The only thing that upset Kairo about this entire situation was that he had missed Skylar. As soon as he was done speaking to Amy, he took off for the parking lot. Sadly, only a small trail of her scent lingered among the spot where she parked her car and entered the station. The day had been unusually windy, and her trail was fading fast. Because Kairo had to wait and get the full story from Amy, Skylar had about an hour head start. As much as Kairo wanted to stay in that spot and inhale her amazing scent, he knew that would draw unnecessary attention to himself. Skylar's scent and the image of her on the aerial ring was still embedded in his brain. She was an unforgettable woman, and in due time, he would find her again. She was meant to be his.

Skylar was such a beautiful creature to him. She was so beautiful, in fact, that Kairo was having a hard time deciding if he was going to keep her as his mouse, his blood slave, or his partner in life. If Kairo was being honest with himself, he wanted Skylar as all three. Needing to bask in her delectable scent, Kairo stayed in the parking lot inhaling the air for as long as he could. Thankfully for him, there was one place where he could go and enjoy Skylar's scent for as long as he needed until he found her again. I-Kandies was Kairo's next destination, because after the club closed last night, her scent was trapped and able to linger and float over every inch of his club. There, he could relive the best parts of the night repeatedly until he decided on his next course of action.

Walking back into I-Kandies was unreal; of all the people who had stepped foot in that club last night, Skylar's scent still overpowered them all. Kairo knew that he would be able to pick up on her scent, but this was more than he could have imagined. In every corner of the club, her scent was found as if she was standing there next to him. Somehow Kairo was connected and in tune with her energy, feeling everything that she felt that night. Her scent took him back home as she smelled of lychees, mangos, and pineapples. Her scent was like a tropical fruit basket made of some of the sweetest fruits on earth. While engulfed in her aroma, Kairo's thoughts were naturally turned to her blood and what it would taste like as well as her sweet center. Thinking about Skylar in that way aroused Kairo, making him hard and needing her in the worst way. Without ever having her, Kairo knew no other woman would satisfy his needs the way he knew she would. Sitting alone in the club was only delaying the search for what was rightfully his, and the sooner Kairo found Skylar, the sooner he could hear her scream, all her screams.

For ten minutes Kairo was in heaven until he determined that inhaling Skylar's scent was not enough. He had to see her beautiful smiling face, touch her soft, silky skin, and make her understand that she was his now and forever. Kairo ached to the depths of his essence with a need to feel her energy, and to taste her. Hiding himself away in his club was not getting him any closer to his goal of finding her. As Kairo thought back on every conversation that she and her friend had, everything came back to him. He remembered she was supposed to be in Romare Bearden Park today setting up for the health fair she was hosting. With a quick sniff of the air, Kairo knew his enchantress was nowhere to be found. The air was empty of her delicious aroma. Knowing that Skylar was not in the area, Kairo started his search for her at the tea house she was known to frequent.

The place was called Herbal Temptation. It was a tea house designed for people who loved to read while sipping on different flavors of tea. The tea house was nice; it was filled with tons of Zen and lots of books. It reflected Skylar's personality well, and Kairo could see why she enjoyed it as much as she did. To his dismay, Skylar was nowhere in sight. Tea was not his favorite beverage of choice, but it was something he learned to drink to please his mother during a much different time in his life. Kairo hoped Skylar would show up, so he sat down at a table and waited.

Reading was also not high on his list of things to do, but he would read every book in the tea house if it meant that Skylar would show up. Kairo ordered a raspberry pineapple luau tea that reminded him of Skylar and her amazing tropical scent while he waited and hoped that she showed up. Had Kairo been looking for just any mouse, he could have had his pick of any woman in the tea house. While they were pretty women, none of them made his body react in the same way Skylar did. All the women had eyes for him, but he only had eyes for her. It was crazy, but in a single night this woman had turned Kairo's world completely upside down, and things would never be the same again. After fifteen minutes of waiting, Kairo knew that Skylar was not going to show up here. It was still early in the morning, only a few minutes after ten, so Kairo hoped that the French pastry shop would be more promising.

Kairo was back in the Uptown area in minutes, and his day was not going according to plan. He was becoming angry and agitated and needed to find Skylar, and soon, to calm both him and the monster that lived inside of him. His search for her was taking much longer than he had expected. To calm his nerves, Kairo needed a few shots of tequila; then everything changed. Seconds before walking through the club's doors, Kairo was taken to heaven. On a gust of wind that blew across his face came the sweetest scent on earth. It was her, and in an instant, Kairo and his monster were put at ease. Catching Skylar's scent was step one, but Kairo still needed to see her and to touch her. Taking off at a speed only slightly faster than a human's, Kairo followed her trail straight to her. He caught just a glimpse of her as she walked through the doors to La Creme, the French pastry shop she loved.

Without ever seeing her face, Kairo knew with everything in him that it was Skylar walking into the shop. It may have taken him longer than he would have liked, but in the end, he finally found her. She had her hair pulled back into a ponytail; she wore dark jean shorts and a red sleeveless shirt with black sandals. Seeing and smelling her put Kairo on edge again when he needed it to calm him down and relax him. Being this close to her only made the monster inside of him want her more. Before doing something stupid, Kairo had to center himself and calm down. He wanted to kill every person inside that shop and take her away. After a few deep breaths, Kairo was able to regain control and enter La Creme to lock eyes with Skylar for the second time.

Skylar had already taken a seat at a small table for two just to the right of the counter when Kairo walked in. He thought she was a thing of beauty in purple, but he was wrong. Her being in purple could not compare to how beautiful she was in red, which was his favorite color. The energy in the room was palpable, so intense it almost made Skylar's hair stand on end. Kairo literally took her breath away when he walked past her to an empty table adjacent to her. More interesting to Kairo was the fact that Skylar tried to act as if she did not have an interest in him. That little-known fact made Kairo smirk and laugh a little to himself. Skylar was just too cute acting as if she were not turned on by him and wanted his hands all over her. Somehow, she regained her focus and turned her attention back to the cinnamon baked apple turnover and jasmine green tea that she had ordered. Even now, her scent overpowered the room.

It flowed all around Kairo making his mouth water once again. It was one thing to smell small traces of her lovely aroma and an entirely different thing smelling her as she sat so close to him. She almost drove him over the edge, pushing him to do something stupid and highly reckless. Kairo could feel his monster trying to claw his way to the surface because he wanted to take control of the situation. He wanted Skylar more than anything and would have risked everything to have her. For Kairo, to let the beast control the situation would have been the dumbest thing for him to let happen as he fought to regain control once more. To match the sweetness of the order Skylar placed, Kairo ordered some cinnamon sticks. From where he was seated, he could see every nervous move that she made, and he loved every second of it. His seat was literally the best seat in the house.

While enjoying their pastries, they both watched but did not watch each other. Kairo could not take his eyes off her. At times, their eyes would lock onto each other and it felt as if time itself had stopped. Knowing that he was watching her, Skylar had to give him another show. She decided it was time to take things up a notch and find out how interested in her he was. Taking her right index finger, Skylar scraped the icing off her apple turnover. In doing so, she had the perfect excuse to lick her fingers in the most seductive way. It was an action that drove Kairo wild. He wanted to take her right there on top of that table. She was playing with fire, and they both were going to get burned. Kairo had to turn the tables on her. He thought, *Two can play that game.* Taking one of his cinnamon sticks, Kairo licked off the icing, making sure to work his tongue into every crevice.

That was too much for Skylar, as she was taken back to the dream that she had. Round one went to him. He had successfully turned the tables on her and became aware of her need for him. All the nervous energy between the two of them was gone and replaced by a sexually frustrated energy. Even Skylar's aura had changed. She now had this amazing glow around her that Kairo loved. With the tables now turned, it was Kairo's chance to walk away leaving Skylar wanting more. He had accomplished the first part of his mission and found her. Setting her on fire was a bonus. Now, for the rest of the day, her mind would be stuck on him. Kairo's plan was to keep Skylar focused on him so that she would drop her guard, making it that much easier for him to take her away. The time to strike was now, since Skylar was going to be his forever mouse.

CHAPTER 17
My Forever Mouse

Seeing Skylar was both a blessing and a curse. Kairo underestimated how much he wanted to taste her blood and controlling the monster inside of him was proving to be extremely difficult. With each passing second, the urge that Kairo had to feed on Skylar was growing out of control. If he did not leave soon, he was going to do something he was going to regret. Kairo left the shop while Skylar was hypnotized by their encounter and circled back around to pick up her scent and follow her from there. Kairo quickly found his bewitching beauty walking over to Romare Bearden Park where she was organizing a health fair. Sadly, for him, the park was crawling with people whom Skylar enlisted to help with the set up. Taking her now was going to be a lot harder than he first expected, and waiting was going to be torture on him. Kairo wanted Skylar badly, more than he had ever wanted a mouse before. She was different, she was special, and she was going to belong to him. From the safety of his hiding spot across the street, he was aware that Skylar had a full day's work ahead of her. Her bossiness and take-charge attitude were such a turn-on to him. Skylar was a woman who knew what she wanted and how she wanted things done. She would never allow for someone to defy her orders. Kairo knew he would have so much fun breaking her if he could bring himself to hurt her in that way. There was a part of him that wanted to feed on Skylar, frighten her, and be the monster in her nightmares. There was another part of him that wanted to protect her because he felt like he loved her. Love was a dangerous emotion for him to have. Dangerous or not, Kairo was going to find out why Skylar made him feel things that no other human had before.

Skylar was stressed out and all over the place. The set up for the health fair was behind schedule since she had to give her statement to the police. In her absence, nothing had been completed, and on top of all of that, she had this feeling of being watched. It did not help her mood that she saw him again, and for the second time, she missed her chance to talk to him. *Why did I not say anything to him?* she thought. He was even sexier than she remembered, and he smelled so good. Everything about him was sexy, the way he walked, talked, and even the way he ate when he was not trying to drive her crazy. The way he started to lick the icing from his cinnamon sticks brought her back to the dream she had about him last night. Skylar wanted him to do everything that he had done to her in that dream and more. She was upset with herself for letting him get away once again, but there was something about him that made her tongue stop working. She just could not bring herself to utter a single word to him, but until she got the set up complete, she had to put him and Dimitri's death on the back burner.

Putting on this health fair was important to her, and that was all that mattered. Like the Montgomery woman that she was, Skylar cleared her mind and focused on making her event perfect and her massive to-do list. The stage had to be put up, tables needed to be set, and the banners still needed to be hung. That was just the start of Skylar's list. Once all that was done, she still had to pass out the hundreds of flyers that she made inviting everyone to come. The purpose of the health fair was to help the uninsured get covered and provide tests and screenings for those that needed it, like the large homeless population that the city had. The health fair was scheduled to be a two-day event. Day one was more of an informational day, while day two was for the free screenings and checkups. The one silver lining was that Skylar had plenty of nurses and doctors who volunteered their services, and that was the only item she could check off her list.

As Skylar delegated her workload for the day, she could not help but notice that she still felt like she was being watched. Every time she looked around, there was no one there, and on top of all of that, her new normal showed its face. Honestly, Skylar was not sure how long her new normal had been present since she had become so good at ignoring it. Like before, the energy around her was off and all wrong. That butterfly feeling was back, and there was this force pulling at her from across the street. The strangest thing was whenever Skylar looked across the street, nothing was there. It may have been wishful thinking on her part, but she believed that it was him that was making her feel this way, but he was nowhere in sight. Maybe I am crazy, she thought as she tried to focus on the many tasks she still had to finish.

When Skylar completed half her work, she needed, and deserved, a break. This was her chance to venture across the street and investigate what that pull of energy was. It was the strangest thing because, as the force got stronger, it would disappear as if it were never there. Then as Skylar walked away, she would feel the pull again. The entire experience was frustrating, as the pull would come and go like the wind. Skylar really was starting to feel as if she was crazy until she convinced herself that she had been out in the heat for too long. That motivated her to get back to work so that she could go home and get some much-needed sleep.

Safely across the street and out of sight, Kairo watched Skylar all day as she worked hard to set up for her event. The sun was beating down on her making her skin glow with tiny beads of sweat allowing for the air to be filled with more of her delicious aroma. Kairo fought hard to remain in control and keep his inner monster from coming out of the shadows and claiming her for himself. The waiting was starting to take its toll on him, and if she was not finished soon, he was going to have to find another way to take her away. Kairo's patience was running out, and to make matters worse, Skylar acted as if she knew he was there watching her. Kairo wondered again if Skylar could feel the connection the two of them shared, and if she could, how and why was that possible? Skylar added to his problems when she took a break and went in search of the energy that connected the two of them. Through that energy and connection, Kairo was able to understand how important this health fair was to her, and because of that, he put her needs above his own. He would give her the chance to finish the set up to ensure that the fair could go on without her. No matter what, at the end of the day, she was going to be his now and forever.

The health fair was important, and that was more than enough of a reason for Skylar to get back to work. This was her chance to use her name and influence to help the people of her city. The homeless and the uninsured needed to know what options they had and all the ways they could stay healthy. Charlotte's first health fair was going to go off without a hitch and be perfect, even if the host could not be there to kick the event off. The set up was taking longer than Skylar had planned for and she still had not processed Dimitri's death. After such a long day, she was just not up to putting on a happy face and smiling for the world. As a Montgomery, she was taught to bury her feelings and to never let the world see her as anything less than perfect. With all that life had thrown at her, Skylar was mentally and physically exhausted.

As her day was coming to an end, she looked over her checklist one last time. Everything had been checked off and was completed. She could finally go home with the assurance that, come tomorrow, there would be no surprises if she showed up or not. Skylar left instructions for the crew tomorrow, gathered her things, and started walking back to her car. It all happened faster than she realized, but out of nowhere in particular, she was hit with that familiar energy. Skylar knew something was off, but she chose to ignore it. Her car was not that far away, and it was still light out, so she was safe, or so she thought. Skylar had been wrong, very wrong about that. Kairo had been patient, and he was about to be rewarded. He kept his monster in check for hours, and now it was time to set him free.

Kairo was just minutes away from unleashing his inner monster to do horrible things to her. The parking lot where she left her car was small and empty and the perfect place for her to be taken. Kairo could not have asked for a better setting than this. Skylar's disappearance would not be traced back to him at all. No one ever saw him stalking her like she was his prey. Quiet as a mouse, Kairo pursued her from the park and back to her car where he made his final move. Sneaking up behind her, he jammed a needle filled with liquid GHB into her beautiful neck.

Before the drug took effect and Skylar's world faded to black, Kairo caught her, allowing their eyes to meet once more. Skylar managed to utter two words. "It's you," she said before passing out in his arms. In that moment, Kairo realized she was even more exquisite asleep, as the sight of her took his breath away. She was the most beautiful and most talented mouse that he had ever taken. She filled him with so much love and affection and hope for the future. With ease, Kairo carried Skylar back to his car and carefully placed her on the backseat for the short drive home.

"Sleep tight, my love," he said as he kissed her once on the cheek and gently on the lips before getting into the front seat and driving away.

Getting Skylar was only half the battle. Now that he had her, his main objective was to keep her away from Malachi. Skylar was his mouse, and she would not be shared with anyone, Malachi included. Kairo expected Malachi to ask him for a taste of her just to see how mad he would get. Somehow, he knew that Skylar was different, and that worried him. He was not sure what Malachi was planning, but he was certain that he was planning something. Whatever his plan was, Kairo knew that it was not going to be good for him or Skylar. As a part of that plan, Kairo knew that Malachi would test his feelings towards her. For Kairo to keep Skylar safe, he was going to have to treat her like she was not special at all, but that was almost impossible to do. The problem was that Skylar was nothing like his other mice. She was special, and she was his.

Kairo was strong and fast, but he was no match for Malachi. If it came down to a fight for her, he would give it his all knowing full well it would cost him his life and possibly her life in the end. Fate, however, was smiling on Kairo again because Malachi was nowhere to be found. As quick and as gently as he could, he got Skylar into the house and safely to the basement. For now, she was safe and would stay that way if Kairo could keep Malachi out of the basement. It still blew his mind that he finally had her and just how beautiful she was.

Until the drugs wore off, Kairo hovered over Skylar waiting and watching her sleep. He placed her on the bed and made her as comfortable as he could. To further frighten her, he relocated the bed to the center of the maze and waited in the shadows to make her think that she was alone. He was so eager to play with her, and at the same time, he wanted to protect her and make her feel at home. The urge to undress her and violate her in so many ways continued to drive his thoughts because he needed to feast his eyes on every inch of her lovely body. As Kairo started to undress her, something inside him forced him to stop. He realized that it was wrong, and he could not violate her in that way because she was just too important to him. This was a first. Kairo never had a mouse mystify him the way that Skylar had, and he found himself in a dilemma. Should he treat her like every other mouse and hurt her, or should he protect and love her forever? How could he hurt her when he would kill anyone who harmed a hair on her head?

Torn, Kairo changed his mind on what to do with Skylar. After watching her and feeling a love for her, Kairo knew that he could not physically harm her. While she was sleeping, he restrained her by the ankle to a hook in the center of the maze. Kairo wanted to be kind to her by allowing her the freedom to move around when the drugs wore off. He still needed her to know that she was at risk of being hurt and hoped that would be enough to frighten her and satisfy his dark urges. It was important for him to see Skylar's reaction when she realized she had been taken by him. More than anything, Kairo was curious to see how their connection towards each other would play a part in how she felt towards him. It was his hope that she would put her stubborn nature aside and give into the fear that he knew she would have.

Skylar was a fighter, and that meant Kairo was going to have to be careful with her. While she would not hurt him, fighting her was not what he wanted to do. Thinking about her fighting spirit and punching Dimitri brought a smile to Kairo's face. She was feisty, and on second thought, Kairo thought he might want her to fight him just a little. With three more hours until the drugs wore off, Kairo still had plenty of time to decide what to do with her. Unfortunately, that decision was taken away from him the second that Malachi walked into the room.

Malachi appeared out of thin air and took one look at Skylar that changed everything.

"My my, she is a beauty and smells divine. Would you agree that I should have a taste of her as well?"

Kairo was furious at the thought of Malachi touching her or anyone other than him touching her again. "No, Malachi, that will not be happening; she is mine, and I will not be sharing her with anyone."

"What a shame," said Malachi. "At least I will get to hear her screams," he said before walking out of the room. Kairo did not like this at all. What did Malachi know about their connection that he was not saying? The fact that he expected for Kairo to treat her like all his other mice was not a pleasant thought. What was worse was the fact that Malachi would be listening and waiting to hear her scream. Skylar was more than a common mouse, and there was no way Kairo could treat her like he did Stacee and all the others. The thought of hurting Skylar with his most heinous devices and breaking her will to live was killing Kairo on the inside. He had just three hours to figure out a way to give Malachi what he expected without causing too much pain to Skylar. Left with an impossible choice, Kairo waited and watched over her like a protective father just in case Malachi came back for her. When she did open her eyes, things were not going to be good for either of them.

Blurry vision and a pounding headache greeted Skylar when her eyes opened. Quickly she realized that she had been drugged and, most likely, she had been taken for ransom. She was a Montgomery after all, and her family was very influential and would pay handsomely for her safe return. Once Skylar fully came to, she discovered she was tethered by the ankle and lying in a bed that appeared to be in the middle of a maze. As she took in her surroundings, she noticed that she was in a room of horrors. Despite being tethered to a chain, she realized she was free to move around and explore her new surroundings. Everything about this situation told her she should be scared, but she was not.

Skylar knew this scene very well. She watched several horror movies, and this scene she found herself in was all too familiar to her. Whoever had taken her was going to be in for a rude awakening. She was a fighter, and whoever this man was, he would not break her that easily. Skylar's senses told her she was not alone. She was being watched by someone who was hiding in the dark corner she was currently facing. Skylar could not see who the person was, but she knew that he was there, as she felt a strong pull of energy in their direction. It was stronger than anything that Skylar had felt before, and she could feel his eyes on her watching her every move.

"Who are you?" she asked. "What do you want with me?" Skylar already had her guesses. She was certain that whoever had taken her only wanted her to be scared and afraid of them. She would not give into them and show them her fear. When she got free, there was going to be hell to pay. Whoever had taken her was going to want her to relinquish all her power to them, and that was not going to happen. It annoyed Skylar that he did not answer her, so she asked him again with more power in her voice. "Who are you, and what do you want with me?"

He still did not give her an answer. Skylar's kidnapper walked towards her stepping into the light and the first thing that she saw was his eyes. They were not the eyes of a human but the eyes of an animal. They were the same golden amber eyes she had stared into once before, but they had changed. It was his pupils that had changed, as they were now shaped like diamond slits. His entire body was muscular, and Skylar knew he was stronger than any human. Keeping his eyes glued to her, he smiled and licked his lips. It was an action Skylar found extremely sexy, and he had fangs, actual real fangs.

This was no human; it was a vampire, and it was him. The mysterious man from the club and the same man from the pastry shop. Skylar was confused. She could not believe her eyes. *How can that be?* she thought. He was not human; he was a vampire, but Skylar saw him outside during the day and eating human food. No, that cannot be right; this is not real, she thought. The man that she wanted could not be a real vampire; they did not exist. Kairo saw and felt the confusion that was written all over her face, and he laughed. Skylar tried to sound bold and brave when she asked again, "What do you want with me?"

In a voice that pulled at her heart, he said, "I want to hear you scream, my little mouse."

That was enough to wipe away any fear that Skylar had. This man, no, this monster wanted nothing more than to hurt her and hear her scream. Well, Skylar was not going to give him that much satisfaction. She was determined to outlast every evil thing he was planning to do to her. In her most bold and bravest voice, she stood tall and said, "Do whatever you must, but I promise you will never hear me scream."

Her defiance was such a turn on to Kairo, but he was left with no choice. Skylar had to be tortured to save her from a much darker fate at the hands of Malachi. That made Kairo be a man of his word even if deep down inside he did not want to harm her. With one look into her brown eyes, Kairo pivoted again and could not go through with his plans to hurt her, but Malachi's words were still floating in the back of his mind. Skylar may have been strong, but she would not resist him or his methods of torture. Kairo would find a way to break her and keep her safe all at the same time. All his devices were too evil for her, so the best he could do was subject her to electric shock.

Kairo grabbed Skylar and chained her to the wall, allowing his hands to freely roam her body. She was not scared of him at all. She enjoyed his hands on her body, but she was more concerned about what he was going to do to her. Unaware of the pain she was about to be put through, Skylar mentally prepared herself for the torture that was about to come her way. Kairo sensed that she craved his touch, but that was not what this was about. Her pleasure would come after her pain. Kairo watched as her eyes narrowed in on him when he took out his two electric rods. To spare her and save her from some pain, Kairo decided not to use the steel wool pads.

The voltage started off light, just enough to agitate the skin. Kairo needed Skylar to understand that this was just the beginning of what was to come. With each pass over her body, Kairo turned the voltage up, but Skylar refused to scream. She was hardheaded and needed more time to learn her lesson. Her refusal to scream broke Kairo and forced him to continue to torture her. This was not what he wanted, and under normal circumstances, Skylar would have given him anything that he asked her for. She loved him, or at least, she felt like she loved him, but she would not allow him to break her. That was not who she was. She did not understand that Kairo was only doing this for her safety since Malachi expected to hear her screams.

"You are one tough, little mouse," he said. "I will break you, Skylar."

Skylar was tough, but she was running out of fight. This game of theirs had been going on for at least an hour or more, and Skylar still refused to allow Kairo the satisfaction of hearing her screams. The pain was finally getting to be too much for her, and she was about to give Kairo what he had been waiting for. Every inch of her skin was red and swollen, and in some areas, her skin was covered in blisters where Kairo left the rods for too long. With one more touch to her body, Skylar was going to scream at the top of her lungs finally making Kairo a happy man.

The long hours were getting to Kairo as well. He could no longer stand what he was putting Skylar through. Every inch of her beautiful skin was disfigured and grotesque. Kairo had to end her suffering without hearing her scream. Kairo had done his best to break Skylar, and she had outlasted him. She earned the right to be left alone to heal and recover. Kairo would fix this for her; all she needed was his blood. Skylar still fought against him every step of the way. Her last words ripped through his heart when she said, "I don't want your blood, just kill me and end this sick and twisted game of yours." Skylar had this all wrong, killing her was not an option. She may have refused his blood, but Kairo could still help her. He gently placed her back on the bed with ice packs for the swelling and antibacterial ointment for the severe burns.

Kairo did not want to hurt her, and in time, he would explain everything to her. This was all Malachi's fault. He only did this to keep him from touching her, to keep him from hurting her. It was all done to keep her safe. What Malachi would have done to her would not compare to what Kairo had just done. In the end, her torture was mild compared to what Kairo had done to his other mice. The ice and ointment were helping, just not as fast as his blood would have, but Skylar did not want his help, and Kairo was going to honor her wishes. He was the one to cause her this pain, so it was only right that he was forced to suffer by watching her slowly heal.

Every slight touch to Skylar's body or move she made caused her to grimace in pain and shattered Kairo's heart. He tried his best not to touch her, but it was hard. Once she was comfortable, she slept peacefully for the rest of the night with Kairo watching over her. Even though he did not achieve his goal of making her scream, Malachi would have heard the torture she had been through. That was going to have to be enough for him, since Kairo would not be hurting her again. "Sleep, my love, I will protect you always and never hurt you again."

CHAPTER 18

Goodbye for Now

Skylar's first night with Kairo had been a painful one because she was such a stubborn woman. She was in more pain than she let on and slept for an entire day. At first Kairo was okay with her sleeping, but the longer she slept, the more worried he got. His hovering got worse by the second as he checked on her like she was a fragile baby making sure she was breathing and that her wounds were healing okay. Kairo hated what he had done to her and wished that he could turn back the hands of time. If he could go back and do it all over again, he would have never brought her here, but Charlotte was her home, and he could not take that away from her. All she had to do was scream just once and Kairo could have ended her pain. Malachi would have been satisfied and she would have been safe. Her torture could have been over hours ago. Kairo was determined more than ever to keep his promise to her. He would never hurt her again and everything would be right in the world if she would just open her eyes.

During Skylar's torture, Kairo caught a glimmer of something hiding behind her beautiful brown eyes. It was something he had not seen in years, but he was positive that what he saw was real. In Skylar's eyes, Kairo saw hope for him; he saw a care for him, and love. Skylar had seen a small portion of the monster he could be, but she loved him all the same. It had been centuries since someone loved and cared for him, but he never forgot what love looked like. Skylar loved him, and Kairo knew he loved her as well, and that was a secret Malachi could never know. Kairo was surer than ever before that Skylar was his, and no one was going to change that.

Midway through their second day together Kairo finally saw a change in Skylar. She was still sleeping, but at least she could move and be touched without being in pain. Skylar's healing was a huge weight that was lifted off Kairo's heart, as he was now able to lie beside her and hold her in his arms. Once Skylar opened her eyes, the two of them could figure out what their next move would be. Kairo had a lot of things to explain to her. He needed Skylar to know that she could trust him and, despite what he had done to her, that she was safe with him. More than anything, Kairo just wanted to tell her how he was feeling and how important she was to him. The problem was that Skylar would not open her eyes and he had grown tired of waiting for her to wake up. Kairo needed a shower so that he could wash away the events of the other night. Skylar was not the only one Kairo needed to have a conversation with. It came as a surprise to him that Malachi seemed satisfied with her level of torture. Kairo was thankful for that, but it was highly suspicious that Malachi had not come back to offer up his opinions. While Kairo was upstairs, he would have a much-needed conversation with Malachi. Kairo needed him to understand that Skylar was his now and that she was not to be touched by him or anyone else. Her torture was over because he would never hurt her like that again.

Leaving Skylar's side was hard for Kairo because he did not want her to wake up alone in that room without him. Kairo wanted and needed to be the one to explain to her why he had to do such a horrible thing to her. It was not his choice, and Kairo needed her to know that and not be afraid of him. Just in case she did wake up while he was gone, Kairo went the extra mile and hid all his devices behind their false walls. It was important for him to make her feel at home and to make the space appear normal. *Normal,* he thought, *what is normal, really?* Nothing about their situation was normal since Skylar had changed his normal. According to Malachi and his definition, Skylar was making him soft and weak, and if Malachi picked up on Kairo's weakness, he would kill him without question. For now, Kairo's feelings for Skylar had to stay a secret.

Kairo had to stop stalling, because he needed a shower and he had to get this conversation with Malachi over with. If he revealed too much information to Malachi during their conversation, it could prove to be dangerous for both him and Skylar. With the hope that she brought into Kairo's life, he held onto hope that something in Malachi would change and he would understand what Skylar meant to him. She was the most beautiful creature he had ever seen, and it was crazy to him how she held all this power over him. With one word she could make him do whatever she wanted and change him completely. If it came down to it, Kairo would give up his life for her. As he kissed Skylar on the forehead, she gave him a little smile that made his heart melt. Even after all that he had done to her, she could still smile at him. "I will return, my love, soon," he said as he locked her in the basement. The shower and the drinks were exactly what Kairo needed. Now that he had a much clearer head, he had a better understanding of what to do. The truth was that Malachi would not change and Kairo had to keep the truth about Skylar to himself. Feeling much better about his decision, Kairo found himself eager to return to Skylar's side. The longer he was away from her, the bigger the hole in his heart grew without her by his side. Kairo's happiness was about to come to an end when he heard Malachi say, "You cannot keep her; return her first thing in the morning."

Those words were like a knife straight to Kairo's heart. How could he not keep her when they were connected; he loved her and was sure that she loved him. In a second, Kairo was standing inside Malachi's room; he did not knock on the door or wait for his permission to enter.

"What do you mean I can't keep her? She is mine, Malachi."

Malachi just laughed; it was funny to him the way Kairo became bold and brave all for this little human of his. It almost made him want to break Kairo and remind him that his strength was nothing compared to his.

"You simply did not follow the rules, Kairo; do you even know who she is?"

Kairo did not care about who she was. All he knew was that he wanted her, and he was going to keep her.

"You obviously know who she is, Malachi, so please tell me, who is she?"

With a smirk on his face, Malachi picked up the remote and turned on the TV. There on his big screen was Skylar, his Skylar, and she had a family that was looking for her. A woman who Kairo assumed was her mother was pleading for her safe return and she even offered up a monetary reward for any information. This was beyond bad; Kairo knew it and so did Malachi. He screwed up royally this time.

"Malachi, she is mine, and I will not be taking her back."

Again, Malachi just laughed and shook his head. "You talk as if you have a choice in the matter; you will take her back, or I will," said Malachi with rage in his voice. This could not be happening; how could Kairo have not found out who she was? There was no way he could take her back, but he could not let Malachi anywhere near her either. By this time, Malachi was standing in front of the basement door. The locked door would not stop him from getting to Skylar, but Malachi chose to wait for Kairo. If he followed his rules, Malachi had no reason to harm her in any way. If Kairo wanted to play games, Malachi would kill Skylar in a heartbeat, make her body disappear, and never return to North Carolina again. The disappearance of a high-profile person like Skylar would pique the interest of the Council, making Charlotte off limits to their kind. "Stop, Malachi, I will handle this."

Kairo was furious at the thought of having to take Skylar back just when he had wrapped his head around the idea of keeping her forever. The world was a cruel place after all. Kairo raced down the stairs and unlocked the door to the basement. There, right where he left her, was his lovely Skylar still sleeping peacefully on the bed. Kairo knew deep down that she was happy here with him and would not want to leave him. He struggled with the idea of admitting it to himself, but he had fallen in love with Skylar. Malachi was standing behind him growing impatient with him by the second.

"For our sake here, you must take her back in the morning, Kairo."

Kairo could not think straight anymore. He woke Skylar up, and she was happy to see him. "It wasn't a dream," she said as she smiled up at him.

Kairo sat next to her on the bed and asked, "Who are you?" Skylar picked up on the anger and disappointment in his voice. For a split second, she was confused before everything came back to her.

She was taken by this man who was not a man at all but a vampire. A very handsome vampire whom she did not want to leave even after what he had done to her. Skylar felt at home here with this person. She knew that once her family learned of her disappearance, they would not rest until she was returned to them.

"I am Skylar Montgomery, and you must return me to my family." Those words crushed both her heart and Kairo's heart. Skylar did not say this out loud, but she would fix this and find a way to return to him, her beautiful monster.

"Compel her now, Kairo, or I will do it for you."

His name was Kairo; she finally found out what it was. It was like sweetness on her lips and she wanted to say it over and over. Malachi's voice changed; he was done playing with Kairo. It was deeper and darker when he said again, "DO IT, NOW." That was the final push Kairo needed. "Fine, Malachi, I will compel her and take her back in the morning." Kairo could not stand the idea of Malachi compelling Skylar even though he did not need to be near her to do so.

This was Kairo's last opportunity to protect her from Malachi. With one last look at her, Kairo memorized every detail of her perfect face. Even though she would soon be forgetting their time together, he would never forget anything about her. Sitting beside her, Kairo looked deep into her eyes, erasing their last couple of days together. Kairo compelled her to forget their night together and their encounter at the pastry shop. His only hope of finding Skylar again would be her memories of him from the club. Those memories had to stay with her and intact to avoid causing too much confusion with her friend. Hopefully, they would meet again one day soon. For now, Kairo was certain that Malachi would make sure that he kept his distance. Kairo was going to get Skylar back, because she belonged to him. She was his other half, the yin to his yang.

When Skylar was left with a blank stare, Kairo was positive that the compulsion had worked. He planted a likely story in her head. When she came back to reality, she would think she had been in search of a homeless man hoping to invite him to her health fair. For now, Skylar would sleep and stay in her dreamlike state until Kairo left her side. Once the morning came, the park was just too crowded for Kairo to leave her there and go unnoticed. It was still crawling with police and people who were helping to look for her. Kairo had to leave her alone on a side street away from the action so that he could make a clean getaway. With one last look and a quick kiss on the lips, Kairo vanished into thin air and Skylar came back to reality.

CHAPTER 19
I Remember Everything

Skylar awoke from her compulsion as if nothing had happened to her. The last thing she remembered was that she was in Romare Bearden Park setting up for the health fair she had been planning for months now. She walked over to a homeless camp to help spread the word about the health fair and get as many of the homeless to stop by. The health fair was for them because they were the ones that needed health screenings and check-ups. The homeless man Skylar thought she saw was nowhere in sight. With tons of work that still needed to be done, Skylar did not have the time to search for him. She hoped that, with enough people spreading the word, he and others would show up. Skylar entered the park from the side street and, she was quickly surrounded by several police officers. Clearly confused, she had no clue as to what was happening. She was surrounded by the police as if she had just issued a bomb threat on the city. The entire scene was crazy and something out of a movie. Detective Cobb approached her to make sure that she was okay. It was his hope that a familiar face would help put her at ease.

"You don't have to be afraid, Skylar, you are safe now," he said.

Totally confused, Skylar thought that Detective Cobb had lost his mind. She knew she was safe. With a bewildered look on her face, Skylar asked,

"What is going on? Did I miss something?" She hoped that nothing else bad had happened. After hearing the news of Dimitri's death, she could not take any more bad news.

Detective Cobb looked at her as if she were the crazy one and needed to be committed. "Skylar, do you know what day it is? he asked.

"Yes, it is Saturday, June third," she said feeling like he was the crazy one.

"No, Skylar, it is Tuesday the sixth."

Skylar's mouth dropped open. There was no way that Detective Cobb was telling her the truth. This had to be a mistake, there was no way it was the sixth. What happened, and why was she missing two entire days? Skylar looked at her watch, and there it was, clear as day, 6/6/2019. It was crazy, but that would explain why all her hard work was nowhere in sight. The last thing she remembered about the setup was that everything was done. Her checklist was completed and she left instructions for Mary on how the informational portion of the health fair should go.

"Skylar, let me take you home and we can sort this all out," said Detective Cobb. He knew Skylar should have been taken to a hospital, but on orders from her mother, she was to be taken home as soon as she was found. It was not smart to upset Estelle any more than she already was.

Skylar finally gave in and let Detective Cobb take her back home. Sitting in the passenger seat of the police car, she found the nerve to look through her phone. She had fifteen missed calls between her parents and her best friend just from the third alone. The only message she could bring herself to listen to was the first message from her mother. Estelle was still calm after calling her three times with no answer. Skylar knew how worried her mother must have been when she did not return her fifth call. In the message Estelle told her to call her immediately, and Skylar could hear the worry and panic in her voice.

The voicemail was hard enough to hear, but Skylar had to take things further. She Googled her name and found the press conference of her mother on the news pleading for her daughter's safe return with a cash reward. Even though Skylar knew that none of this was her fault, she still felt bad for putting her family through all this worry and fear. To make matters worse, Skylar could not recall anything about her disappearance, and she was concerned about the questions she was going to get.

As Detective Cobb turned down the street to Skylar's house, she noticed that her mother had managed to turn her cute little bungalow into Fort Knox. From the outside it looked as if the entire police force was camped out at her doorstep. A part of Skylar could not believe that her mother managed to do all of this in forty-eight hours or less but, then again, a part of her could. The Montgomery's knew people in high places, and when they called, they always got what they wanted. If anyone could have gotten the entire police force to stop what they were doing and search for her, it was most definitely Estelle Montgomery. When the car finally pulled into the driveway and the door opened, Skylar was not sure if she was ready for what awaited her inside.

When Detective Cobb opened Skylar's front door the scene that she was looking at was unimaginable. As far as she could see, every square inch of her house was occupied by detectives and officers looking at video and still photos trying to piece together what happened to her. In all the chaos, it only took Estelle a second to realize that Skylar was standing there in the doorway. It was true, her baby girl was finally back home where she belonged. Without thinking, Estelle dropped her cup of tea to the floor and ran to Skylar. Estelle wrapped Skylar in her arms tight and would not let her go until she grimaced in pain. Skylar still had some soreness and bruising from her day with Kairo. Estelle quickly noticed the bruises along her arms and wondered what happened to her child. She would get to the bottom of that, but right now she was thankful that Skylar was finally home and was mostly in one piece.

Just as Skylar thought, the questions started one after another once her father and Angelina realized that she was also back. All the attention was starting to make her head spin. How could she explain what happened to her when she had no clue that she was even missing in the first place? Skylar's mind was moving a mile a minute as it tried to process and piece everything together. Imagine being told that you have been missing when you have no memory of it.

Fed up with all the questions, the only answer Skylar could give them was "I don't know." She knew it was a lame answer and one that was going to be unacceptable for her mother, but it was the only answer that she had. Estelle did not understand that Skylar had only found out that she had been missing an hour ago. Skylar's head was still spinning, and all the questions did was give her an even bigger headache. What she needed was some peace and quiet and

159

sometime to herself to figure all of this out. Unfortunately, her "I don't know" was not the answer that her mother wanted to hear.

"What do you mean you don't know what happened? Tell us everything that you remember, Skylar," she said calmly. Skylar tried to the best of her ability to retell what she knew. She started at the beginning.

> *First thing Saturday morning I met with Detective Cobb to clear my name of any involvement in Dimitri's murder. Our conversation lasted for about an hour when he told me I was free to go. I was already an hour behind schedule and I still needed to go by the printers and pick up my flyers for the health fair. Since it was still early and I was starving, I stopped by La Creme to get something to eat. I ordered my usual, a cinnamon baked apple turnover and jasmine green tea. I even sat down at my favorite table by the bar and enjoyed my meal. I finished eating and walked straight over to Romare Bearden Park where I was furious to learn that nothing had been done since I was not there. I quickly got everyone on task and worked hard for almost eight hours when I noticed a homeless man I wanted to invite to the fair. As I went in search of him, he disappeared, and the next thing I knew I was surrounded by the police. Detective Cobb told me that I had been missing for two days and he brought me home. That is the end of the story, so like I said, Mom, I do not know what happened, I cannot remember anything.*

Skylar's account of what happened did not put her mother at ease; instead, it made her more curious about what was done to her daughter.

After Skylar retold her story, Estelle insisted she go to the hospital and get checked out at once. Estelle needed answers her daughter could not provide, and she wanted to know what drugs her daughter was given. She did not want to think about it, but she also needed to know what else may have been done to her. Estelle was extremely worried that her child had been violated in the worst possible way. Too exhausted to argue, Skylar gave her mother what she wanted and went to the hospital where she was given a clean bill of health. Thank God she was not raped like her mother had suspected; however, she was drugged. With her tox panel getting expedited, Skylar was informed that she did have trace amounts of liquid GHB in her system and that the bruises and sores on her body were from some type of electric shock. They were healing nicely because someone had given her medical attention.

None of this made any sense to Skylar. She was a fighter and would have fought to save her life. Did she escape on her own, or was she released? *Why give me the date rape drug and not rape me?* she thought. Whoever had taken her did not ask for a ransom and they did not hurt her badly, so why did they take her in the first place? Skylar's so-called "kidnapping" was not making any sense at all. Now, more than anything, she wanted to be left alone. She had been poked and prodded and questioned enough and all she wanted was some peace and quiet to think.

With the help of her father, Jericho, Skylar was able to finally get her mother to at least clear the house so she could have some peace and quiet. Unfortunately, Estelle was not going anyway any time soon. She was terrified that the person or people that had taken Skylar were going to come back for her. Skylar felt exhausted, but that night's sleep would not come. She tossed and turned all night long. Her lack of sleeping worried Estelle because she was sure that Skylar was remembering all the terrible things that were done to her. It upset Estelle even more when Skylar refused to talk to her about what was really going with her. Every time she asked, Skylar just said she could not sleep.

After a few days of being the center of attention, Skylar was over everything that happened to her. All she wanted was for her life to get back to normal and for her mother to stop hovering and worrying about her. She could not remember what happened to her, and it was somewhat of a blessing. Skylar was holding onto a secret; while she put on a brave face. She had a huge hole in her heart, and she did not know why. Since the night of Dimitri's death, she had not felt that pull of energy, and now she felt as if a part of her was missing. After a week of being lost in a fog, even that was getting old to her. Like she was taught as a child, she buried all her negative feelings and put on a happy face. It was time for her to move on with her life. Estelle was playing a much different tune; while she too put on a brave face for the world, she never stopped worrying about Skylar. Skylar's disappearance was hard for Estelle to handle, and for her safety, Estelle was not going to let her out of her sight. Skylar may have been her oldest child, but she was going to protect her no matter what. From this day forward, Skylar was going to be watched around the clock.

For two weeks Estelle stayed with Skylar, never leaving her side. When Estelle was not able to be there, she made sure that Skylar had twenty-four-hour, around-the-clock security. It was perfectly fine for Skylar to reclaim her life, but Estelle was going to make sure she was always closely watched. Skylar may have moved on and gotten past what had happened, but something about her kidnapping still concerned Estelle. Something about it did not make any sense at all. Again, with the help of her father, Skylar was finally able to be set free. He convinced Estelle that smothering Skylar was not helping anyone. What she really was doing was upsetting Skylar and making her continue to relive that night. It was time for her to let Skylar be an adult and get back to living her life as it was before she was taken. That was music to Skylar's ears. Her father was the best; he always came through for her when she needed him the most.

For the first time since Skylar was taken, she was finally able to be alone in her house. She was thankful for the peace and quiet and for what her mother was trying to do. Skylar had not realized just how much she missed having her house all to herself until it was given back to her. After soaking in the tub for over an hour, the weight of the world hit her like a ton of bricks. Before her kidnapping, she was already finding it hard to sleep, and nothing changed after her kidnapping. While the situations were similar, what she was feeling now was completely different from what she was feeling before. Skylar hoped that her lack of sleeping was due to her mother's overprotective attitude, since she treated her like a baby. Estelle would check on her every time she made a noise, and it was just too much for Skylar to take. She wanted more than anything to finally be able to sleep through the night. She just needed one good night's sleep, just one night.

For the first part of the night, Skylar was able to sleep without tossing and turning. She was right, this was going to be the best sleep that she had in weeks, until everything changed.

It all started out like a dream with her at La Creme. She was sitting at a small table in the pastry shop, and then he walked in. Without a shadow of a doubt, it was him, the same man she saw at I-Kandies. He literally took her breath away. He sat across from her at a small table for two. From there, he could see her, and he watched her every move. He watched her like she belonged to him or as if he wanted to take her away with him. Skylar was not afraid of him; in fact, she wanted to be with him. He left before she did, and for the rest of the day, she had this strange feeling like she was being watched.

Every time she turned around, there was nothing there except that strange feeling. Even when she took a break to follow the energy, she was left with nothing but an empty void. For the rest of the day, Skylar worked on the health fair as she stated before. She remembered approaching her car at the end of the day when she was sure everything for the health fair was completed. Suddenly someone with strong hands grabbed her and a needle was jammed into her neck. Everything faded to black fast as her body went limp and she was caught by someone.

When her eyes opened again, she was in a room, a basement, with him. He was not human; he was a vampire. Those last words made Skylar jump out of bed. She was completely out of breath and could not wrap her head around what she had just uncovered. Skylar remembered everything, every little detail about what happened to her while she had been missing. It all came flooding back to her. He was a vampire, yet she saw him out in the sun, she even saw him eating human food. They were real; he was a vampire, and he was the one that took her.

That night, he tortured her wanting to scare her and hear her scream. Skylar fought him, not giving him what he wanted even when the pain became more than she could bear. He could have done more, but he held back; something was stopping him from hurting her more. When Skylar's torture and pain ended, she refused his help, and that broke him. For the rest of her time with him, he watched over her and cared for her. He protected her and loved her deeply. Her body had been allowed to heal itself, but he was angry at her because of who she was. He had to take her back, but he did not want to, and she did not want to leave him. She felt at home with this man, this vampire who had taken her and tortured her for his own gratification.

His name came flooding back to Skylar. His name was Kairo, and he was a different kind of vampire from what was portrayed in the movies. He wanted to torture her, and he did torture her. It was her screams that he was after. That fact was funny to Skylar; everyone always thought she was your typical female, delicate and soft. The fact that she resisted him made him more intrigued by her. Skylar could tell from his eyes that she changed his perception of her. There may have been a part of him that wanted to hurt her, but there was another part that wanted something entirely different.

For some strange reason, Skylar felt that he was trying to protect her from something, or someone else, but she could not remember. He kissed her before leaving her alone both at the house and when he brought her back to the city. His name was like sweet honey on her lips. *Kairo, Kairo, Kairo*, just saying his name made Skylar feel happy inside. Apart from the torture that he put her through, Kairo did things to her no other man had ever done before. Skylar was furious at Dimitri for hitting her, and this man had done something ten times worse, but she would have forgiven him. In truth, she had already forgiven him.

Skyler knew one thing for certain, and that was that she had to find Kairo again. She did not remember the drive, but she had this nagging feeling that she was taken to a house on the lake. She could smell the water and the dampness of the grass; it was a house on the lake. It had to be a house on the lake, but on which lake? That meant it could have been Lake Norman, Lake James, or even Lake Wylie. Unable to fall back asleep, Skylar could not let this go; she had to find Kairo at once. She needed answers and hoped that he would fill the void in her heart.

That night Skylar jumped into her car with Lake James in mind. She did not know what she was looking for, but she hoped that something would jump out and spark her memory. She was hoping to feel that same familiar feeling that she could now associate with Kairo. Once she felt their connection again, she would know she was in the right place. From that point, she would follow that force straight to him. This time, she would be running towards him and not away from him. Lake James was an hour and a half drive that turned out to be nothing more than a dead end. Skylar drove around for hours searching every inch of the lake and came up empty. Eventually she got tired from her search and vowed that she would not stop until she was reunited with Kairo.

The next day was more of the same. Skylar continued her search for Kairo in and around the Lake Norman area. She was determined to find him and, at the same time, keep him a secret. Just as she had done on Lake James, Skylar searched every inch of Lake Noman for any sign that Kairo was there. She left no stone untouched as she started to feel like she was unraveling at the seams. Finding Kairo and feeling whole again was the only thing that mattered to her. For the second time, her search came up empty. Nothing stood out to her, and she was getting frustrated. Even though her searches were coming up empty, she was more determined than ever to find Kairo again. Every time she closed her eyes, an image of the lake was always there to greet her. One way or the other, Skylar was going to find her beautiful monster even if she had to search every city in North Carolina. Sadly, her searching was going to have to be put on hold until the following weekend. Skylar's forced vacation because of her kidnapping was coming to an end. Living with what she had uncovered was hard, as she was forced to act as if her life was normal. Knowing what she knew meant that she was never going to be normal again. Until the weekend, Skylar would put finding Kairo behind her as she pretended to get back to her everyday life.

CHAPTER 20

Unleashing A New Kind of Monster

Kairo was not himself. It broke him to have to let Skylar go, but in the end, he did not have a choice in the matter. Without Skylar around, Kairo suppressed all his emotions and the true essence of who he was. Nothing in his world mattered without her, not blood, not his cat and mouse game, not even Malachi. Life was not worth living anymore, but with some time, Kairo would pick himself up and live again. Until he got Skylar out of his system, it was best for him to not feel anything at all. Skylar's absence in his life left a huge hole in his heart, which he hated. His problem stemmed from the fact that he did not know or understand why Skylar affected him the way that she did. Kairo promised himself that once the dust settled, he would find a way to get Skylar back. Until that time, he just had to find a way to exist in this world without her. Once he had her back, then and only then would he live again and enjoy all that this world had to offer with Skylar by his side forever and always.

Kairo had to be the one to compel Skylar. Letting Malachi do it would have been a huge mistake. With his power of suggestion, Malachi could have planted anything in Skylar's head without Kairo ever knowing. If Malachi really wanted to, he could have had Skylar wait a week and commit suicide and no one would be the wiser. He had an evil streak that ran so deep, it would have given him great pleasure to hurt Skylar out of spite. While Kairo was unaware of what his connection to Skylar was, he was certain that Malachi knew, and that would have given him enough reason to hurt her. Kairo could only hope that, with time, Malachi would let him in on the secret and tell him why Skylar had this hold on him. Either way, the reasons to let her go outweighed the reasons Kairo had to keep her. He knew it was for the best and for Skylar's safety and wellbeing. Without a body to bury, Skylar's loving family would never let her disappearance go until they had proof that something bad happened to her. With that type of thinking, they would become a problem for him in the future even if his plans changed and he kept Skylar alive.

Skylar's ongoing story would have gotten too much news coverage and brought the Council to Charlotte. That was not what Kairo, or Malachi needed. The members of the Council were the only humans who knew ethereal beings existed and how to kill them all. Finally getting their hands on Malachi would have been a great accomplishment for them. Kairo had come to enjoy this city, and he had hopes of returning one day. Now that he had his club here, he could not let the Council ruin this city for him. Charlotte was becoming his home because it was home to Skylar. *Taking her back was for the best*, Kairo said over and over in his head. If he said it enough, maybe he would start to believe it himself. Once he got past the sadness, the anger, and the hurt, he would figure out a way to get Skylar back. When he did, no one, not even Malachi, was going to take her away from him. She may never come to fear him like he had wanted, but she would love him. Kairo was positive of that. When he got Skylar back, she would become just like him, and they would be together despite Malachi. Skylar meant more to him than anything in this world. She was more than just a mouse, much more than just a plaything to him.

Malachi knew losing Skylar was hard on Kairo, even though he was trying hard to act normal. Malachi saw through the facade he was putting on. Long before Kairo had ever seen Skylar, Malachi knew that someone was keeping

Kairo here. Malachi knew the signs; he had seen the same look in Kairo's eyes. Since his arrival in Charlotte, there had been a small glimmer of light in his eyes, and that could only mean one thing. It disgusted Malachi and, more than anything, took him back to his past, the one place he never wanted to revisit. Kairo had finally found his soulmate, even though he was unaware of what was happening to him. Since the beginning, Malachi made sure to keep the soulmate bond a secret from all his transformed creations for one reason and one reason only, love.

Love was not meant for their kind and only made them weak and clouded their judgment. Love was reserved for the good and pure of heart. According to humanity, "vampires" were evil and undeserving of love. Malachi's beloved Rose may not have been his soulmate, but her death still broke him all the same. The way Malachi saw things, removing Skylar from Kairo's life was his way of saving his son from a pain that he could not handle. Once their bond was completed, losing one would almost kill the other. Malachi had seen it hundreds of times before. It was his hope to spare them both that type of unbearable pain. With that said, Skylar had to be removed from Kairo's life and their bond could never be completed.

For just over two weeks now, Kairo had been lying with his claims that he was going to the club and feeding. Kairo was barely eating, and soon that would work out perfectly for Malachi. In another day or two, he would have Kairo feeding the monster inside of him. He would let go of Skylar and all his weak human emotions. When he was done with him, Kairo would return to what he was raised to be, an evil and vicious monster driven by blood and destruction. Malachi could sense that all Kairo's emotions were off. He was angry and upset and, dare he say it, sad and depressed. It appeared that Kairo wanted to die without Skylar, and under no circumstances was Malachi going to allow that to happen. Their kind was not made for this type of sadness. That was another feeble human emotion, an emotion that would get them all killed.

Everything that happened that night was all a part of Malachi's plan. He wanted to see how far Kairo would go to hide his secret while doing what was necessary to keep Skylar safe. Even if her family never looked for her, Malachi was going to find a way to take Skylar away from him. For his plan to work, Kairo had to be a broken shell of the man that he was. The compulsion was just another trick. Unbeknownst to Kairo was the fact that soulmates could not be compelled. In a few days, Skylar would remember everything about her night with Kairo, but by the time that happened, it would be too late for her.

What Kairo did not know was that he would be seeing Skylar again soon, very soon. Skylar was a cancer Malachi had to cut out of Kairo's life, and the best way to remove this type of cancer was in person. Kairo thought that he was keeping Skylar and their connection a secret, but he was wrong about that. When Kairo took her, all he did was put a much bigger target on her back. In their short time together, Kairo allowed for Malachi to know without a shadow of a doubt who she was to him. Before Malachi could set his plan into motion, he had to fix Kairo. First, he had to relearn how to be the monster he was created to be. Kairo needed a lesson in how to become a real monster.

Malachi needed Kairo to be filled with so much anger and rage that the monster inside of him could be unleashed to blaze a trail of death and destruction onto the world. Kairo needed to relearn what humans were good for. Kairo needed a new game to play, a much darker game to play. *Buckle up, Kairo*, thought Malachi *because school is about to be in session.*

Kairo had his secrets and so did Malachi. He managed to keep the lake house he acquired from Karen a secret from Kairo for over a month now. He had not been back to that house since his time with Max two weeks ago. For Max, the house was fine, but for what he had in store for Skylar, it needed some serious upgrades and additions. The only room that would be touched was the master bedroom. Malachi had some incredibly special plans for it because Skylar was an incredibly special woman. When the time was right, Malachi would let Kairo in on the secret of who Skylar was. Tonight, was only about Kairo and the new lesson that he needed to learn. When he was restored to his true self, the real monster in him would take care of Skylar himself. That beast would take control, making sure that Kairo was never weak again.

To fix Kairo, Malachi needed an endless supply of blood, which meant that he needed an endless supply of pretty women. What Kairo needed was his very own blood donation center, and that was exactly what he was going to get. Malachi had only been in the city for a short time and he had already learned everything that he needed to know. Charlotte was like any other large metropolitan city. It swallowed up the little guy and spit them back out onto the streets after breaking them of all their hopes and dreams.

Just on the outskirts of Uptown, the city had a large homeless population ripe for the picking. All they needed was a bath, some clean clothes, and food to make them perfect for unleashing the monster that Kairo was. Malachi started with fifty unsuspecting women who needed a hand up after the city chewed them all up and spit them out. After picking out the fifty Kairo would find appealing, Malachi cleaned them up and took them to a starving and blood thirsty Kairo.

With the sun setting, Kairo was aware that he needed to leave the house. His tale of him feeding at the club only worked if he left his home. Tonight, Kairo just did not have it in him to keep up with his lie. Malachi could read him like the back of his hand, so he knew Kairo was lying. All he wanted was to be left alone and not have to talk or answer to anyone. He was starving and was about to lose the last bit of control he had over his inner monster. While Kairo wanted to feed, he just did not want anyone's blood. He only wanted Skylar's blood, but soon his inner beast would take whatever blood he could get his hands on.

The second that Kairo smelled Skylar he knew that no one in the world would taste as sweet as she would. Since she walked into his life everything was different. Skylar confused him, and he no longer knew which path to take. He could become a "weak vampire" living as a human, or he could live as Malachi in the dark and alone forever. Kairo had an important decision to make. One path gave him everything he never knew he wanted, and the other path left him in a world void of light. Kairo's dilemma was the age-old battle that his kind wrestled with for centuries, Good versus Evil or Light versus Darkness.

A life of darkness was what Malachi had always wanted for him and the rest of their kind. Light once lived in Malachi until he was consumed by so much hate and darkness. Since the first day of Kairo's transformation, Malachi pushed him to a life of darkness, and for his entire existence, he was happy with that darkness, until now. Malachi never taught him that there was another way to live, and now Kairo was confused. Skylar gave him a small taste of what a life in the light was like, and without her, he had no hope of seeing that light again. Skylar was the total opposite of Malachi and his teachings. She was Kairo's sun on a cloudy day, and she gave him a brand-new life to live. She gave him purpose and a reason to turn away from everything Malachi had taught him.

Malachi was gone again; he seemed to never stick around anymore, as he only wanted to feed his dark nature. That was fine with Kairo since it was time for him to leave as well. For three hundred years, he let Malachi groom him and mold him into who he was today. Now that he had met Skylar, he wanted to change for her. With each passing day, he thought more and more about who he wanted to be. Malachi could watch the club or put someone else in charge until he came back. Some time away and some distance was what Kairo needed. With a clear head he could decide who he wanted to be for himself. With a small bag packed and the keys to his favorite sports car, Kairo was ready to walk away from a life in Charlotte when something stopped him dead in his tracks.

Suddenly Kairo heard the sound and smell of fifty different women downstairs. At first Kairo assumed Malachi was entertaining and feeding his dark nature yet again. Those women were of no concern to him since none of them were Skylar, but Kairo could not shake that smell. It was blood, fresh, rich, succulent, blood. The smell was divine, even though their scent was nothing compared to Skylar's. The monster inside of him was salivating at the thought of having fresh blood again. It had been weeks since Kairo last fed, and he wanted every drop of their blood. He was pushed over the edge when he heard Malachi say "Come, Kairo, and feed; they are all here for you." That was like music to his ears. He could no longer deny the hunger that he was now feeling.

Once downstairs Kairo was taken aback by the overwhelming smell of blood in the room. Malachi was clever and compelled them all to stand in a straight line while Kairo did as he pleased with them all. They all were primed and ready for him to take possession of and drain them dry. Things were taken to the next level when a lovely, petite brunette took a straight razor to the left side of her neck. Kairo came undone and was completely submerged in the darkness as he transformed and lunged towards her. It was one thing to smell them, but to see her beautiful red blood was another thing entirely.

Right before Kairo was about to devour his first victim, Malachi stopped him and took control of the situation. "Easy, Kairo," he said. "I know how hungry you are, but listen to me, choose one and drain her slowly." It was important that Kairo slowly lost control and allowed his monster to lead the two of them. Once he could take control, there would be no going back for Kairo. The darkness would win out, and Skylar would be eliminated for good.

Kairo did as he was told. He chose the brunette simply because she was closer to him and already bleeding. Kairo grabbed her, pulling her closer to him, and plunged his fangs deep into her carotid artery. Her blood was so rich and fulfilling. It did what it was supposed to do, erasing his hunger, but that was not enough. Kairo's inner monster wanted Skylar and her blood, and since she was not her, that made him angry. Malachi saw the look in Kairo's eyes and knew it was time to feed the beast. He needed to shatter every trace of light Skylar had awakened in him.

While Kairo was busy feeding, Malachi was in his ear telling him that the brunette woman was not what he wanted and that it was her fault Skylar was taken from him. This revelation took Kairo to a new level, and this woman had to be punished. Once Kairo drained her of all her precious blood, he took one look into her eyes and ripped her head off her body.

"Yes, Kairo, make them all pay because they are not her," said Malachi as he watched from the couch enjoying the show that was playing out in front of him. This was better than any American TV show he had ever seen. Kairo moved onto his next victim and did the same exact thing. He fed from her, careful not to waste a single drop of her blood, and ripped her apart limb from limb. With each woman Kairo did the same thing repeatedly until there was nothing left but a pile of body parts. Kairo looked to Malachi and said one word, "More." That was what Malachi was waiting for. The monster inside of Kairo was now in control and ready to punish the world for taking his love away from him.

Malachi had succeeded in pushing Kairo into the darkness, and now it was time to push him past the point of no return. The Kairo that he had been was gone forever. Without Skylar, it was much easier to push his buttons and un-leash the monster he was. Now, with the two of them focused on the darkness and by having I-Kandies, Charlotte was the perfect hunting ground. Part one of Malachi's plan went off without a hitch. Kairo was one step closer to being the man Malachi had wanted him to be for years. With a little more of a push, Malachi would eliminate all those feeble human feelings Skylar had awakened in him, as he was about to embark on a lesson of pure evil by the greatest teacher of them all.

CHAPTER 21

An End to the Light

Things were going better than Malachi could have expected. Kairo was seeing red and fully accepted the darkness that he was pushing him towards without any fight. With time, more blood, and more rage, Malachi would eliminate Skylar and all the weakness she awakened in him. Soon he would have Kairo seeing and fully understanding what his true potential was. Skylar had awakened a softness in him that took Malachi back to a long time ago, and it was that softness he could not accept. That same softness once lived in him, and it was forced out of him in a similar and equally brutal way. For once, Malachi saw himself as the good guy because he was saving Kairo from having to live centuries with that same hurt and pain he was still living with today. The pain Malachi was forced to live with would be nothing compared to what Kairo would have to endure if he lost Skylar.

Under the cover of darkness, both Malachi and Kairo preyed on the city's easiest targets. The city's homeless and transit people were ripe pickings, as they were easily manipulated into coming with two perfect strangers willingly. They both promised each of their unsuspecting victims they would make all their dreams come true. To toy with their victims and make their night more entertaining, Malachi insisted all their victims be cleaned and treated to the finer things in life before it was all taken away from them. Kairo's interactions with each victim was only about fulfilling his thirst in the beginning. As the night progressed and Kairo's inner beast grew stronger and took over control, everything changed for him. His focus turned towards destroying one human after another.

In Kairo's eyes, and with the help of Malachi, every human he came across was responsible for taking Skylar away from him, and they all had to pay for that injustice. The old Kairo was on the verge of being gone forever, and when that happened, there would be no more room for weakness in his life. With a few more kills, the old Kairo would never emerge from the dark path Malachi had set him on. He would be like the man who created him, a monster who did not care to be fragile ever again.

They were more powerful, the more superior species, and tonight they were letting it show. For tonight, nothing else mattered but their kills. Malachi did not care about their number one rule or the Council. Tonight, he was creating a monster, and he would deal with the consequences of their actions in the morning. Kairo was only five kills away from fully giving into the dark side as he slaughtered each human like they were nothing at all. This had become more than just a game to him. This was who he was and what he was created to do. Kairo was thankful to Malachi for all that he had taught him. He finally saw humans through his eyes. They were nothing more than vile creatures who were meant to be their food. Oh, how the tables would turn in their favor if more of their kind gave into and embraced a life of darkness.

Kairo did not only have Malachi to thank for his new lesson, as the entire human population played a part in his transformation. They were the ones responsible for pushing him to the darkness, and they brought this evil on themselves. Malachi was right, feelings were meant for humans and humans alone. Kairo was no longer human, and therefore, their feelings did not apply to him. All they did was make him soft; she made him soft, and Kairo could no longer allow that to happen. It was weakness that got them killed, and Kairo vowed from this day forward to never be weak again. He made a promise to himself to never die by their hands.

During the night, Malachi stopped his destruction of humanity and let Kairo do his own thing. Malachi thought that it was important for Kairo to develop his own techniques of destruction and to make his own rules to this new game he was now playing. This was his lesson to learn, and he was excited to watch. Kairo truly was a master of destruction, and Malachi was loving every minute of it. The way he dismembered each one of his victims was textbook. He drained every drop of blood from their bodies, so when he ripped them apart, the clean-up was minimal. It was as if Kairo had been doing this for his entire existence. Once he fully gave into his darkest nature, Kairo no longer needed to toy with his victims. He no longer took the time to clean them up as he snatched them off the street and killed them on the spot.

While Kairo continued his murderous dance, Malachi waited in the shadows to gather up the pieces and dispose of them later. As Kairo continued to feed the monster, the homeless were not enough to satisfy his urges. He needed new blood and turned his attention to all the poor souls who came to the city looking for a fresh start. Like the homeless, they were easy pickings and satisfied the growing itch that Kairo had. Each new busload brought with it a new group of people with a light Kairo could not wait to extinguish. He had become just like the monsters portrayed in pop culture, hiding in the shadows waiting for his next victim to arrive. Kairo had fallen so deep into the darkness that he no longer cared about the physical appearance of his mice. The way they looked, smelled, or tasted was not important to him anymore. Male, female, young, or old no longer mattered because none of them were Skylar. Kairo had become a one-man killing machine, and he was loving every minute of it. There was no turning back now that he had found a new purpose in life.

When the sun started to rise high above the clouds, Kairo's time of owning the night was coming to an end. Malachi had changed his mind, and that night had been his most thrilling and best night ever in Charlotte. With the help of his mentor, Kairo found a new side of himself that he not only loved but enjoyed being. Malachi opened his eyes to a new world and freed him. Charlotte truly was the perfect playground, and with the addition of I-Kandies, Kairo had the potential to surpass his teacher. This new lesson Malachi taught him combined with his torture devices made Kairo a very destructive creature. He was on pins and needles anticipating all the fun that awaited him once the sun set on another glorious day. Malachi was right; this was a much better game to play.

Kairo's night of fun ended in a blur. His victims blended as he moved on from one to the next. More impressive was Kairo's body count, as it climbed into the hundreds and was the highest that he had in one night. The scene in Kairo's living room and kitchen was something straight out of a movie. From the front room to the kitchen, everywhere Kairo's eyes went were the remains of his victims. Malachi had a few bodies sprinkled in the mix, but most belonged to Kairo, as this was his lesson to learn. He was the one that allowed love and light into his heart making him fragile. More importantly, he felt free now that he had become the monster the world would fear. The monster he was now would have broken Skylar, making her tremble with fear, giving him everything he wanted.

Thinking of Skylar almost derailed everything Malachi had taught him. The hold she had on him was unreal. No one, let alone a human, had ever had this kind of control over Kairo. To push Skylar and the weakness she created in him away, Kairo returned his focus to the masterpiece that lay before him. The remains of his victims reminded him of what he was, and if he could, Kairo would have left the pieces scattered around as a reminder of what he was capable of. It was in the middle of the summer, and his masterpiece would start to decompose bringing with it one of the worst smells in the world. A smell Kairo would not be able to hide, so his artwork had to be cleaned up until he could create a new art piece.

Malachi insisted Kairo leave the mess for him to clean up because he needed to rest before phase two of his plan went into effect. Unknown to Kairo, Malachi's phase two was going to be the hardest thing he had ever faced. There was still so much for Kairo to learn, and Malachi still needed to see where his head was at. After the rage had settled, would Kairo regret what he had done, or would he continue to be ruled by his new dark nature? Where Malachi was concerned, this was a simple choice between strength and weakness, and he hoped Kairo would make the correct choice. Either way, Malachi was going to go through with the second part of his plan. With a speed unmatched by anyone, he had all the body parts cleaned up and hidden behind the false wall in the basement. Once the drum to the promisson device was filled, with the flick of a button all the evidence from the night was ground into dust. With the night erased, Malachi checked to make sure Kairo was asleep before leaving the house again, because he had a mouse to catch.

While Kairo was in full blood lust and focused only on feeding the darkness, he completely missed Skylar's scent. Had Kairo been thinking clearly, there was no way he would have missed her delicious aroma. Malachi was fully alert and did not miss a thing. Skylar did smell divine, and Malachi was curious about how she was going to taste. Malachi caught her scent easily, as it stood out like a rainbow after the storm and followed it back to her bungalow in NoDa. When Malachi arrived at Skylar's house, she was already in her car leaving for work in the early hours of the morning. Malachi could have taken her right then and there, but he chose not to do so. He knew where she lived now, and when the time was right, he would be back for her. *See you soon, little mouse*, he said to himself as he turned to vapor and vanished.

Malachi rematerialized back on Lake Wylie at his residence. He had to prepare the house for Skylar's arrival. Phase two of his plan would involve cutting out the last traces of weakness in Kairo. Skylar was that weakness, and if she chose Kairo, she would eventually be responsible for breaking him. Malachi had seen it many times before, and he did not want Kairo to have to experience that type of pain. As a human, Skylar was already stubborn, and as a newly transformed vampire, she would continue to be stubborn and put herself in harm's way. Should she die, she would take Kairo with her, as he would not be able to live without her. Malachi was only doing his duty as Kairo's creator. He was protecting him from himself and from Skylar. For that reason alone, she had to be eliminated, and Kairo was going to be the one to do it.

Two days was all Malachi needed before he went back for Skylar. Since Kairo had a love for his medieval torture devices, Malachi would use them against him. Kairo once claimed to want to hear Skylar's screams; well, Malachi was going to make that happen. He was torn between two popular medieval devices, the iron chair, and the pear of anguish. Both devices would be equally successful in ripping the screams from Skylar. For Malachi, it was a matter of which one would cause her more pain. While he decided on which device to use, he prepared the master bedroom for Skylar's arrival ensuring that they would have all the privacy they needed.

All the windows were blacked out, the bed was removed, and the entire room was soundproofed. Skylar could scream all she wanted to, and no one would hear. Opting to cause the most harm, Malachi decided to use both devices on her. He decided he would strap her to the iron chair and, later, stretch her mouth open with the pear of anguish. He wanted to see Kairo's reaction to her blood and his reaction to her being tortured, for real this time. Since

Malachi only wanted to hurt Skylar and not kill her just yet, the iron chair was going to need to be modified. For starters, several spikes had to be removed while the remaining spikes were dulled to gently pierce the skin. Nowhere in his plan was Skylar dying of massive blood loss before Kairo had the chance to see her. Kairo's reaction to her was important; it would tell Malachi which Kairo he was dealing with.

The pear of anguish was another nasty device that would muffle Skylar's screams, but she would scream. Malachi was sure of that. The last piece of the puzzle was to set a trap for Kairo, since he loved his game of cat and mouse. This time, Kairo was the mouse, Malachi was the cat, and Skylar was the cheese that would be used to lure Kairo in. The cherry on top of Malachi's brilliant plan was the addition of a tungsten door, the one material that would block all Kairo's senses. Malachi's plan would not work at all if Kairo sensed Skylar before walking through the door to the master bedroom.

Skylar went about her day as normal, unaware of the monster lurking in the shadows. To ensure she could keep up with her nightly activities of searching for Kairo, she changed her work schedule. The change was hard on Skylar since she missed her morgue at night. The day shift was boring, and Skylar missed the vibe and energy she got from working at night. Things were not the same, but it was what she had to do if she was going to find Kairo again. Finding Kairo and that house had become her new obsession, and she had no plans of stopping until she found him again. The only bright spot Skylar had was the fact that her life was starting to get back to normal. Her coworkers had finally stopped hugging her and watching her every move to make sure that she was okay. Somehow Skylar even managed to get through Dimitri's homegoing service without completely falling apart. It was hard to believe someone had killed him and that the investigation had gone cold. Skylar felt certain she knew why his murder had not been solved and why the trail had run cold. That was just another reason why she had to find Kairo. She needed to look him in the eye and confirm that he was the one who had killed Dmitri.

Today, Skylar's work was simple; she only had three bodies that she had to process. In each case, the causes of death were simple and straightforward. Two of the remains died from natural causes, and the other one was from a single gunshot to the chest. Skylar had not seen any more bodies like the ones she had a few weeks ago, and that was curious to her. She wondered if the "serial killer" had moved onto another city now that Dr. Hayes was gone. With such a light workload, Skylar was done early and quickly realized that simple was exactly what she needed. With so much free time on her hands, she laid out her search plans for Lake Wylie. This was it, the last lake on her list to search. If this final search came up empty, she was going to be left with no other option than to camp out at I-Kandies. She had not been back there since that night.

Five o'clock finally rolled around, and when it did, Skylar was just not ready to go home. It was still too early for her to start her search on Lake Wylie, so drinks were a great idea. Angelina had plans with James, so Skylar invited a few of her coworkers to join her at the Wine House. Skylar was happy for Angelina and James and hoped something good would blossom out of that tragic night. Skylar hoped Angelina would be able to get past the reservations that she had about James, because they made such a cute couple.

The Wine House was close to work, so it was decided that they would all walk over together. With a cold front blowing in, the humidity had finally broken, which made for a nice night to enjoy a walk through the city. A night out was just what the doctor ordered. With the rumor mill settling down, Skylar was finally able to go out without the stares and side conversations. For everyone one, else her kidnapping was a thing of the past, but for her and her mother, it was always in the back of their minds for completely different reasons. The evening was great; Skylar had an amazing time catching up and hearing the news about someone other than her. As the hours ticked away, Skylar remembered that she had some important plans to attend to. With the setting sun came the urge for her to get home, get changed, and find Kairo again. The void he left inside of her heart was starting to be unbearable. Living just a short drive away from Uptown, Skylar quickly made it home. As she exited her car, everything seemed fine until her world faded to black for the second time in a matter of weeks.

Hours later, Skylar awoke in a poorly lit room strapped to a chair with spikes that dug into her back, arms, and legs. The spikes were not very sharp, but they broke the skin on her body all the same. She could feel the trail of blood running down her back and the back of her arms and legs. It was a feeling that caused her a great deal of concern. For just a second, Skylar thought that Kairo had found her again. The hope that she had quickly turned sour as she realized that she did not feel that pull of energy towards him. Things were indeed different this time around because she did not feel safe like she did before. The vibe and energy were completely off, and that scared her.

Whoever this person was, they wanted to hurt her and were already doing a rather good job of it. This was not the work of Kairo; he would never hurt her in this way. Skylar knew that as clearly as she knew her name. She took in her surroundings as best she could while trying to move as little as possible to keep the spikes from getting deeper. Next to her on a table was further proof that this was not the work of Kairo. The table contained some nasty medieval devices that she prayed were not meant for her. She was scared out of her mind, but she had to remain calm. She could figure a way out of this, she just had to think.

Quickly, things went from bad to worse when she heard someone calling her name and this dark and twisted laughter. It was by far the creepiest thing she had ever heard, and horror was her thing. Skylar knew this was no horror film, and whoever had taken her this time wanted her dead. She could feel their evil intentions deep down in her gut. The seconds seemed like hours as the mystery man finally came into view. Just as she suspected, this was not her beautiful and loving Kairo. This was someone else, a more sadistic monster than Kairo was. He was also a vampire, and he was extremely handsome. He was just not her Kairo. He walked closer to her, smelled her, and smiled. "Our friend does have great taste," he said. "He will be here shortly, but until then, I think I should sample you first."

Malachi grabbed Skylar by the neck and plunged his fangs deep into her. As this vicious creature took more than a sampling of her, Skylar screamed at the top of her lungs hoping that someone nearby would hear her and help. She knew her odds were slim, but she still hoped someone would hear her and come to save her. Skylar did find solace in her mother. Estelle would have the entire police force looking for her if she went missing again. All she had to do was stay alive long enough and she would be saved.

When Malachi was done with his taste, and he was right, Skylar did taste as sweet as she smelled, he laughed at her. "Scream all you like, my precious; no will hear you and come to save you. You belong to me until he comes for you."

"Until who comes for me?"

"What type of game are you playing? she asked.

"You make him weak; you bring light back into his life, but you will lie to him; your kind always lies. I taught him the truth, and when he comes, he will end you and live in darkness with me, with our kind, where he belongs."

As this man was talking, Skylar searched her mind, taking her back to the night she was taken. She was almost positive she knew that voice. She had heard it once before, but she could not remember where she heard it last. *Think, Skylar, think,* she thought, *you know that voice.* Who was he talking about; who was coming for her? And then it all made sense. He was talking about Kairo; he was there the last time she was taken. Finally, Skylar remembered everything from that night; all the pieces fell into place. *Malachi, his name was Malachi. He was the one who made Kairo take me back.*

Malachi was different from Kairo. He looked at Skylar with pure hatred and disgust in his eyes. He hated humans, and it showed on his face. He would kill her, no doubt about it. When Skylar looked into his eyes, she saw something deeper there. Behind the hatred, she could see there was pain in his eyes. She wondered if the pain she saw in his eyes was the reason why he was doing this to her. Pain or not, Skylar was at the mercy of this vampire, and she could tell his plans for her were not going to be good. Hopefully, she would be able to break through whatever spell or hold that he had on Kairo. *What has he done to him that makes him so sure that he will end my life?* Skylar needed to get herself out of this situation, and fast, but how? She hoped that by getting Malachi to talk, he would reveal something helpful.

"Why do you hate humans so much? What did they do to you?"

"You are a funny little mouse; I can see why Kairo likes you so much, but that is not going to work."

"What am I trying to do besides have a conversation with you?"

"You may be cute, and you even smell delectable, but you do not entice me." He was across the room in the blink of an eye and was standing in front of her. Skylar knew that vampires were fast, but fast did not even come close to describing how quick he moved. Malachi eyed one of the devices that was on the table, and it looked heinous. Skylar had no clue what it did or how he was going to use it on her. As he twirled it around his finger, the most cold-blooded smile came on his face.

"This is called the pear of anguish, and during the Middle Ages, it was invented exclusively for the torture of women to punish those accused of inducing a miscarriage. It was also used for blasphemers, homosexuals, and liars like you, my sweet."

The sight of that device made Skylar's blood run cold, "Please," she begged, "don't use that on me." Malachi eyed her luscious mouth as he turned the screw on the device to close it. Skylar tried her best to prevent him from inserting that thing into her mouth. She clamped her mouth closed as tightly as she could to stop him, but that did not stop him at all. He may have been small, but Skylar quickly found out the hard way that he was much stronger than he looked. He grabbed her jaw, nearly breaking it as he forced her mouth open.

"This is all your fault; you insisted on continuing to speak," he said.

With tears in her eyes, Skylar tried once again to beg and plead with him not to do this. She made him understand why Kairo loved to hear his little mice beg. All the fight and defiance she gave Kairo was gone. Malachi knew he would eliminate all that fire in her soul. Skylar proved to him that she was nothing more than a weak human after all. Once he had her mouth forced open and the pear of anguish inserted, he twisted the dial, stretching her mouth open wide. Malachi stopped before he ripped her mouth open because he wanted to keep her beautiful face intact. With the addition of a lead blanket to add more weight forcing the spikes deeper into her skin, Malachi left Skylar there waiting for Kairo to come. The quicker he got there, the sooner their fun would begin.

CHAPTER 22

The Power of Our Connection

*T*wo days after Kairo's lesson, the power Skylar had over him appeared to be gone. Kairo was the same man he had always been but with a much darker streak in him. He thoroughly enjoyed his nights out with Malachi and understood what he was trying to get him to learn. The darkness was amazing, but it could not stop Kairo's love and connection to Skylar. He still blamed the people of Charlotte for taking her away from him, and he was hellbent on making them all pay. Malachi had successfully convinced him that humans and their emotions did make them weak. As much as Kairo wanted Skylar, she still made him weak, so for now, there was no place for her in his world. For now, Kairo would be the monster Malachi groomed him to be, and when he was stronger, he would have Skylar by his side. What Malachi had done for him was unleash a new monster in him, one that craved the utter destruction of the entire human race one little mouse at a time. With this new beast in him, Kairo's methods of torture had to change. He still needed to hear his mice beg and plead for their lives. Their screams would remind them that he was the dominant force in the room. Before his lesson from Malachi, Kairo's methods focused on the fear in his mice, but now he needed more. Their fear and screams were not enough; they had to be destroyed.

With this new outlook on the world, Kairo had to tweak a few of his devices, starting with the iron maiden. In its previous state, the spikes were dull to cause his mice to slowly bleed to death. Before, he only wanted to hurt them instead of killing them with this device. He had always loved his games, even when killing his mice was not a priority. With his newly acquired lesson, their screams would continue to be important, but now their deaths would take center stage. Keeping his mice for weeks on end would be no more; they would be lucky if he allowed them to live for longer than a few hours. With this change in tactics, Kairo's hunting habits would also change. Now, like Malachi, he, too, would have to set traps to catch more than one mouse at a time. With his thirst in check, Kairo spent the next two days adjusting several of his favorite devices for maximum destruction.

The iron maiden would now do what it was designed to do hundreds of years ago and kill its victims in a matter of minutes. Kairo spent the better part of the day sharpening all the spikes on the iron maiden to the sharpest they had ever been. While he was inventorying his devices, he decided to keep the breast ripper in play, since it was one of his favorites, and add the Judas cradle. Apart from just adding new devices to his torture chamber of pleasure, Kairo had some adjustments to make to better enhance the basement layout. Now that he would be entertaining more than one mouse at a time, the basement had to be segmented to provide the mice that were not in play the perfect place to wait. To increase their fear, they needed to believe that they were trapped and alone until it was their turn to play. By the time he had finished everything, night was approaching, and he had to freshen up. Tonight, he would be hunting a different type of mouse.

Malachi's idea of going after Charlotte's homeless population was a brilliant idea. The homeless turned out to be the perfect food supply, with the expectation that they all needed a bath. The humans paid no attention to them, so they would not be missed in the slightest. For Kairo's activities tonight, going after the homeless was not going to cut it. He needed more excitement and more fight from his food. He already had the perfect playground where he could sit back and have the time of his life. At I-Kandies, he would not have to wait for his victims to be cleaned before he was able to play with them. Some of his mice would be lucky enough to make it back home and live to see another day. For the ones that pleased him the most and could go missing, they would not be so lucky. Their lives would be ending before the sun rose on the next day. This was the real reason Kairo acquired the club in the first place. The club had no cameras and a new fully stocked bar that kept his guests drunk and easily manipulated. With a few rounds of free drinks and a live party atmosphere, most of his guests forgot all about their phones and their love of social media.

Tonight, Kairo only cared about having fun and, for the moment, putting Skylar and the hold she had on him out of his mind. All the blood Kairo had consumed after his lesson meant that blood was not his priority. Tonight, was all about fun and destroying a race of people who wanted to destroy him and his kind. While Malachi was nowhere to be found, Kairo was sure he would meet him at the club. With two monsters hellbent on destruction, no one in I-Kandies was safe. *Game on*, thought Kairo as he raced up the stairs to his room.

On the nightstand he saw a note from Malachi. *That can wait*, he thought, feeling like the note was only Malachi telling him of their plans for tonight. Little did he know, but Kairo had already made his own plans for the evening. Whatever Malachi had planned for the two of them tonight was not happening. Kairo would not be letting Malachi interfere with his plans. He decided to keep his dress casual tonight. He wanted to blend in more with the locals instead of standing out and being the center of attention. Instead of relying on his money to win over his mice, Kairo wanted his looks and charm to sweep the women off their feet. He was a new Kairo indeed. After he was dressed, the note on the nightstand caught his attention once again. The note read:

I have a gift for you.
Come to 54843 Lake Wylie Rd

Malachi

Interesting, thought Kairo. What could Malachi have for me? The note also raised a few questions for Kairo. He was eager to find out when Malachi acquired a property on the lake and why was he keeping it a secret. After thinking about his actions over the last few months, things started to fall into place and make a lot of sense. This explained why Malachi was always disappearing. He had his own house filled with his own little mice. The fact that he had a gift for him was enticing, to say the least. The house was just around the corner on the other side of the lake. Kairo knew of the house; it was probably the second-best piece of property on the lake. The property had been owned by someone, but Kairo was not sure who it was. He had purchased the last available house on the market, and there were currently no homes listed for sale. There was only one way that Malachi could have gotten that house. After thinking through everything, it finally hit Kairo. The house had to have belonged to Karen, the lonely older woman Malachi killed during his housewarming party.

As Kairo approached the house, it was empty. His senses did not pick up on Malachi's energy or anyone else's. The front door had been left unlocked, so Kairo walked in and was prepared to wait for Malachi to show up with his gift. Nothing about this house said that Malachi was planning on staying here. Karen had been killed a while ago, and Malachi still had not put his flare on the place at all. He had not removed any of her belongings, her furniture, or her photos. *What is he planning on doing with this house?* thought Kairo. Knowing that he was not there, Kairo still called out to him. Kairo had planned on waiting, but he had much better things to do than sit in a dead woman's house. He was about to leave when he heard a creak in the floorboards from upstairs. *How strange*, he thought. There was someone else in the house with him, but why could he not sense them? Feeling hopeful, Kairo sped up the stairs to collect and unwrap the gift that Malachi had promised him.

Malachi had gone to great lengths to keep Kairo's gift hidden from him. The once wooden door had been replaced with a metal tungsten door. Tungsten, the strongest of the metals, and the one and only material that blocked all Kairo's senses. *Clever, Malachi, what are you up to?* he thought before opening the door. He was eager to see his gift; knowing that Malachi went to all this trouble, she had to be something special. With just a small crack, the overwhelming scent of blood made Kairo's mouth water and his fangs release. It was succulent and sweet, and he had smelled it before. The scent was delicious; it was her, but how and why was she here?

That made Kairo pause because he was utterly confused. Malachi had found Skylar, but why would he do that when he told him she posed too big of a risk to be kept? This was a game Kairo was not about to play with Malachi. On the one hand, his love was just on the other side of that door. On the other hand, Kairo knew that this had to be a trap. None of this made any sense to him. Skylar could not be the gift Malachi was giving to him. Her scent was undeniable, and with a second deep smell of the air, Kairo confirmed it was her. The proof was in the air, and he could not deny what he knew was the truth. Skylar really was on the other side of that door. *How could she be here; who brought her here?* thought Kairo. Malachi would never risk the safety of their kind for him to have this gift. That could only mean that this "gift" was not from Malachi. Kairo started to walk away when that smell hit him once again.

It was that unforgettable scent of lychees and mangoes mixed with blood, her sweet blood. The scent of it was too rich and too overpowering to him. That could only mean one thing, she was hurt and bleeding just beyond that door, and that angered Kairo. The note said that it was from Malachi, but was it really him or someone else? Malachi had an interesting sense of humor, but would he really do this? Kairo slowly pushed open the door, and the sight before him stopped his heart. There, in the middle of the dimly lit room, was his Skylar. *What the hell did Malachi do to her?* She was strapped to an iron chair with the pear of anguish in her mouth. Kairo was so stunned at the sight of her that he missed the small trail of mist that was hovering behind her.

The sight of Skylar in that chair broke Kairo and froze him in mid step. Skylar was in pain, crying and begging him with her eyes to save her. Kairo was torn. What was the right thing to do? There was a big part of him that wanted to save her, take her into his arms, and love and protect her with everything that was in him. At the same time, she was the cause of his weakness, the reason why Malachi needed to teach him a new lesson. She could single handedly destroy him and everything Malachi put in him. *Was this Malachi's doing, or was this a trap?* thought Kairo again. Humans were great at lying and manipulating a situation for their own gain. This had to be the doings of the Council. *How did they find out that we were here so fast?* This had to be them, and Kairo had to get away before they took him and Malachi down for good. Kairo looked at Skylar one last time before he turned to leave her behind for good.

Before he made it out the door, Malachi materialized in front of Skylar. As soon as he was back in a solid form, Kairo picked up on his presence and was furious. "What is the meaning of this, Malachi; why have you brought us here?"

"This is my gift to you, Kairo. I just want to watch as you destroy the last bit of weakness that lives in you."

"You, it was you that did this to her, hurt her in this way?"

Knowing that the Council had nothing to do with this and that it was Malachi all along made Kairo even more furious. He forgot all about the lesson Malachi tried to teach him. His Skylar was hurt, and she needed him to save her. How could he touch her? She was his and his alone. "Your plan was to use her as a pawn in this game of yours, why, Malachi?"

"You still don't get it, do you? Because of that right there; she makes you weak, and that disgusts me. I can see it now all my hard work has been undone by her, this frail human who keeps you weak."

Malachi circled around Skylar and extended his nails to cut her open from her wrist to her elbow. That awakened a force in Kairo he had never felt before. Malachi was out of his mind; how dare he continue to hurt her. For that he was going to pay. Faster than Kairo, Malachi was behind Skylar before he had the chance to get her out of his grasp. The force that Kairo was giving off intrigued Malachi because it was a force he never felt in him before. It was as if his strength had been increased, but Kairo was still no match for him. The force Kairo was giving off was something that Malachi was going to have to keep an eye on.

"Careful, Kairo, I will snap her neck like a twig with one finger." Kairo had just told Malachi all he needed to know. The connection between them was a lot stronger than he expected. Their bond was rare and should not have been this strong, not yet. Kairo had not even tasted her blood yet. This was a first; together they had the potential to be an extraordinarily strong pair. Skylar was indeed a special little mouse; maybe she was not a weak human after all. This was not how Malachi saw things going when he devised this plan.

"Let her go, Malachi, and I will give you what you want. I will be the monster you created and do as you want, just give her to me."

Malachi gave that some thought and decided to release Skylar from the chair, but he kept a hand on her just in case Kairo had any ideas. Even if she was his soulmate, Kairo was no match for him. Malachi did not trust him, and he saw the truth in his eyes the second they connected with hers. Kairo was going to allow love and all the rest of his human emotions to control his life. Malachi knew he was never going to be the monster he needed him to be. He was not going to end Skylar's life. That was just another lie among so many that he was telling him. Malachi still had the upper hand, but he could not allow Kairo to taste Skylar's blood. Once that happened, he would know the truth about the connection they shared. There was no way Malachi was going to let that happen. Skylar was a problem, and he knew how to solve problems.

Kairo refused to take his eyes off Skylar and Malachi. If he knew what was good for him, he would keep his word and let her go. Seeing her hurt, bleeding, and scared by the hands of his friends made the monster inside of Kairo grow in strength by twenty. Malachi had always been stronger and faster, but now Kairo felt as if he had a fighting chance, if a fight was what he wanted. The look in Skylar's eyes annoyed and infuriated him as Malachi held her tightly in his grasp.

"I said to release her, Malachi."

"I did release her from the chair, but I do not trust that you will end her as you promised. I know what she means to you, Kairo, and you will not end her like you said, so I am afraid that I will have to do it for you. I promise you that this is going to be for your own good."

Kairo was losing it as he was clinging to the edge. There was no way he was going to stand by and let Malachi touch another hair on her head. He had already done too much to her. The problem was that Malachi still held Skylar close to him, preventing Kairo from lunging at him. Skylar was still in a dangerous position, and Kairo would not risk her life even in the slightest way. She was weaker from the blood loss due to the chair and Malachi's feeding. That angered him more than anything else. His so-called friend, his creator, had the balls to feed from her even after he knew that they shared a connection with each other. For that and that alone, Malachi had to pay.

Kairo did not want to kill him. He just needed to make sure Malachi understood that she was not to be touched by him ever again. Kairo had to play this right since she was still in danger. If he missed, Skylar was most definitely going to be the one to pay, and she would be paying with her life.

"Looks like we are at a standstill, Malachi; you don't trust me, and I don't trust you, so how are we going to handle this situation."

Kairo paced back and forth in front of them both. He was trying desperately to find an opening to get Skylar out of Malachi's hands. Malachi was also busy calculating every possible move Kairo could make. He was not going to release Skylar until he was satisfied that there was no way that Kairo could save her. When he was certain of that, he did the unthinkable. With Skylar still firmly clutched in his hands, Malachi threw her out of the second-floor window.

Kairo was shocked, heartbroken, and reached a level of anger he had never known. He was forced to watch as Malachi threw her out the window and to her death. Kairo knew there was no chance she was going to survive that fall. Malachi was a great planner and had thought of everything. Just below the window to "cushion" her fall, Malachi placed iron spikes to pierce her body. Skylar was dead, and Malachi's laughter pushed Kairo to a very dark place. It was a place he had never gone before. All he saw was red and the sound of laughter coming from Malachi.

"That is what we do, Kairo; you said you were going to destroy her, and I wanted her destroyed, so problem solved."

Kairo turned on Malachi in full transformation with blood-red eyes. He felt a new surge of power running through his veins. Before, he just wanted to hurt Malachi, but now a part of him wanted him to die. Malachi wanted him to turn to the dark side, and that was what he was about to get. Killing Skylar was never going to be a part of Kairo's plans. With time, he hoped that Malachi would come around and understand how important Skylar was to him. While Malachi was distracted, he never saw Kairo coming for him. Kairo had the upper hand and managed to land several swift punches to Malachi's face and body before he was able to turn the tables on him. Kairo was relentless as he fought Malachi to avenge Skylar. Malachi was going to put an end to this fight and threw Kairo across the room, because a fight was not what he wanted.

"Are you sure a fight is what you want, Kairo?"

"You will die for taking her away from me!" he shouted.

Kairo lunged toward Malachi for the second time and rammed him into the wall. Again, Malachi laughed.

"So be it, Kairo; if a fight is what you want, a fight is what you will get."

Malachi was done playing around with Kairo. His eyes turned to a haunting white. His fangs lengthened as his facial features changed making him appear like a vicious lion. His already muscular body transformed making him even more muscular. It appeared as if his muscles had muscles as his arms and chest expanded. Even his hands changed as his fingernails elongated. Malachi transformed into a being Kairo had never seen before. In all his years of existing, Kairo had never seen this type of transformation in Malachi or anyone. Malachi was extraordinarily fast and strong. Kairo's connection with Skylar may have increased his strength, but he was still no match for Malachi. In the blink of an eye, Kairo was rethinking his decision to try Malachi in this way.

Malachi tossed him around the room like he weighed nothing at all. Each punch came harder and faster than the last. There was just no way Kairo could keep up with the assault Malachi was putting on him. Kairo's only option was to try and protect himself from the beating as best he could. This beating was reminiscent of the beating he gave to Dimitri. Malachi was going to kill him; there was no doubt about that in Kairo's mind. With each blow, Kairo was suffering from broken bone after broken bone. His breathing became labored and impaired as he started to cough up blood. It was a myth that vampires could not die.

They could die from massive blood loss, decapitation, and if their hearts were ripped from their bodies or crushed into a thousand pieces. Kairo was sure that one of these scenarios was going to happen to him. Malachi was growing tired of this one-sided fight. Clearly Kairo wanted to die now that Skylar was dead; otherwise, he would not have crossed him the way that he did. Kairo chose this since he wanted to be weak like the rest of the human population. There was no room for weakness in Malachi's kind. He grabbed Kairo by the throat and placed his other hand over his heart. Malachi broke through his chest to reach inside and crush his fragile human heart.

This was going to be the end, and Kairo welcomed every second of it. This world was not worth living without Skylar in it. Kairo closed his eyes as he felt Malachi's hand wrap around his heart. Malachi squeezed his heart to show him he was in charge and had the upper hand. This was fun for him. He almost wanted Kairo to beg him not to kill him as he reached his hand back into Kairo's chest and slowly squeezed his heart again. This time there was no stopping Malachi. He squeezed and squeezed until he was hit with a bright white light. The force behind the light was so strong, it made Malachi drop Kairo to the ground, but the damage was already done. Without blood to heal himself, Kairo would be dead in a matter of minutes.

Magic, Malachi was hit and stunned by an enormously powerful beam of magic. The blast was strong, much stronger than Malachi would have expected. The blast came from across the room, just behind him. As he tuned to see who the beam of magic came from, he was shocked beyond words. Standing in front of the window was Skylar, alive and well. She should have been dead, but she dodged that bullet. There was this glow of white light surrounding her entire body and a wind that only she could feel. Malachi could not believe his eyes. *How had I missed the fact that she was a witch?* he thought. Her power was incredibly strong and out of control. Malachi always knew Skylar was different and special, but he never expected this. While Malachi was shocked at the recent turn of events, Skylar was able to keep the upper hand. She blasted him with another hit of her white-hot magic that sent him crashing into the wall. Skylar hit him again and again with her magic, breaking him down the same way he had just broken Kairo down. Malachi was getting a taste of his own medicine, this time from a girl and a so-called "weak human."

Skylar had Malachi in an unfamiliar situation. She would have never been able to get the upper hand if she had not caught him off guard. All that changed when Skylar heard the faint wheezing sounds of Kairo dying on the floor. This entire time she thought he was already dead. In her anger, she turned all her attention towards Malachi. He had been responsible for taking Kairo away from her, and that meant he had to die. Kairo being alive changed everything. Skylar was wasting time on Malachi when her attention should have been on Kairo. That split second distraction was all the time Malachi needed to plan his escape. He was severely injured now and needed to get free of this house. More importantly, he needed to get his hands on some fresh blood and heal. With his small window of opportunity, Malachi transformed into vapor and disappeared.

Kairo was alive just barely, but he was still alive. The damage Malachi had done was hard to look at. Kairo was covered in his own blood, suffering from several broken ribs and a massive hole in his chest exposing his heart. It was a miracle he was still alive.

"You are alive; you saved me ; why would you do that?"

Skylar did not have an answer for him. She did not know why she saved him or how she managed to save herself from the spikes. Stopping Malachi was one thing, but she had not saved Kairo yet. He was still dying and would die for sure if she did not do something fast. Malachi was gone for now, and Skylar was not sure that he would not come back for her. He may come back and try and kill her for what she had done to him, but none of that mattered right now. Kairo was the only thing that she cared about. He was a broken, bloody mess. Somehow, she was able to save herself, so she hoped that she could save him as well. Skylar hoped, prayed, chanted, and did everything that she could think of to try and save him. Kairo was fading fast, and Skylar feared losing him for good this time.

"I don't know how to help you, Kairo; please tell me what I am supposed to do."

"Blood," he uttered, "I need blood to heal, but I can't feed from you."

"Why?" asked Skylar. "Is it because I refused your blood before?"

"No," said Kairo, "it is because I will kill you. Since I first laid eyes on you, I have wanted your blood, and I am afraid that I will not be able to stop once I taste it. Let me die if I must feed from you."

Letting Kairo die was not the answer. It finally hit Skylar that she loved this man, and there was no way that she was going to let him die. Kairo was more concerned about her life than his own life. What he did not understand was that she was more concerned about him and his life than her own life. Something inside of her changed, and instantly Kairo became the single most important person in her life. He was her world, and she would not be letting him die. With his body bloody and broken the way that it was, Skylar failed to realize that Kairo was, in fact, a vampire. He needed her blood, and he was going to get it even if he killed her. Skylar placed her wrist in his mouth and urged him to drink from her.

"Here, Kairo, drink," she said, "please drink and stay with me."

Kairo could not resist her offer, and with his last bit of strength, he released his fangs, sinking them deep into her wrist. He had waited a lifetime to taste blood as sweet as hers, and just as he expected, she tasted like heaven. As he plunged his fangs deep into her wrist, his body began to shake and convulse. Through each shake of his body, he forced his fangs deeper into Skylar's wrist, taking more of her blood than what he needed. Her blood was the sweetest thing that had ever graced his lips. He needed more of her; he needed all of her. The blood does not lie; now Kairo understood their connection. Why he would throw away everything that Malachi taught him to be just for her. Kairo was right; Skylar was his and only his; she was his soulmate. They belonged together, and she was going to have to change and become just like him.

Kairo had to force himself to stop feeding from her before he changed her without her knowing who she was to him. He had to explain everything to her before she was transformed. Unlike with him, Kairo wanted Skylar to have a clear understanding of their connection and what transforming meant. The monster inside of him knew all along who Skylar was to him, and he fought to change her right then and there. Skylar was new to this world; she needed to know what she was and who she was to him first. Kairo loved her deeply and owed her an explanation before he turned her world upside down and inside out. Kairo fed from her until she passed out. He had gotten caught up in the taste of her blood and taken more than he wanted to take. Skylar was still alive but weakened from all the blood loss and amount of magic she used. Finally, Kairo could take her home where she belonged.

CHAPTER 23
We Must Become One

*T*he last twelve hours had been rough on both Kairo and
Skylar, and the entire night had taken a lot out of them.
Thankfully Kairo found the strength and control to stop himself from injecting
her with his venom when she passed out from his feeding. The last thing he
wanted was for her to wake up as a vampire-witch hybrid. That would have
been a lot for anyone to handle. Before telling Skylar anything, Kairo had
to let her rest and recover since her body had been put through the ringer.
In her attempt to not only save herself but to save him as well, she used a
great deal of magic. Add in the blood loss from the torture and his feeding
all made her extremely exhausted. Once again, she was sleeping longer than
Kairo would have liked, but for now, he was just thankful for the little
things. She was alive and safe back at home with him, and this time, no one
was taking her away from him. To ensure that, Kairo sent her parents a text
letting them know that she was staying with a friend, and he even sent a
message to Angelina so she would not worry. It had taken Kairo three hun-

dred years to find her, and now she was where she belonged, where she was going to stay forever.

As Skylar slept like a peaceful baby, Kairo was awestruck by how beautiful she was. She was dressed in one of his shirts, wrapped in his soft white sheets with her dark hair spread out over his pillow. With each passing second, he wanted to touch her, kiss her, caress every inch of her body, and love her for all eternity. Throughout his entire existence, Kairo had never been happier than he was right now, and it was all because of Skylar Noelle Montgomery. She had become the light in his world of darkness, a light he would die to protect from Malachi or anyone who posed a threat to her in any way.

In Malachi's defense, though, Kairo understood why he wanted to remove Skylar from his life, but he was completely wrong about her. Skylar did not make him weak, and in time, he would make Malachi understand that. Kairo wondered how much Malachi knew about Skylar. With his gifts, Malachi did not miss much and always knew more than he let on, because he was the master of secrets. Kairo quickly realized that it was not Skylar, per se, that Malachi wanted to cut out of his life but love. It was through their connection Kairo learned that love was a powerful emotion. It was his love for Skylar that gave him a fighting chance until Malachi changed forms. It was Skylar's love for herself that awakened her powers so that she could save herself and her love for Kairo that allowed her to save his life. It turned out love was more powerful than Malachi or Kairo had known. Love made him feel all kinds of emotions he never felt before. *Who did Malachi love that left him with this giant hole in his heart?* thought Kairo. It was funny how things changed so fast. One minute Kairo was ready to turn his back on the light and live as Malachi had wanted him to. He was ready to live totally in the darkness with Malachi, and one look at Skylar crushed everything Malachi tried to put into him. Skylar was a light Kairo would not live without ever again.

For Kairo to allow love and light into his heart was a big deal. At the same time, it did not mean that he was stupid or weak. He understood that just because he was changing, did not mean the world was changing. The Council and those that followed their teachings were always going to see a monster if they knew what he was. Accepting light into his otherwise dark world did not mean that he wanted to live as a human. Kairo loved who he was and what he was. Skylar had seen a small portion of the darkness that lived inside of him, and she did not run away. A part of her wanted to be with him despite the darkness that he lived with. While watching her sleep, Kairo vowed that he would find a way to balance the darkness and the light that existed in his life. Hate was a choice, a learned behavior Malachi taught him the day he was transformed. Kairo had chosen to follow Malachi's lead and live in hate for the past three hundred years because it had come in handy. Malachi's way of thinking had saved his life more times than he could count, and Kairo could not picture his life without some part of that dark side remaining inside of him. The world could be a very ugly place, and he was going to need that dark side in the future to keep Skylar protected.

The same way Malachi had taught him to hate, Kairo hoped Skylar would be able to teach him to love and live with love in his heart. Living in a world of light was going to be an uphill battle for him. Until Skylar learned and understood how to use her powers, she was vulnerable. She was at risk of getting taken by the Council or by one of the many enemies Kairo had. Kairo would move mountains to protect her and unleash an evil this world had never seen before if harm ever came her way. Skylar was all that mattered to him, her safety and her happiness.

Skylar had slept the morning away and woke up around noon. Waking up for the third time in a strange room, in a bed that was not her own, caused a confused look to appear on her face. Unlike the last time, Skylar had no fear in her body at all when she woke up in yet another strange room. She felt right at home, and for the first time in months, she had a good night's sleep. Kairo was by her side in less than a second to reassure her that she was safe and with him. One look into his beautiful golden amber eyes and everything from the night before came back to her. Skylar remembered how she almost lost him and the sensational feeling she had while he was feeding from her. He was her world, and he was a vampire. Skylar still could not believe that they were real. She broke the silence between them with the most obvious statement.

"You have some beautiful eyes," she said with a smile.

Kairo smiled at her, fighting back the urge he had to take her in his arms and kiss her passionately on the lips. He was concerned that, in doing so, he would scare her and make her feel uncomfortable, so he forced those urges to the back of his mind. In time, he would have the opportunity to kiss her and more. It was their connection that increased his passion for her, and until they had a conversation, he had to control his urges. He also had no way of knowing if she was aware of their connection. Kairo had never heard of their kind having a soulmate, let alone one that was a witch. He had so much to tell her, and he did not know where to begin. To avoid freaking her out, he thought that it was best to start with a safe question.

"Did you sleep okay, love?"

"Yes, like a baby. I can't remember when I have slept so good in my entire life." Since she did not know how to respond to his 'love' comment, she acted as if she did not hear that part.

"Well, you did have quite the ordeal last night," he said. Again, Skylar remembered everything that happened and had a lot of questions, but only one mattered the most to her.

"Are you okay?" She easily recalled the events from last night and just how close she came to losing him. She would be able to breathe a little easier once she knew for sure he was okay. He looked okay; in fact, he looked better than okay. He was drop-dead gorgeous, and he was hers all hers.

"Yes, I am okay, better than okay, actually, thanks to you." As Skylar breathed a sigh of relief, Kairo heard the growl of her stomach.

"I will be right back; promise me that you will stay right here," he said.

"I promise, Kairo, I will stay right here until you come back."

With a smile and a kiss on the check, Kairo disappeared from her sight faster than the speed of light. Skylar was finally able to take in her surroundings now that Kairo had left her alone. This room, the bed, it all looked so familiar to her, but why? This was not the room she was in last night or the last time Kairo had taken her. As Skylar climbed out of the massive four-poster bed and over to the French double doors, it all came rushing back to her. She knew why this room was so familiar to her. It was the same exact room from her dream. *This is so strange*, she thought. *How can that be?* Skylar had never met Kairo before nor had she ever been inside his room at any point in her life. The view, however, was breathtaking. It was much more serene and relaxing in person and was another reason why Skylar never wanted to leave this house. While she was lost in thought and bewitched by the view in front of her, she never heard Kairo walk back into the room.

Kairo was taken aback by her standing in the doorway, totally mesmerized by the view in front of her. Without making a sound, he set the tray of food on the bedside table and he walked over to her. He placed his hands on her shoulders and whispered into her ear saying, "It's such a beautiful view but pales in comparison to your beauty." Skylar jumped, startled by the fact that she never heard him when he reentered the room. She was not sure she would ever get used to how quick and quiet he moved.

Even with her dark complexion, Kairo was aware of how his comment made her blush. "Yes, it is a very beautiful view, but I don't know if it pales in comparison to me," she said.

"Trust me, it does," he said with a smile as he took her hand and escorted her back to the bed.

"I made you something to eat; I hope you like it," he said with a mischievous smile. That made Skylar very curious. *He can cook*, she thought. There on the bedside table under a silver platter were homemade cinnamon rolls and jasmine green tea. "I would have made apple turnovers, but I do not have any apples." Skylar could hardly contain herself as the memory of their encounter at the pastry shop came flooding back to her.

"Interesting, a vampire who cooks food that he can't eat."

"There are a lot of things about me that you do not know, love, but I assure you, you will learn everything you need to know in due time. I will give you some privacy to eat in peace and get dressed. I have some clothes for you in the bathroom just through that door," he said before allowing her time to eat alone.

Kairo left Skylar alone for only the second time since he had her back, and it was still hard to let her out of his sight. Their connection made it hard for him to stay away from her now that he knew she was his soulmate. The fact that they had not completed their bond was another reason why it was hard for Kairo to leave her alone. He had to explain everything to her soon, because he was not sure how long the monster in him would wait before he forced her into her transformation. They belonged together, and Skylar had to understand that and accept it. To fight it would end badly for anyone who got close to her, touched her the wrong way, or even looked at her wrong. What he did to Dimitri was nothing compared to what he would do now that he knew she was his soulmate.

Skylar belonged to him now, and there was nothing she could do about that. Her time away from Kairo seemed like an eternity, even though it was only forty-five minutes. After what seemed like hours, Skylar finally came downstairs and almost knocked Kairo off his feet. It was one thing to see her dressed up, but in her natural state, she was utterly breathtaking. When Kairo thought she could not get any more beautiful, she always seemed to find a way to silence him and prove him wrong.

"What?" she said. "Is something wrong with me or what I have on?"

"No, love, you look absolutely amazing." *Love, he said it again*, thought Skylar as her heart melted. *Does that mean I am special to him, or does he call all his women 'love'?*

Skylar was still looking at Kairo confused. All she had on was some simple dark jeans and plain shirt, so how could she look so amazing in that? Kairo picked up on her confusion. "Come with me, love; we have so much to discuss." Skylar agreed with him. She had some questions of her own she needed answers to.

Before taking a seat on the couch, Skylar had to ask, "How did you get me my clothes?"

While taking a seat, Kairo explained, "I am a vampire; I have ways around locks to get what I want when I want it." *Of course*, thought Skylar. Kairo being a vampire was going to take some getting used to.

Skylar decided to sit across from Kairo on the couch since she needed to be looking in his eyes as he explained everything to her. She had tons of questions, and he was the only one who could answer them. That butterfly feeling that she could now associate with him was firing on all cylinders. Skylar knew in the pit of her stomach that what Kairo had to tell her was going to be huge, so she insisted he start the conversation. She had no clue how right she was. Kairo did have a lot to tell her. He was just not sure how she was going to take it all. Their conversation could be a great one, or Skylar could see the ugly side of him he had been trying to keep from her.

The minute Kairo tasted her blood, everything changed. Her free will was completely gone and a thing of the past. Not having a choice in this next chapter of her life was not going to go over well with her. Skylar was not the type of woman who was used to a man, or anyone for that matter, telling her what she was going to do. Kairo could only imagine how her life was growing up. He knew that she was bossy, and that was such a turn on to him, but to deny him what was his was not a good idea. Once Skylar was transformed, he would give her everything that she wanted and needed. When they were bonded to each other, Skylar could have the world on a silver platter, or neon green if she wanted it. This was going to be the hardest conversation Kairo had ever had.

"Before we get into what happened last night, love, I have something to explain to you. For the last one hundred years or so, I have developed this love of torture towards my victims, or my mice, as I like to call them. That night at the club when I first laid eyes on you, I wanted to hear both your screams of pain and pleasure. I was determined to have you at all costs. When I took you from the park, my intentions changed, and I could not hurt you because I had this overwhelming need to protect you. The pain and the torture I inflicted on you was because of Malachi. He knew who you were to me, and he wanted to see if I would hurt you. What I did to you was for your safety from him. I will never hurt you like that again, love. I need you to know that.

That night came back to Skylar quickly. The pain Kairo put her in was unbearable, but somehow, she knew that it could have been worse. Deep down, she knew Kairo did not want to hurt her. She looked Kairo in the eyes and said four words that put him at ease. "I forgive you, Kairo." Skylar did not know why, but despite all that he had done to her, she truly did forgive him for all his actions that night. Kairo could relax a little; that was one conversation that was over and done with. Now, on to more pressing issues.

"Do you remember everything that happened last night?"

"Yes," answered Skylar. "What do you have to tell me, Kairo? Just spit it out, please."

"Love, I am eternally grateful to you for saving my life, but that act has changed not just my life but yours as well. You see, when you allowed me to feed from you, I learned why we have this connection to each other."

Skylar tried to act like she did not know what he was talking about, but she knew; she always felt that pull or connection towards him.

"I am sure that you have felt some type of pull between us, there is no need to lie about that. As I was saying when you allowed me to feed from you, I now know what that connection is all about. Love, you are my soulmate, and that means you must transform so that we can become one. You do not have a choice in this. It will happen, and it must happen soon. The last thing I want to do is force this on you, but if you make me, I will do so. I will be left with no other choice, because you belong to me, we belong together, and there is no changing that."

For a split second, Skylar thought she was dreaming. For years now she had been obsessed with vampires and the supernatural world. Never in a million years would she have thought they were real and that she would turn into one. Skylar did not understand how she, a normal human being, could be the soulmate to a vampire. *She was a human, right?* but then again, *she could do magic.* No other human whom Skylar knew of could perform real magic. Since she had unleashed all that power on Malachi in order to save Kairo, she felt it still just under the surface of her skin. It was only a flick away. The minute she focused on her magic, Skylar had this overwhelming need to unleash all that power. She realized she could control the urges she had if she did not focus on all the power that was just a flick away.

"I don't understand," said Skylar, "how can I a simple human be your soulmate."

"First of all, Skylar, there is nothing about you that is simple. Humans refer to what you are as a witch, and what I am as a vampire. Humans have tainted who and what we are simply because we are different than they are. Malachi is one of four full-blooded ethereal beings. That is what we are, love, not a vampire, a witch, or a werewolf; we are ethereal beings. As far as we know, our kind was here on earth first. We coexisted with humans until they turned on us, making us out to be these evil monsters. They created this hatred in us and forced us to hide in the shadows. They wanted us to be monsters, and over time, that is what we became but not who we truly are. I cannot explain how or why you are my soulmate. I just know that you are. Our soulmate bond was never explained to me, and it came as a shock to me as well. It seems Malachi wanted to keep me in the dark about the bond because he despised love due to some events from his past. I do not know that story, and he never talks about it. I can understand why he wanted to do that. I will kill anyone who hurts you, even if it means losing my life or upsetting you in the process. When I say anyone, love, I mean anyone, even someone you may love and care about."

Skylar was having a hard time believing what she was hearing. What did Kairo mean that she was not human? How could that be possible? Her parents were her parents; she had already investigated her family tree. Wherever Kairo was getting his information from, he was mistaken. He had to be wrong; there was no other explanation. Okay, so she could do magic, but that did not mean that she was a witch. She was still Skylar Noelle Montgomery. She did not know how to process the fact that she was supposed to be mated to a vampire. "What do you mean I am a witch? How do you know all of this?"

"The blood does not lie, it revealed to me your true self. I know who you are through your blood. You are my soulmate, and you are a witch. I am only guessing, but some or all your family members are witches. If you have never heard this before, then someone in your family has been lying to you. Over time, witches learned to hide in plain sight by hiding their powers until they became dormant after generations of no use. Again, I am only guessing, but I would have to say that this is what happened to you and your family. The fact that you are connected to me and this world brought out your powers. In order to save yourself and me, your soulmate, your powers were awakened. By the look of them, you are from a powerful line of witches."

This was all too hard for Skylar to process. Kairo was sitting there acting as if all of this was not supposed to affect her the way that it was. In one night, her entire life changed, and he acted as if it was all normal. Well, it was not normal to her. She did not know this world nor did she belong in it. "Did I kill Malachi when I attacked him? If I did not, will he be coming after me?"

"No, love, you did not kill him. You are strong, and we are stronger together, but our powers are nothing compared to his. That form you saw him in when he almost killed me has been the strongest form I have ever seen him in. You severely injured him, but he will recover. All he needs is blood and some time. Both of which I am sure he has found by now. We will see him again but not in the way you are thinking. He will not come for either of us again. Once you are transformed and bound to me, you will become a part of the family, so to speak. Malachi is a bit of an enigma. As you saw, he hates to see weakness in our kind again due to his past. He is haunted by it and concerned that history will repeat itself. He will not come for you or me simply because we are family. I am aware it did not look that way to you last night, but I challenged him because I believed that he had killed you. Had I backed down, that fight would not have happened. He says on several occasions that he will not hesitate to end me, but that is only true if I expose our kind and put us at risk or if I betray him. Malachi created me, and it will take a lot for him to destroy the last of his creations. He is not as bad as he seems;

his only goal is making sure his people are safe, because we are the only ones that we can depend on and trust."

"Well, that is good to know," said Skylar. "I am glad that I will not have to look over my shoulder for the rest of my life. I am not sure how to tell you this, Kairo, but there is no way I can transform. I have been obsessed with vampires for a long time. I have even dreamed about what it would be like to become a vampire, but that was all fantasy. I cannot live in this dark place with you. I do care for you, Kairo, I will not lie about that, but I care about my family, my friends, and living more. I do not believe all humans are evil, and I do not want to kill them for my survival. That I cannot do. I do not want to die, Kairo."

Skylar did not know just how bad those words were to Kairo. She angered him to his core. Before speaking again, Kairo tried to control himself so that he would not frighten her or hurt her simply because she was playing with fire.

"Skylar, you have to understand that talking like that is not good. I am not joking when I say that you have no choice in the matter. You will transform, Skylar, and that will be the end of that. I am giving you the chance to do so voluntarily, but if you push me, I will force you. Please do not make me have to do that, love. The only thing you do have a choice in is how you want to treat the rest of the world. I have lived this way for three hundred years, and I have never found one person who would allow me to live once they knew what I was. The same will be true for you. You will be free to try and get humans on your side without letting the world know we exist. Secrecy is our number one rule, and that cannot be broken. I cannot save you if that rule is broken. All you know about my kind is a myth told to you through American cinema. We are not dead; I am not dead, Skylar. My heart beats the same as yours. There is a reason why we call the change a transformation. Our hearts never stop beating, like in the movies. The process is more like a human going through a blood transfusion. I will feed from you, taking most of your blood into my body while leaving enough to keep you alive. Think of it like this: your weaker human blood will be replaced with our stronger special blood through our venom. You know that I am different because you saw me in sunlight, and you even saw me eat. That was real and not some vampire magic to fool you. Until we transform, we appear human, we blend into that world seamlessly for our safety. Humanity taught our kind to hate first; they created the monsters we became, and now they want to punish and kill us for being the monsters they created. Malachi was only doing to them what they do to us, what they taught us."

Skylar was at a loss for words. At some point in the conversation, Kairo moved from the chair to sit next to her on the couch. It was strange feeling, his heartbeat, which was almost in rhythm with hers. Since Kairo could hear her heartbeat, he assured her that once their bond was complete, their hearts would beat as one, rhythm for rhythm, because they would be forever connected. Kairo was an amazing creature who was easy on the eyes. If he were human, Skylar would have been all over him right now, but he was not. He was a vampire, and she could not get past what his intentions for her were. Skylar just could not wrap that one fact around her mind. Her being a witch did not change the fact that she was human her entire life. Nothing Kairo said was going to change that fact. Skylar was thankful to him for all the information he had given her. She now had a better understanding of why he and Malachi were the way they were. She knew humanity firsthand and could agree that humans loved to create their own monsters and later play the victims, because they made up the rules.

Skylar could clearly see that Kairo was not joking about forcing the transformation on her. While she was talking, she saw a flicker of the monster he was talking about. She had already seen a glimpse of that monster once before, and it was not pretty. She needed some time to process all of this. Her life literally changed in less than twenty-four hours. Somehow, she was able to convince Kairo to give her the time that she needed alone. As a man of his word, Kairo was determined to give Skylar what she wanted. When it came down to it, he could not say no to her when she looked at him with those beautiful brown eyes. It was going to be hard, but he was going to give her the time that she needed. Throughout their conversation, Kairo had been honest with her about everything, but he did have a secret. With her blood running through his veins, he could pinpoint her location easy. All he had to do was focus on her, and somehow, through their connection, he would be able to locate her. Skylar had a few more questions to ask him before he took her back home to process everything that he told her. "Are all of the stories about New Orleans true?"

"Yes, love, most of them are true. New Orleans has a rich history in supernatural lore. As the story goes, when the world changed and our kind were forced to move on, some of them settled in New Orleans. Until they were forced to hide their powers, vampires, witches, and shifters did not have to hide. They lived free lives until the killings began. We are hard to kill, but with the proper tools, we can all die just like humans. The mass killings forced us to hide in plain sight as we tried to rebuild our numbers. For a while, our numbers were high, but as the world continued to change, so did several of our kind. They became tired of the lies and living as monsters. Most of them turned 'weak' and were killed while the rest chose to hide their true nature and live as humans. As the years went by, humanity turned our history into their entertainment. Almost everything about our kind became twisted and unreal. Many our kind live in New Orleans and live great lives. They have learned to hide and, at the same time, live free lives, but it is not a safe city to be in. The Council of Truth Seekers, a vigilante group, has their base of operations there. It is their number one goal to kill us all and rid the world of all ethereal beings. Anything that happens around the world that is strange and weird gets on their radar. They will investigate the story while setting up a new base of operations in that city. Love, that city is not the fairy tale that you think it is; it is dangerous. You must understand that everything we do now has to stay off their radar. It is not wise for us to draw attention to ourselves now that our numbers have severely gone down once again."

Wow, thought Skylar. The supernatural capital of the world was just that. That helped to explain why her powers started to awaken on her family trip. The power in that city made her come alive. Skylar wanted to talk to Kairo about what she experienced there, but something stopped her. Maybe he could give her some insight about it, but could she trust him? She had just told him she could not transform for him, and she wondered if that fact made him alter the truth to make her feel better about changing.

Skylar had just one more burning question she had to ask him. "Are you and Malachi the ones draining humans of their blood and leaving their bodies at dumpsites all over the city?"

This time it was Kairo's turn to be stunned into silence. "I have no clue what you're talking about. While we have taken and had our way with several victims here, no one would ever find the remains. Long ago, Malachi came up with a way for us to be who we are without a body ever being found."

"Interesting," said Skylar. She was positive she had solved her serial killer angle. "Are there more of your kind here in the city?" she asked.

"No, love, the only vampires that are here are Malachi and myself. While my senses are heightened, Malachi's are even stronger than mine. Neither of us have picked up on anyone else, but I will investigate the matter for you."

"Thank you, Kairo." Skylar was relieved the killer was not him, and she hoped she could trust him. For now, her only option was to trust him and believe what he was telling her.

Their conversation had taken longer than Skylar and Kairo had planned. While Skylar did not want to leave Kairo for a minute, she did need some time to process all of this. Truthfully, what Skylar needed was a drink and to talk this through with Angelina, someone she trusted completely. Kairo had agreed to give her twelve hours alone and not a minute longer. Come tomorrow morning at eight, he would be coming back for her.

Kairo drove Skylar back to her house, gave her a passionate kiss, and let her know he would see her in twelve hours. "Good night, my love; I will see you soon," he said as Skylar got out of the car. Like any overprotective man, he watched and waited until she was safely inside her house before he left. For now, Kairo would keep his word, but this was going to be the longest twelve hours of his life.

CHAPTER 24

Is This What I Really Want?

The news Skylar had just received was both unreal and amazing. Vampires were real, and she was a witch. The icing on the cake was that she was the soulmate to a very sexy and handsome vampire. That was a fact Skylar still could not wrap her head around. Her head was spinning out of control, and she did not know what to do. Literally, her life had just changed right before her very own eyes. In one night, she went from living a very normal life to being thrown into the twilight zone. *It was all real*, she kept saying repeatedly in her head, *it was all real*. Who would have thought that the supernatural world existed, and that she was a part of it? If Skylar was truly honest with herself, this should have made her happy and not have stressed her out the way that it did. She admitted to herself that she had an unhealthy obsession with vampires and vampire lore. For crying out loud, she had always said that she wished that vampires were real because she dreamed of becoming one. *Well, God answers prayers*, she could hear her mother's voice saying that in her head. The extremely popular saying *be careful what you ask for because you might just get it* was also a true statement, and one Skylar had learned loud and clear. She had begged the universe for this gift, and the universe delivered. The real question she had to ask herself: was this a gift, or was it really a curse? Only time would tell, but what she needed right now was tequila, and lots of it, or even a shot of moonshine. Thankfully, she had some of both chilling in the freezer from her last ordeal at the hands of Kairo. Hopefully, a drink would help to clear her head and help her to make sense out of all this.

After a few drinks, Skylar still could not believe it was all real. She was a witch, and there was no denying that. She could feel her magic and could call upon it at the drop of a hat. Unfortunately, it was highly dangerous for her to use her magic. Whenever she would attempt to try it out, she quickly lost complete control of it and busted the glass out of the mirror and left a large hole in her living room wall. Even through the mishaps, Skylar was starting to get used to the idea that she was a witch; it was kind of cool to her. It was the other news she was having the hardest time dealing with. Being the soulmate to a vampire and having to transform, now that took some time getting used to. She saw Kairo's reaction when she told him she could not transform, and it was not a pretty sight. Kairo was terribly upset, even though Skylar could tell he was trying hard to not let her see that side of him. His facial expressions made it clear to her he was not playing around with her. What would he do when she was forced to refuse him again?

Bad attitude or not, Skylar could not deny that she felt something for him. Maybe he was right and it was love Skylar was feeling, but transforming for him was a huge deal. Love was a powerful emotion, but it was not that powerful. Literally, Skylar had just met this man and he expected her to change her entire life just to be with him. This situation would have been much easier if he was human. *Why did he have to be a vampire?* Skylar only asked Kairo for this time away to think just to buy her some more time. No matter how cool she thought the idea of being a vampire was, she could not turn into one. It was just a joke and not something that she wanted to do.

What Kairo did not understand was that she had a family she loved and who loved her deeply. In just a short time, Kairo had managed to get his hands on a large piece of her heart, but love was not enough. Even now, Skylar could feel the void being away from Kairo left in her heart. However, Skylar's family held onto a much bigger piece of her heart. She had to think about them and put their feelings first. Kairo had more to gain from this situation while she had more to lose. Transforming meant that she would have to give up her lifestyle, her family, and her friends. How would they all handle this? Her own family locked Ester away because of the things that she said and saw. Ester had been right, and Skylar had the proof to back their story, but would that be enough for her family? Skylar was spiraling out of control fast; how could she stop Kairo from forcing her to transform? He was strong, much stronger than she was without the use of her magic. The million-dollar question Skylar had to ask herself was, could she use her magic on him? She had a huge and almost impossible choice to make.

The only thing Skylar could focus on was having to kill an innocent person just so she could live. That was not the type of existence she wanted for her life. Aside from having to kill an innocent person, she could not even fathom the possibility that she might kill someone she loved, like her parents. The same people who gave her life. Without them, Kairo would never have found his soulmate. The more Skylar thought about her situation finally brought her to a reasonable solution.

Kairo would have to be the one to change for her if he could. If he loved her, he would change his lifestyle for her without question. Was it at all possible for him to become a "vegetarian" vampire and find another source of blood to satisfy him for the rest of their existence? Blood was blood if it kept him strong and alive. Who cared where it came from? The more questions that Skylar had only pushed her closer and closer to having to tell Kairo that she could not transform to be with him. She hoped they could find a way to be together without her having to be the one to change. If that was not the case, then he was going to have to live without her. It was getting late, and Skylar could use someone to talk to and bounce ideas off. She really needed Angelina and hoped that she would be willing to come over now.

It had been a few weeks since Skylar talked to her simply because life just happened. They both were processing things differently and just needed some time to get their own lives back on track. Now they both had a lot to talk about and catch up on. Angelina was Skylar's best friend; if there was one person she could trust with Kairo's secret, it was her. Skylar knew that she would take that secret with her to the grave no matter what. Angelina heard the stress in Skylar's voice and knew her friend needed her. Within an hour, she was knocking on Skylar's front door ready to hear what was troubling her. When Angelina saw her best friend, she knew immediately that something bad was going on with Skylar.

"What is going on, Skylar? Tell me everything," she said.

Skylar started at the beginning, telling Angelina what really happened the night she was taken. She told her everything and knew how strange it sounded. Vampires were real and living here among them in Charlotte. Angelina reacted the same way Skylar did when she finally realized that this fantasy world was true. Angelina's mouth fell open, and she could not believe what she was hearing. Not only were vampires real, but Skylar was also positive Kairo was responsible for killing Dimitri because of her. He all but admitted it when he told her he would kill anyone, even someone she cared about, if they hurt her. On top of all that was the fact that she was Kairo's soulmate, and he was going to force her to transform so they could be together. Skylar explained to Angelina about the connection they shared and that she wanted to be with him despite everything that he had done to her. He was her fairytale and made her heart skip a beat.

When Skylar was done retelling her story to Angelina, she looked to her best friend for some sound advice. Angelina did not know where to begin or what to say. She needed a drink and normally would never touch tequila, but tonight it was going to have to do. This was beyond crazy, and Angelina did not have any advice for her best friend. Vampires were real, and Skylar was the soulmate to one. *What am I supposed to say to that?* thought Angelina. Her continued silence only caused Skylar to become even more stressed. *Why is she not saying anything?* thought Skylar. She really was looking to Angelina to help her make some sense out of all of this, but that was not happening. Her silence was not the reason Skylar called her over here. She wanted and needed Angelina to give her some advice. More importantly, Skylar desperately needed Angelina to say something, anything at this point. She would have been happy if Angelina started screaming at the top of her lungs as long as something came out of her mouth.

Skylar gave in, and for the next hour, they sat there in silence trying to process all this new information and this new world that they were living in. While Skylar was busy trying to come up with a solution to her problem, Angelina was busy processing the fact that vampires were real and wondering what other supernatural creatures existed in this world. Sitting in silence only forced Skylar to think about Kairo and what he was doing. She missed him like crazy, and it just did not make any sense to her. As the minutes ticked by, that void in her heart grew bigger and bigger. Every time Skylar thought about him or said his name, there was this urge inside of her that needed to see him and be near him as she was drowning inside without him. It was starting to be utterly painful for Skylar to continue to be away from him. She wanted nothing more than to get up out of her chair and run straight to him. That was not the best idea that she had, as she knew that once she was back that Kairo would change her against her will. She was not the type to give into a man, but Kairo had this weird hold on her, and all she wanted to do was make him happy. With a look and a simple ask, Kairo would be able to get her to do whatever he wanted her to do. With that said, it was dangerous for her to be around him.

Finally, Angelina broke the silence with her great big idea. She thought that, somehow, Skylar could convince Kairo that they could be together. The main piece to her plan was that Skylar had to sell Kairo on the idea that she had to stay human. They could have a wonderful and happy life together. According to Skylar, Kairo loved her and promised to make her happy. He had already lived a long and fulfilling life, and when Skylar died, he could end his life as well. The two of them would have been together in life and death. *Problem solved*, thought Angelina. To her, it was that simple, but she did not know Kairo and could not see the giant hole in the middle of her big idea. It could have been a win-win for them both. They would be together, and Skylar would be able to stay human and continue to have her family and best friend in her life without the threat of killing someone that she loved.

For what it was worth, it was a good idea, but Skylar did not believe that this plan would work for Kairo. She could not be certain, but she felt like Kairo enjoyed living way too much and he would not agree to this plan. Now that Skylar was a witch, what did that mean for her; how long would she live? The other problem with Angelina's plan was Skylar did not want Kairo to die, not now or ever. With each tick of the clock, hour by hour, minute by minute, time was running out. Skylar had to come up with a plan that was going to make both her and Kairo happy. She knew that once her twelve hours were up, Kairo would be coming back for her. Skylar wondered if the transformation process would be painful like it was in the movies. She hoped that was a myth, too, and that it would be painless and lovely. There was still the idea of her having to kill for blood and for her survival. If by some chance Skylar decided to let Kairo change her, the thought of drinking blood made her skin crawl. With more time to think, Angelina came up with another brilliant idea.

She said, "Maybe you just need to take some time and learn about this new world you now belong to. You just found out you are a witch and the only supernatural beings you have ever talked to were Malachi and Kairo. Maybe you need to be around more supernatural beings so that you can get a better understanding of this new life of yours. With more of an understanding about them and their world, then maybe you will feel better about transforming. You never know, there may be a way for you to have your old life while making a new one with Kairo. You just told me he walks in sunlight and eats food. I am sure that Kairo would give you the time to learn about all of this if what he feels for you is true. Let's face it, Skylar, everything you thought you knew about vampires and this world was a myth."

"I knew I could count on you, Angelina," and with a smile on her face, Skylar ran to her room.

Angelina sat in the living room confused. She wondered what she said that made Skylar so happy that she jumped up and left the room. After realizing Skylar would not be coming back any time soon, Angelina went off to Skylar's room to look for her.

"What did I say that made you so happy, Skylar?" Skylar was busy packing her bags like a mad woman.

"What are you doing?"

"You just gave me the best idea, and I only have a few hours to make this work."

"Okay, Skylar, slow down and tell me what's going on."

Angelina had just saved the day, and Skylar could have kissed her. She was right; all Skylar needed to do was learn more about this new world for herself on her own terms. Skylar could only do that if Kairo was not around. He would continue to cloud her judgement and tell her only what he felt like she needed to know. He would have the power to control the narrative, and she did not want that to happen. All throughout Skylar's life, she was sheltered from the truth. Her family had to know they were witches, and they kept her in the dark on purpose. Well, not anymore; from this day forward, Skylar was going to be in control of her own fate. She had made up her mind, and her decision was final.

She was going to learn all that she could starting with where it all began, in New Orleans.

"It is all real, Angelina; everything that you hear about New Orleans is all real. Kairo told me that a large population of supernatural beings currently live there, and they all are not evil. If I take your advice, which I am, that is where I must go. It was in New Orleans where it all started. That is where I am going, and I have to act fast before Kairo comes back for me."

Once Skylar filled Angelina in on everything, she asked Angelina to come with her. Skylar knew that she was going to need her friend on this new and exciting journey she was about to take. Angelina had always wanted to visit New Orleans, and this was her chance to do something for herself and get to be there for her friend once again when she needed her. With nothing to lose, Angelina agreed to go and raced home to pack her bags.

They decided to meet at the airport to avoid running into Kairo should he come for Skylar earlier. Skylar felt like that was a real possibility. She could feel that he was coming undone without her the same way she was coming undone without him. The difference was that Skylar had a reason to push those feelings down for just a little while. She was determined to understand this new world on her own terms. When she got settled in New Orleans, she would contact Kairo and tell him not to worry. *What will he do when he finds out that I am gone?* thought Skylar. Whatever Kairo did truly did not matter if she was able to find out the truth. Right before she walked out the door, Skylar called her parents to let them know not to worry and that she needed another vacation. Something inside of her made her keep her real travel destination to herself, because after all the lies, she no longer trusted her parents.

Skylar was on pins and needles as she waited for Angelina to arrive at the airport and for the plane to board. They both were excited for vastly different reasons, but both shared the same anxiety that Kairo would catch them before the plane took off. The hole in Skylar's chest grew bigger as the pain of leaving Kairo slowly set in deeper into her heart. Leaving him like this was what she had to do for herself. She knew that one day they would figure this all out and find a way to be together that made them both happy. Right now, she was determined to learn everything that she could while on this trip as she pushed the pain aside and welcomed the excitement of a new adventure.

CHAPTER 25

Until We Meet Again

*L*etting Skylar out of his sight was harder than Kairo ever thought. The soulmate bond was new to him, and it was hard as hell to deal with. The stronger his connection got, the more he could understand why Malachi wanted to keep him in the dark about it. Kairo now knew, in his own twisted way, Malachi was only trying to protect him and save him from this type of heartache and pain. It was hard to focus on anything other than Skylar. Having a soulmate was already hard; having a soulmate who was fragile like Skylar was turning out to be even harder. Even though Skylar was a witch, magic was new to her, and she did not know what she was capable of or how to use her gifts to defend herself and save her life. This new world Skylar found herself in was not a fairy tale or anything like the books that she loved. It was wonderful and amazing, but at times, it was hard and dark and extremely dangerous. Kairo did promise to give her twelve hours to get used to the idea that her life was about to change forever. Their time apart was a struggle, but he would keep his word no matter how hard it was for him to do so. Lying to Skylar was something he would not do. They both had been lied too enough already. It was just twelve hours; he could do this. He had to do this for Skylar's sake.

Before Kairo knew it, Skylar would be back in his home by his side and in his bed completing their mating bond. Kairo could tell that she was having as hard of a time being away from him as he was being away from her. He could sense Skylar more easily now that their connection was growing stronger due to her blood flowing through his veins. As far as Kairo could tell, Skylar's energy was all over the place. At times she was fine, and at other times she was upset, angry, and even sad. Her emotional state made him worry. Maybe letting her process all of this on her own was a huge mistake. *What was she doing right now, thinking right now?* he wondered. In a single night, Skylar had become his everything now. She made his world go round, and nothing else mattered except her. If Skylar's emotions did not level out soon, Kairo was going to break his promise and bring her back home with him where she belonged.

Sitting and watching the hours slowly tick by and connecting with Skylar's energy was not good for Kairo. He needed to do something else to take his mind off Skylar and all the ways she could be in danger. Thinking this way was only making him crazy while the monster inside of him tried to force him to go back on his word. He wanted Skylar back. More than anything, the monster inside of Kairo wanted to complete their bound. He wanted to taste her blood again and have it fill his body, making him stronger. Thinking about her blood made Kairo transform, as he was starting to lose control.

Skylar was a newly discovered witch in a world that would chew her up and spit her out like she was nothing. She was not human and did not fully understand this new world she now belonged to. No matter what she believed, she was different, and the world was going to treat her as such. It was this type of thinking that continued to drive Kairo crazy, because Skylar was headstrong and did not like to be told what to do. She refused to believe she would be seen differently. In his world, there were several ways in which she could be killed. In this new world, she was not strong enough to be left alone, and he had left her alone. He was such an idiot. *How could I let her out of my sight for such a long time?* Malachi would have been furious with his show of weakness and stupidity towards his soulmate.

It was easy to look at Kairo and see a monster. He knew what he was, what Malachi taught him to be. Skylar did not understand, but everything Malachi taught him was for the safety of their kind. Malachi may have been a monster on the surface, but he was nothing more than a wounded man hurt by humanity. Kairo could understand where he was coming from. Should something ever happen to his Skylar, the world would pay ten times over. All the thoughts of something happening to Skylar made Kairo more and more uneasy. Thinking about all the harm that could come her way was a bad idea. In theory, how much danger could she be in? She was at home, and he was the only person who knew she was a witch. Him and Malachi, but he was gone, wounded, and needed to recover. If any harm came to Skylar, it was going to be his fault. He was the idiot who left her alone in the first place.

Kairo needed a distraction, a true distraction, because the alcohol was not working. Maybe it was a good idea for him to beat out all the pent-up frustration and aggression that was building up inside of him. Hopefully, a few rounds with the punching bag would be enough to level him out and help him get through these last hours without Skylar. With all his pent-up frustration, Kairo did not bother with changing out of his clothes before attacking the bag. As he pulled his punches, he landed blow after blow on the bag until he busted it open at the seams allowing the sand to spill out onto the floor. With it went all Kairo's frustrations and fears about leaving Skylar alone. After what felt like an hour of punching that bag, Kairo was covered in sweat and needed to shower. What felt like an hour turned out to be seven hours later. This was the distraction he needed, and now he felt better about his decision as he searched deep inside himself to check on Skylar. In doing so, Kairo noticed that she was still on edge, but her emotions were settling down, and that pleased him.

With only five hours before her time was up, Kairo was close to having her back. After a quick shower that brought him some much-needed clarity, Kairo knew what his next move needed to be. He was over waiting alone and would bring Skylar back kicking and screaming if he had to. He would honor his word and allow her to have her final hours to process her changing world without interference from him. Soon he would have Skylar back in his arms and he would feel much better. They both would feel much better, as their closeness would put them both at ease. Kairo could sense that Skylar's anxiety and frustrations were gone and replaced by a nervous excitement. Something had changed in her, and Kairo was not sure if he liked it or not. *Soon, my love, we will be back together soon.* Traveling by vapor would have been faster, but his goal was to return with Skylar, and that meant that he had to drive.

Minutes later, Kairo was pulling up in front of Skylar's home, and his feelings had been correct. Something had changed; in fact, something was wrong very wrong. Skylar was gone; her energy and presence were nowhere to be found around her home. She was not there, and the real question was, did she leave on her own, or was she taken from him? That would have been a bold move on Malachi's part. Malachi knew who Skylar was and what she meant to him. Before Kairo let his mind go there, he had to be certain that Skylar was missing and just did not leave on her own. The only energy he was picking up was hers and another human. It was familiar to him, so it had to have been Angelina's energy.

Skylar's trail led him to the end of the driveway where her signature essence faded away. It was clear to Kairo that she left him on her own as she took a car somewhere. Kairo was angry, mad, and, most of all, hurt. How could Skylar leave him the way she did? Clearly, she was not listening when he told her she had no choice in this. She belonged to him now, and she was flirting with danger. Kairo had to calm himself down so that he could create a clear picture of what happened here. For Skylar's sake, he hoped that she was taken instead of deciding to leave him on her own. Once inside the house, things were not going the way Kairo wanted them to be going. There was broken glass and plaster all over the floor. From the look of things, Skylar was testing out her magic. It was unpredictable and unstable because they were apart, and it would stay that way until her emotions were back under control.

Kairo's worst fear had not come true, not yet at least. Skylar was not taken, but she left on her own. She was running away from him and the bond they shared even though it was clear that she was planning on returning. That angered Kairo all the same because she was still running away from what they shared. He tried to be subtle about what would happen if she refused him, and now, she was about to find out just what he was talking about. She would not leave his side again until they were bonded. If he had to restrain her until she understood where he was coming from and their bond was completed, then so be it. That was what he would do. Concentrating on her energy, Kairo was able to pinpoint her location. She was at the airport, and her emotions had changed yet again. Happiness, Skylar was happy and excited to be leaving him behind. *You can run, my little mouse, but I will find you; I will always find you, my love.* Kairo transformed to vapor with the airport as his new destination to recover what was rightfully his.